DARK
ZONE

TOM CLANCY'S OP-CENTER NOVELS

WRITTEN BY JEFF ROVIN

Op-Center	Balance of Power	Mission of Honor
Mirror Image	State of Siege	Sea of Fire
Games of State	Divide and Conquer	Call to Treason
Acts of War	Line of Control	War of Eagles

WRITTEN BY GEORGE GALDORISI

Out of the Ashes	Into the Fire	Scorched Earth
(with Dick Couch)	(with Dick Couch)	

ALSO BY JEFF ROVIN

Vespers	Rogue Angel
Stealth War	Conversations with the Devil
Fatalis	Zero-G
Dead Rising	(with William Shatner)
Tempest Down	

ALSO BY GEORGE GALDORISI

FICTION

Coronado Conspiracy	Tom Clancy Presents:
For Duty and Honor	Act of Valor
	(with Dick Couch)

NONFICTION

The United States and the 1982	The Kissing Sailor
Law of the Sea Convention	Networking the
Beyond the Law of the Sea	Global Maritime
Leave No Man Behind	Partnership

Tom Clancy's
OP-CENTER

DARK
ZONE

CREATED BY
Tom Clancy and Steve Pieczenik

WRITTEN BY
Jeff Rovin and George Galdorisi

St. Martin's Griffin ⚞ New York

This is a work of fiction. All of the characters, organizations, and events portrayed in this novel are either products of the authors' imaginations or are used fictitiously.

TOM CLANCY'S OP-CENTER: DARK ZONE. Copyright © 2017 by Jack Ryan Limited Partnership and S&R Literary, Inc. All rights reserved. Printed in the United States of America. For information, address St. Martin's Press, 175 Fifth Avenue, New York, N.Y. 10010.

www.stmartins.com

Designed by Omar Chapa

The Library of Congress Cataloging-in-Publication Data is available upon request.

ISBN 978-1-250-02689-7 (trade paperback)
ISBN 978-1-250-02688-0 (e-book)

Our books may be purchased in bulk for promotional, educational, or business use. Please contact your local bookseller or the Macmillan Corporate and Premium Sales Department at 1-800-221-7945, extension 5442, or by e-mail at MacmillanSpecialMarkets@macmillan.com.

First Edition: May 2017

10 9 8 7 6 5 4 3 2 1

DARK
ZONE

CHAPTER ONE

"It is said that a diplomat is someone who is able to deceive his friends but never his enemies."

Douglas Flannery brushed windblown strands of gray hair from in front of his sunglasses as he looked up at the speaker. The sixty-two-year-old former ambassador was sitting on a bench near South Street Seaport, watching the late-morning sun play on the East River, mesmerized by the shards of light leaping and stabbing constantly as water taxis and ferries shot by. He was thinking back to the last time he had sat beside a river, waiting for her. It was on the older, western right bank of the Dnieper River, in a park with winter-bared trees and lean squirrels emboldened by hunger. There were squirrels here, too, but they were well fed.

He stared briefly at the woman who had spoken, took her in with surprising equanimity—surprising, given how they had parted—before turning back toward the hypnotic water. She looked well, and he was glad of that; but it was the woman's accent that had stirred an immediate and overpowering rise of emotions. The inflection was Ukrainian, starting far back in the throat and possessing a somewhat nasal quality. It was an accent Flannery had grown accustomed to during the eight years in which he served as the United States ambassador in Kiev. Though he was fluent in the language—he held a master's degree in translation from NYU—he had never quite mastered a precise accent, since most of his contacts had been in writing.

"I have heard that said," Flannery replied. "Which is why, after thirty-plus years, I've learned that a good diplomat treats everyone equally—as a potential adversary."

"Even an old friend and ally?"

"Everyone," he said, his body tensing, the word sounding harsher than he had intended. He relaxed his shoulders. The conflict in Crimea had done that to all of them—made them callous, or worse.

"I see," the woman replied quietly.

"Events change us, alliances challenge us," Flannery said in an apologetic tone. "In our work, 'old' doesn't mean settled. You still have to start over again."

"What is the saying? 'Everything old is new again'?"

Flannery nodded and took another look at the familiar figure as she sat easily on the opposite end of the bench. The woman was in her late thirties. She had dark eyes, a long neck, and a broad, open face framed by black hair worn in twin ponytails. Her powder-blue jogging suit was speckled with perspiration. Swallowing a mouthful of water, she began to text as she spoke.

"I suppose even friends and allies want something, often without knowing it," she said.

"Inevitably," he agreed. "Though I continue to believe that there may be rare exceptions. People who just want to say hello or reconnect. Otherwise, I might become a cynic."

She gave him a sidelong look. "You know what I remember best, Douglas? I remember watching you with the Australian ambassador when he called after Malaysia Airlines Flight 17 was shot down. So many of his countrymen lost, and you could not have been more sincerely compassionate. You will always be a humanist."

"That was three years ago, another life," he said. He met her glance, and then they both looked away.

In 2011, three years before the hostilities began in Crimea, Galina Petrenko—who had been relocated at age two from Chernivitz after the Chernobyl nuclear disaster—had secured a mission position as an ADC, an arrivals and departures coordinator who helped orient and acclimate American staff. Flannery had been impressed by her work ethic, her patriotism, and her courage: after two years at the embassy she had been drafted, but was turned down when a medical exam revealed Stage 1 thyroid cancer. She went back to the mission, missing only a few days of work to undergo treatment. Risking her job and her freedom, Galina had spied on her employers to transmit any potentially useful scrap of information to the ZSU, the Zbroyni Syly Ukrayiny—the Ukrainian military. Flannery was forced to have her dismissed, though he checked on her through mutual acquaintances. He heard that she had gone to work for a lieutenant general at the

Sluzhba Zovnishn'oyi Rozvidky Ukrayiny, the Foreign Intelligence Service, and was now working as a translator for the Permanent Mission of Ukraine to the United Nations. He was not surprised to hear from her after his appointment as a fellow of the York Organization for Peace had been announced two weeks before. The think tank was located on Pearl Street, in a three-story-tall manor-style building from the Revolutionary era. Financed by wealthy Eastern European expatriates, York was deeply involved in analyzing and guiding the politics of the region.

"How is your health?" Flannery asked.

"Two years without remission, three to go," she said. A brow went up. "Unless you're referring to something else?"

"I meant the . . ." He touched his throat as if he were loath to say the word. "Though there is a rumor that you are involved with Russians here," he added. "Buying information?"

"We buy from them, they buy from us—it is an honest arrangement, no one is deceived," she said.

"That also lets you watch each other," Flannery noted.

"Yes, which is why I asked you to meet me on the river," she said. "A short walk from your office but a decent run for me, and it will take a monitor at least another ten minutes to catch up."

Flannery made a point of not looking north. It would indicate a level of confidence that could put him in jeopardy. "Do you have any backup?" he asked.

"Not today. He is pursuing his own contacts."

Flannery felt an old, familiar feeling. The Galina he once knew—warm, smart, attentive—was still very much in evidence, though those qualities had a newly burnished edge. They were not enough to be off-putting, but they were enough to make him wary.

"So what do *you* want, Galina? I'm due back at a symposium at noon."

"For lunch?"

"For peace."

"Most of the people are there for the free food," she said. "You know, Douglas, I never knew which you disliked more in Kiev, the borscht or the small talk."

"Neither. As much as I dislike a slow verbal massage like the one I'm getting now," he said. "You and I did not part on the best of terms, but I always appreciated your directness."

"Fair enough," she replied, setting her smartphone in her lap and taking another swallow of water before continuing. "I phoned, Douglas, because we need someone inside Suhoputnye Voyska Rossiyskoy Federatsii. Our people undercover in the Kremlin have disappeared amid rumors that six armored columns are being readied as the spearhead for a renewed invasion force. The ZSU wants information on the tanks and their deployment to make a preemptive strike."

Flannery turned to her abruptly. "You want to attack Russian troops and tanks *in* Russia?"

"We don't want them setting a foot deeper in our soil," she replied.

"How—*where* have you been preparing for this?" the diplomat asked. As far as he knew, his own nation's Department of Defense was unaware of any such preparations.

"Do you really want to know?" she asked.

"If I'm to believe you, yes," he replied.

"All right. It's very ingenious," she said. "We use VRS in a secret facility. Only a handful of people know of this training center's existence."

"Virtual-reality simulations?" Flannery said, openly astonished.

"It's the boot camp for the next generation of soldiers," she said. "You'd be surprised. Some of our new recruits suffered PTSD without ever leaving their chairs. They had to be replaced."

"'New recruits,'" he said. "Are you talking about regular military, or paramilitary?"

Galina was stubbornly silent.

"And this facility," he said. "At least tell me where it is?"

"I'm sorry, I cannot do that," she replied.

"That is madness," Flannery said. "All of it. You understand that this will provoke a *massive* retaliation."

"We understand that if the ZSU never takes the fight to them Putin wins by attrition," she said. "And—there are other precautions we are taking. Please. Before we can do anything, we need intelligence."

"Then count me out," he told her. "I don't want to expedite a reckless suicide."

Galina stared thoughtfully out at the river. "Douglas, if you won't help, then our people will be forced to proceed under the assumption that such an attack is being readied," she said bluntly. "Participating, you have the ability to prevent needless bloodshed."

"Or help trigger it by confirming your fears," he said.

"In that case, helping us end this quickly may save lives."

If Flannery had possessed an appetite, he would have lost it. Imagined scenes of combat filled his mind, the grainy green tint of night-vision goggles sparked by the crisp cries of gunfire and screaming—shouted commands, agonized injuries. The region had never been a bed of tranquillity, with ancient ethnic and religious strife, two World Wars, and then the decades as Soviet Socialist Republics. But York was working hard with the heads of local governments and relief groups to try to sow at least the seeds of peace.

"I have to think about this," Flannery said. "How much may I share with my colleagues?"

Galina checked the time on her smartphone and stood. "As much as you see need to, though time is obviously critical."

"How soon do your people plan to move?"

Galina briefly looked down at him. "It will be this month," she said. "That is all I can say." She waggled the phone she was holding. "I have a burner the Russians haven't hacked. Call me on it? You have the number."

Flannery nodded noncommittally.

The woman sent the number to Flannery's phone and, with a lingering look at him—an expression of resolve—ran off to the north, back toward the United Nations.

Be careful, he thought, not daring to speak aloud in the event someone was nearer than she suspected.

The toot of a tugboat brought the diplomat back to the moment, and he rose on suddenly unsteady legs. He stood for a moment, smelling the salty sea air of the harbor. He didn't want this responsibility, but it was his nonetheless. Redacting and forwarding intelligence that helped forge U.S. policy in the region had been stressful enough, which was why he'd left the diplomatic corps. But this . . .

He didn't feel like attending a symposium on the real and existential risks facing Belarus, Lithuania, and Latvia, but he had to get through that before he could discuss this with his colleagues.

And, as if to underscore the fact that even a man of nearly three score years could still learn new ways, the idea of small talk suddenly seemed vitally appealing.

His lean face pulled in a familiar scowl, his careful eyes tired and itchy from the high morning pollen count, Andrei Cherkassov was definitely ready to go home.

When he left Moscow in 1986, it was expensive for a young man—even a former *kapitán* who had been an honored Spetsnaz officer in Afghanistan but who had been retired due to tinnitus, of all things, a six-foot-three-inch young man who could only get work as a security guard at the Cosmonautics Memorial Museum, where he didn't have to hear very well because most of the visitors didn't speak Russian. All he had to do was make sure no one touched the space capsules and satellites.

That job had lasted a year. One of his former superiors, Polkóvnik Birman, had been leading a group through the facility and recognized him, asked him to come and see him at his new post in the Main Intelligence Directorate. Eighteen months later, after a shakedown period in South Africa, Cherkassov was as-signed to London, then New York. He remembered, with a smile, the jealousy of his colleague, Georgi Glazkov, who had really wanted the post. Instead, he was sent to Mongolia to keep an eye on the many members of the Mongolian Revolution of 1990, the "Democratic Revolution," which threatened the country's exten-sive border with southern Russia.

"You may be killed in a very dangerous position," Glazkov had said, "but at least, Andrei, you will not die of boredom!"

His job was surveillance with occasional *zvetchenya*—termination up and down the Eastern Seaboard. It was just like being back in Afghanistan, only civilized. The truth was, Cher-kassov preferred assassination to the Spetsnaz or to working at the CMM. The hours were shorter and the clothes were less re-strictive.

But now, after more than twenty-five years in New York, that city had become much too expensive. Even Moscow was preferable, especially since he could get into one of the flats open to individuals over sixty-five. In just a few days, he would turn sixty-six. Birman was gone, but his successor had promised Cher-kassov a plane ticket . . . and a big party. Cherkassov hadn't had a birthday party since he was six, living in what was still Leningrad.

After receiving the call from Olga confirming the route his target was apparently taking, Cherkassov had taken an Uber to South Street, just north of the Brooklyn Bridge and below the FDR Drive. The highway cast the area in darkness and the col-umns that supported it provided ample cover. He had arrived in time to see Olga pant her way south, after her quarry—the woman was in very good shape, but she was not young—and then he saw Olga again, running the other way. A look from her told him that the other runner had finished her meeting early and was already on the way back. The runner would see Olga, of course. Olga was there to be seen. She would not, however, see Cherkassov.

The killer was dressed in jeans and a New York Mets T-shirt. Both had been freshly laundered; she couldn't see or hear him, and he certainly didn't want her to smell him. Many homeless people lived under the highway. People who ran here were alert to odors, the scent of potential danger.

Cherkassov had chosen this particular spot across from Beekman Street because the road to the west was little traveled and there were parked cars to block the view of anyone to the east. Traffic passing overhead created an irregular, rattling beat; he wouldn't be able to hear her footsteps, but he would see her shadow. The sun was over the harbor and would throw her elongated shape well forward, right in front of him. As it happened, he saw the shadow, heard the footfalls on dirt left over from a recent street excavation, and saw a cloud of that dirt preceding her. His hand went into his pocket and he took out his wallet. He used two fingers to remove his preferred weapon—one that never tripped alarms, attracted the attention of the TSA, or broke any laws: an American Express card, one corner sharpened to a razor's edge. He pinched it between the thumb and index finger of his left hand.

As the woman jogged past the large, slightly rusted stanchion, Cherkassov's right arm shot out toward her. It stretched

across her breastbone, circled her throat, pulled her toward him
back first. She did what everyone did: she reached up with both
hands to try and dislodge the biceps that were thicker with flesh
than muscle but still held her fast. In the shadow of the highway,
the credit card flashed across her throat, drawn firmly and steadily
across the arm that restrained her. It was a guide, a way of making
sure he sliced both her windpipe and her carotid artery. As soon
as the blood began to shoot out, he leaned her forward so she'd
bleed out on the street. She gurgled and gasped, but only for a
moment, as her throat filled with blood and drowned her—which
caused her to lose consciousness that much quicker. The hands
stopped struggling within moments. She was unconscious within
seconds. Though blood continued to flow and pool, she was dead
when he let her flop to the asphalt.

It was a relatively clean kill: there were only a few spots on his
jeans and shirt. The denim quickly turned those speckles brown so
they wouldn't attract attention. The shirt was blue and, to anyone who had ever been to Citi Field, the splatters looked for all
the world like smudged ketchup.

Crouching and wiping the credit card on her jogging suit—
where the blood did look very red—he put it back in his pocket,
retrieved her smartphone, and pressed her dead thumb on the
screen. The phone unlocked. Then the killer slipped deeper under
the highway and headed south for several blocks before turning
toward the sunlit streets and the omnipresent security cameras.

CHAPTER TWO

Op-Center Headquarters, Fort Belvoir North,
Springfield, Virginia
June 2, 12:30 PM

Chase Williams arrived at the office six hours later than usual.

He had been working—a semiregular meeting at the White House with the president and the top bureaucrats at Homeland Security—and, as a result, had been in the heart of the nation's capital shortly after the sun came up.

That was a magical, uncommonly calming time in Washington, D.C.

The older he got, the more Williams valued the late-spring mornings. The mix of floral scents, the sounds of countless birds, the sense of rebirth that came so vividly with spring, especially early in the morning, not long after sunup—these made him smile. There were many qualities that defined living, but these were the foundation of life.

And as the fifty-nine-year-old swung his Escalade into an unmarked parking space at the National Geospatial-Intelligence Agency at Fort Belvoir in Springfield, Virginia, he acknowledged something else with that smile: each year marked a very real passage of time. He was not morose about it; on the contrary. The fewer springs that remained, the more he cherished them.

Challenges, too, he admitted as he eased his six-foot frame from the car. Those challenges were as grave as they had ever been. There had been the Great War in the teens and rampant gang crime in the twenties. Then a Great Depression in the thirties, from which the world saw no possible exit. A World War broke that fever but started another: an escalating fear of Communism. There had been the heavy shadow of nuclear war in the fifties, civil unrest in the sixties, and drug epidemics were always with us like a toxic cloud that moved from city to city, group to group, without the abundant patience of the Devil himself.

But the retired Navy four-star, former combatant commander for both Pacific Command and Central Command had seen enough, experienced enough in his thirty-five years of active duty to believe that right prevailed and that good systems worked. The older he got, the more comfort he took from that belief, too. As the head of Op-Center, the nation's leanest and most effective rapid-response security agency, he was in a position to make sure that American values were preserved in accordance with our greatest traditions. While that spared him the impotent fear that a lot of people felt, it was also a burden: when he made a mistake, even a small one, people died.

Williams leaned into the backseat to grab his backpack. In it was a laptop and his lunch; right now, the latter was what he needed. The president served a decent cup of coffee in the meeting room adjacent to the Oval Office, but the croissants were as buttery as Midkiff's rhetoric. He preferred to hold out for apples covered with organic peanut butter.

The smell of history, fuel, and asphalt swiftly replaced what was left of the scent of rose blossoms. Williams moved easily through the lot heavy with SUVs and Humvees. His dark-blue suit was sharply tailored but conservative, a look as close to a uniform as he could get without it actually being his old, familiar attire. A crisp white handkerchief tucked carefully into the coat pocket was the only concession to civilian style as he headed toward the facility that many on the base didn't even know was there. The parking lot had been expanded when the location for the revived Op-Center was installed in the basement levels of the NGA. The lot still had reserved parking spaces that were emphatically marked for senior NGA staffers. But Williams had insisted that there should be no stenciled names for Op-Center personnel, or any Op-Center logo displayed on the building's façade or directory of tenant commands. One of the most accomplished military officers in a generation and a consensus choice to be the next chairman of the Joint Chiefs of Staff, he had been passed over for that post—and for other essential, good-fit jobs like defense secretary, national-security adviser, and director of National Intelligence, in favor of political appointees by a politically insecure commander-in-chief. Though he was aggressively courted by industry, think tanks, and academia—all very high-paying, high-prestige jobs—Williams had accepted this command because he was, above all else, a patriot.

But he had his demands, and one of them was being guaranteed a high level of autonomy for himself and his carefully picked team. The president had agreed, since Op-Center was autonomous by charter. They moved to action only when the normal levers of U.S. national security—the military, the intelligence agencies, law enforcement, and the numerous organizations that made up the nation's security bureaucracy—couldn't act quickly enough or were compelled by statute or oversight to function within strict legal protocols. Besides, what President Wyatt Midkiff bestowed with a handshake, Congress could undo with the stroke of a budgetary delete key. But with a budget of less than half of one percent of the NSA, the president could afford to take a chance on the man and his vision.

A cornerstone of that was anonymity, not just from other agencies and career bureaucrats but also from other agencies competing for intelligence—and, thus, funding—and from the press. As Williams told Roger McCord, his intelligence director, in their first interview, "Only in the movies does an operative stroll into a bar, announce his name and affiliation, and survive the evening. Not in my world."

In Williams's world, just letting someone know you held an American passport could be a death sentence. That was the reason Op-Center's presence at Fort Belvoir was kept secret, and why it was housed in a sub-basement of the NGA instead of in its own building—which the secretary of Homeland Security had pushed for, since that would have added to the annual budget and to his own power base.

Williams hadn't cared about any of that during his military career, and he didn't care about it now. Only the mission mattered, and, right behind that, the people.

He passed through the double glass doors, showed his NGA badge to the guard at the counter—a young woman who always seemed uncomfortable returning the smile of a man who was just a name and a face—and continued to the leftmost elevator in a bank of elevators. Officers emerging from an adjoining elevator acknowledged him with tight nods. Williams nodded back as he opened an app on his smartphone—doing so notified the staff that the chief was on his way down. Williams held the device to the scanner at the right of the elevator and the door opened. The code was a signal and it changed daily, sent only to Williams's secure, government-issued phone. A swift, quiet three-level descent later, he was in a small antechamber. After submitting to a retinal scan beside the single door, he was admitted to the subterranean bunker that was Op-Center's main compound.

Anne Sullivan was waiting for him just inside the door. The fifty-seven-year-old deputy director was dressed in a red blazer with black trim on the collar and red slacks. She wore a locket with a photo inside that she never shared but which was a source of much discussion throughout the ranks. The current consensus was "girlfriend," though no one knew for sure what Sullivan's sexual orientation was. She had never been married, but that meant nothing to a woman who came of age in an era when a woman couldn't always have a successful home life and a career.

Anne held a tablet cradled to her bosom with one hand, her smartphone in the other. "How was the meeting, Chase?" she asked with just the hint of an Irish brogue and a much larger dose of irony.

"It was polite," he replied as they walked side by side around the circle of cubicles toward their adjoining offices. "They like to make sure the tight suit isn't all that's holding me together. Though this is the first time they asked about you by name."

Anne grinned. "My review isn't for another four months. Am I being considered for something?"

"Not after what I told them." Williams laughed. "You think I can afford to lose you?"

It was a statement, not a question. Anne Sullivan was a former General Services Administration official, a Washington insider who navigated inside the Beltway with a balance of hard work, organizational skill, and a healthy dose of intimidation. She was personally acquainted with everyone who had a skeleton buried somewhere between 1600 Pennsylvania Avenue and Capitol Hill, and also at the Pentagon. That last was particularly useful, since Op-Center had enemies there, officials who knew what a smart high-ranking officer could do with both direct access to the president and to top security secrets. Their acquired paranoia didn't factor into the character of the man they feared, the ally they had—only into his strength as a potential adversary.

They reached Williams's office, and he threw an informal, habitual salute at a framed color photo on the wall, showing General Douglas MacArthur in Manila, in 1945, smoking a corncob pipe. It was signed crisply in fountain pen—not to him, but the great man's hand had been laid upon the photo, and that was enough.

"What did I miss?" Williams asked.

"The lunch with Brian," Anne informed him.

"No, no," Williams replied, shaking his head. "I texted him from the West Wing. Didn't he get it?"

"Not if you sent it from the Oval Office."

He shot her a perplexed look.

"They have the new Closed Whisper Sec System," she said. "Nothing flies without a code. I sent you the alert."

"When?"

"About two months ago," she replied.

"Didn't see that update," Williams said as he sat behind his desk. "There are so many damn alerts."

"There are so many damn crises," Anne replied. "I let Brian know where you were, though he's still at Texters Barbeque. Met an old girlfriend."

The way she had said it—Williams shot her a look. "Carolina?"

Anne nodded knowingly.

"He's gonna need a drinking buddy or a crisis," Williams said.

Brian Dawson was the forty-year-old operations director and a bit of a loose cannon—which was what Williams liked about him. What the former Army man lacked in discipline he made up for with impulsive surges tempered by instinctive good judgment. He also possessed bagfuls of charm, a fact that stood him in good stead with the three-to-one ratio of single women to eligible men in the district.

"We did just pick up one interesting item from the NYPD," she said, looking at her tablet and resuming the briefing. "They found a female murder victim identified as Galina Petrenko, a Ukrainian operative who worked at the embassy there. Her throat was cut, and only her phone was taken."

"Operational specialty?"

"Not known," Anne replied. "But she used to work for our ambassador in Kiev and had been on a KGB watch list since 2011. She was dismissed, charge of espionage."

"Prosecuted?"

Anne shook her head.

"Intimate with the ambassador?"

"Unknown," Anne said.

"Who was she spying for?"

"On the books, Kiev," she said. "They were gathering intel on Russia. Fairly well-known dance they do out of the U.N."

"Anything *off* the books? They don't suddenly start killing embassy employees, even spies."

"Not that we were aware of," she replied. "But you're right, something like that seems likely. Done in daylight, on a morning run—sends a signal."

Williams shook his head slowly. It was hell having enemies, but worse when you didn't trust your allies. "What was the name of our ambassador there?"

"Douglas Flannery," Anne informed him.

"Name's familiar."

"He works for the York group in Manhattan now," Anne said. "It was in the—"

"HUMINT resource update, yes," Williams said. "I *do* read some of what you send around."

"Their offices are a half mile from where the woman was killed," Anne continued. "Tenuous connection, but the NYPD's counterterrorism task force is checking security footage along that route."

"Let's get Paul on this, see what he can come up with," Williams said.

"Starting with Quantico and the usual channels or—?"

"His call," Williams decided. He liked delegating, not because he was lazy but because the alternative was to become a micromanager. He had selected his staff based on competence first, self-reliance second, and team-playing third. As former military, he could get any personnel to mesh as long as each member had the fundamental skill set.

Anne acknowledged with a nod and texted the new international crisis manager. Paul Bankole was recruited after the previous ICM, Hector Rodriquez, was killed in an assault on an ISIS compound in Mosul. Raised in poverty in Atlanta, Bankole was a former senior chief with the Navy SEALs who had served under Williams early in his military career. The young man had left a strong impression as a confident individualist who was also a team player. Wounded in a firefight, Bankole spent a year recuperating, during which time he became a computer specialist. He had a natural genius for all things technical, and after going to work for the ROTC program at the University of San Diego he came back on Williams's radar. He was the only candidate the Op-Center director considered to replace Rodriquez.

"Where's McCord?" Williams asked as he unzipped his backpack.

"At his weekly lunch with Allen Kim," she said.

"Right, right." Kim ran an FBI division out of Quantico that served as Op-Center's domestic wing. Ordinarily, the research into the murder of Galina Petrenko would have begun with his team. That's where Williams would have started. But the director also wanted to see what the new man came up with. "Have *you* eaten?" he asked.

"Fasting today," Anne said. "Annual physical after work."

Williams frowned. "Sorry. Could I have talked about lunches more?"

"I can take it," she said. "The rest of the briefing is on file—nothing exceptional in it, though you might want to think about the reports from Crimea, given this morning's developments. I'm going to review the West Coast files, see what's up in Asia."

Williams thanked her and waited until she had shut the door before setting two apples on his desk and going to the mini fridge to get the jar of peanut butter. He sat down and went right to the joint CIA Crimea Report while he ate. The comprehensive report on Russian and Ukrainian troop strength, deployment, communications, and forecasts was refreshed each morning with HUMINT, ELINT, and satellite surveillance.

The news was all on the factions opposing Russia. NATO was beginning a buildup that had previously been announced by SACEUR, the supreme allied commander in Europe, who was nearing the end of his three-year term.

Legacy move, Williams thought as he saw where the four battalion-size groups were being sent, a total of four thousand troops. They were reinforcing existing positions well within Romania and Poland, put in place to show that NATO took its self-defense responsibilities seriously if Russia moved first. The key word was "if." The orders linked to the deployment were what the DOD was now describing as "resistance-postured." The two words, compounded, was a forceful way of saying they were strictly peacekeepers.

Naturally, Russia was opening new installations near the border for its own "peacekeepers" and their ordnance.

Of more concern was the Polish defense minister's approval of an additional two thousand paramilitary personnel to join the four thousand already stationed in Estonia, Lithuania, and Latvia. The designation meant the troops had received a total of thirty days' military training. The numbers were bad, and the map itself seemed absurd on the surface: between NATO and the Polish paramilitaries, the new array looked like fingers pinching the tip of the nose of the Russian bear. It was even worse when the latest response from Moscow was factored in: in addition to the new bases and the existing thirty thousand troops, the Russians were mobilizing three motorized rifle formations of ten thousand troops each and had another two thousand paratroopers based in Ivanovo. The latter were apparently earmarked to bolster the forces that were manning the Iskander-M nuclear-capable missiles long entrenched in the region. Fortunately, there was no indication of warheads being moved to any of those locations.

"This is why the old days will not be returning," Williams said to himself as he crunched an apple slice. Not that he was nostalgic: classic trench-style warfare would result in widespread destruction, even if NATO's F-16 were a match for the Russian Su-27 fighter jets. The planes were; Williams wasn't so sure about the pilots. Aerial supremacy would lead to a Russian rout and decades of geographical ruin if the situation went all to hell. In addition, the U.S. would be pulled in, responsible for far more than the six hundred troops already on the ground there with NATO. The physical cost would be compounded by a financial cost that was untenable for both sides.

"Special Ops," he said softly. "Surgical strikes."

Remove the hardware, pluck the screws from the hardware, and men and materiel could go nowhere.

Williams closed the file and was just about to start on his second apple when the phone rang. It was Aaron Bleich, the intelligence director's networks leader.

"Go," Williams said.

"Sir, I just picked up something you should see," the thirty-two-year-old Bleich told him. "A game. Well, maybe not. It's a virtual-reality program. And not all of it, just pieces."

"You got it in the tank?" Williams asked, referring to the Geek Tank where the tech genius worked.

"I do."

"Be right there," Williams said, wiping his mouth as he strode toward the door.

CHAPTER THREE

New York, New York
June 2, 12:40 PM

In one hand Vladimir Eisenstein held a plate of uneaten cherry pie à la mode, ice cream melting over the sides. In the other, the young journalist held a smartphone, which he jabbed at Douglas Flannery.

"Surely, Mr. Ambassador, the Russians' claim to Crimea is no less legitimate than the Muslims' claim to Mecca or the Italians' to Rome."

"Muhammad is now on the same footing as Remus and Romulus, then?" Flannery asked.

"Roots are roots, sir, are they not?"

Flannery took a moment to stab a fork into the plate of melon he had taken from the buffet table. He had expected an earful from Eisenstein. Thirtysomething Putin-era journalists had suckled on nationalism. It was pure oxygen to them. Eisenstein himself had coined the "Make Russia Soviet Again" slogan and social media-ed the hell out of it.

"Mr. Eisenstein, I heard the 'Outstanding Forebear' argu-

ment many times while I was in Kiev," Flannery said. "I addressed it on the occasion of—"

"My first roundtable, and a solid but flawed position state-
ment," Eisenstein interrupted. "Crimea is not your state of Texas.
Local reverence for the heroes of the Alamo is a historical
usurpation, an emotional starting point, not a historic claim. San
Antonio is not the ancient city of Chersonesus, where Grand
Prince Vladimir, my namesake, was baptized in AD 988."

"A debatable point," Flannery said with a diplomat's patience. "Your selective, reductive recap ignores my government's
basic thesis, which is the danger presented by the clash of just
such emotional claims. Passion distorts fact, perspective, tram-
ples the compromises that are necessary for our global existence."

"A very pretty ideology," Eisenstein remarked. "You grew up
in Oklahoma, yes?"

"That's right."

"How would you have felt if Santa Anna had defeated General Houston at San Jacinto? Would you not have wanted Texas
back?"

Flannery grinned slightly. "Is this on the record?"

"Always," Eisenstein remarked, holding the phone toward
the former ambassador.

"On our farm in Oklahoma, I used to watch the big reapers
cut through corn," Flannery replied. "When I was old enough,
my father told me about Okinawa. He was with the Sixth
Marine Division. After he described what those landings were
like, I never looked at a reaper the same way. Cutting people down
that way must be a last resort. Longing for freedom is one thing.

Longing for ancestral territory—that's just not good enough, Mr. Eisenstein."

Flannery's mind flashed back to Galina's face as she departed— the hard, determined set of her mouth only slightly tempered by something softer in her eyes. He thought, at the time, that it was sadness, but now he wondered if it was fear. Almost as if they were begging him to get her the information she wanted . . . or to fix the situation by some diplomatic miracle before the machine of war became unstoppable.

"With respect, sir, I say that those pretty words fit a pretty ideology that has no footing in reality," Eisenstein said. He glanced to the left and right, where pockets of symposium attendees clustered nearby. "But I am keeping you from others who wish to wring their hands. Thank you for your time."

"Thank you for your views," Flannery said. "I do like to hear them."

"That is your job," the other man replied frankly.

Eisenstein smiled and turned away, setting the pie on a windowsill as he left. The man was smug, without the background to support it—only the indoctrination of his society and his professional affiliations, which gave heft, if not legitimacy, to his words.

Communists! Flannery thought. He wondered, abstractly, who the dessert belonged to: the Russian, the York group, or the glazier who made the china. There are too many Eisensteins, he thought dejectedly. Ideas were only as sound as the willingness to field-test them, not ram them down the throat of a population.

A reporter from the Cuban newspaper *Granma* turned toward Flannery. The ambassador was delighted when his smartphone sounded the chimes of Big Ben, since he wasn't in the mood for another Communist just then. It was Galina. He held a finger up to the man, who was approaching, and turned toward the windowsill. The Brick Rockies towered before him—the name his father had coined for Lower Manhattan when his troop ship sailed into the harbor.

"Hello, Ga—"

"It is not Galina Petrenko," a hard voice said at the other end. The voice was not female, and it also was not Ukrainian. It was Russian.

"I'm listening," Flannery said, instinctively hunching his shoulders and lowering his voice—an old diplomatic habit.

"You are American," the voice said.

It was a statement, not a question. Flannery did not respond.

"Galina is dead," the voice went on bluntly, but not quite casually. "I want to know why you were her last call."

The words made no sense, and then suddenly they did, hitting Flannery like a long, slow push against his belly. He was glad that he was already bending. He set his own plate beside Eisenstein's. It took him a moment to recover his breath and another moment to find his voice. He didn't use it, yet. He did draw a long, audible breath through his nose to let the caller know that he was still there . . . and to buy himself another moment.

The caller knew Galina, or, at least, who she was. Confirmation of her death—her murder—would come soon enough, either from the NYPD or from his own sources. There were other details: the caller had not yet had the time or the opportunity to trace Flannery's number or he would have addressed him by name—though that trace would be easy to accomplish, since the caller did not bother to ask for his identity. And one thing more. Flannery was accustomed to interpreting nuance in people's voices. There was an urgency in this one. He assumed it pertained to the tinderbox that Galina was helping to ignite—and that, being Russian, the caller was presumably trying to uncover and suppress.

Flannery raised his shoulders. "Did you put that question to her?"

"Be careful," the voice cautioned. "This is not a conversation."

"No, sir, it's an interrogation, but only if I participate," Flannery replied. "If I terminate the call—?"

"I will come for you."

"That costs you time."

"Not much."

"Enough that you did not want to waste it and risked this cold call," Flannery said. "I wonder if you will risk killing me when you know who I am."

The caller was silent now, but only for a moment.

"You didn't end the—*conversation*," the caller said. "What do *you* want?"

"I cannot speak now," Flannery replied. "I will call this phone in an hour."

Flannery knew that it would take anyone except American law enforcement at least that long to trace his private cell-phone number and dispatch personnel to where he lived and worked. It would probably take this individual considerably longer.

"Take no longer than that," the caller warned.

"I understand," Flannery said in a conciliatory tone—one that came with effort, with practice, with experience in talking to murderous despots and those who represented their interests.

He ended the call with a push of his thumb. And allowed the sickness he felt to rise.

Promising the Cuban reporter that he would return, Flannery moved with skillful steps through the crowd, left the reception room, and hurried to his office.

CHAPTER FOUR

Washington, D.C.
June 2, 12:53 PM

"I didn't think the food was *that* bad," Brian Dawson said, adding, "or the company."

Carolina Smith grinned as she slid from the booth. "Brian, some of us don't have government jobs. We *work* for a living."

"Ow."

"And some of us love what we do," she added. "You hated the gallery because of how much time I spent there. No reason to spoil a powerful dynamic now that we're not together."

"'Powerful dynamic,'" Dawson repeated as he signaled the waitperson. "That's artworld-speak, putting a layer of gesso on what some of us just call 'irreconcilable differences.'"

"Technically, that term only applies when you're married," the African-American woman said with a little smile. "At least my work was local. You weren't happy unless you were infiltrating hostile territory." She shook her head. "Now you're in—what did you call it at the Trade Rep's Christmas party? A rabbit warren. The universe does have its whims and ways."

Dawson glowered at the cloth napkin crumpled on the table. Damn her, she was right. In his brain, he was angry at the napkin for being just white cloth and not a flag.

"It was nice catching up," Carolina said, "but it reminded me why our assemblage didn't work."

Another art term. Had she always done this and he just hadn't heard?

Carolina smiled sweetly as the check arrived. "Thanks for lunch."

"Anytime," he said as she turned and walked away. "I mean that!" he added, but she was already checking her email.

Dawson was forgotten—again. Dumped by his current boss, dissed by his former "boss," he wondered why, at a time in life when most people really begin to flower, he could only smell the fertilizer.

Oh, to be in the field, bribing enemies, gathering intel, and planning the takeover of small countries, he thought. He was reaching into his sports jacket for his billfold when his phone beeped. It was a blocked caller. Ordinarily he would let it go to voice mail, but he was in the mood to snap at someone, even if it was a telemarketer. He clicked on Answer, then said nothing.

"Mr. Dawson?"

"Yes?" he answered tentatively. It *could* also be business. Not the president, but no one he wanted to piss off with an opening salvo.

"My name is Douglas Flannery. I got your number from Deputy Chief of Staff Matt Berry."

"I see. Are you his second?"

"I'm sorry?"

"Squash rematch. I killed him on—"

"Mr. Dawson, I am a former ambassador and I need to speak with you and your colleagues in a secure location as quickly as possible."

Dawson quietly thanked the universe and gave the waiter his American Express card as the mental tumblers began to fall into place. Ambassador Douglas Flannery—Ukraine, under the previous administration.

"I'm about to head back to my office," Dawson replied. "It should take me a half hour, traffic willing."

"I don't have much more time than that—" There was a heavy sigh at the other end. "Dammit."

"What?"

"A news item. A murder here in New York. He was telling the truth." There was another sigh. "I can't say more over an open line. As quickly as possible, please? At the highest levels?"

"I'm on my way," the Op-Center operations director replied. "I'll get everyone I can."

"Before a quarter to two, if possible," the ambassador reminded him.

Dawson checked his phone. It would be close, but it was doable.

The operations director phoned Anne as he made his way toward the Lafayette Park side of the restaurant. He felt a familiar rush from loins to chest, the kind he'd experienced often in the Army as Fifth Special Forces Group commander. A feeling that could be summed up in a single word: "Charge!"

It was also an attitude that had made him a lot of enemies in the service, like the time he was coordinator of the takeover of a small Central Asian country and was almost cashiered for setting himself up as the interim ruler.

"Annie—I need a meeting of the big boys and girls," he said, then added, "Threatcon high."

"Can you talk?"

"Negative. I'm about thirty minutes out."

"I'll set it up."

Dawson waited impatiently for the valet to bring his vintage Mustang, then turned onto Constitution Avenue NW and took it to U.S. 50 West. As he drove, Dawson asked the car tablet to bring up public data on Ambassador Flannery. He didn't want to call Matt Berry; if this were a setup, he could be revealing the private number of a White House chieftain, not to mention the fact that they wouldn't be able to discuss anything substantive, in any case.

He used the voice function to have the information read to him. He got the biography, a summary of eight years' service in Kiev—*l'affaire espionnage,* as his pre-Carolina French girlfriend Marie would have put it, a matter involving a Ukrainian staffer. He looked up the staffer's name.

She was dead, found with her throat cut in Manhattan at 12:55. The same time he was on the phone with Flannery. That probably explained the "Dammit."

By the time he'd finished his research, Dawson was on I-95 headed toward Richmond.

With an increasingly heavy, impatient foot, the OD made

the trip in just under twenty-five minutes. He was downstairs and walking briskly toward the boss's office less than a minute after that. Anne was at her post, dependable as the Statue of Liberty.

"They were already in the tank," she said. "The director wanted you to see something there when you got back."

"I love it when objectives dovetail," he said in earnest as he blew past.

Anne fell in, following him without seeming to hurry.

The Geek Tank was centrally situated in Op-Center's oblong maze of belowground offices. Anne had once referred to it as "a brain center located where the heart should be"—a comment that, to Dawson's schooled relationship ears, had carried some personal bitterness. Young experts and a handful of veterans cataloged and analyzed everything from weather patterns to maps so granular that mole hills could be charted; a chemist worked on ways to detect explosives packed in everything from hair weaves to the stuffing for plush animals; a duo known as Remus and Bombulus studied firearms and demotions. It was a busy concern even when there were no emergencies pending.

The two were allowed entrance by a palm-print reader beside the door and a facial-recognition monitor just above it. Inside, the layout was a smaller version of the Op-Center complex itself. The space was large and open, with low-walled cubicles. These were adorned with images of tech gods like Steve Jobs, Albert Einstein, Bill Gates, Stephen Hawking, and the occasional World of Warcraft or Warhammer 40K gaming posters. The workers here could discuss international conflict with intellectual cool, but bring up multiplayer online role-playing games versus tabletop miniature war games and you reignited, fittingly, Armageddon-in-progress.

An Adele song drifted across the room. The desks and occasional card tables were cluttered with pizza boxes, granola-bar wrappers, empty Slurpee and coffee containers, and notations in ink, grease pencil, and, in one spot, dried ketchup applied with a finger. The staff of eighteen eclectically dressed, twenty- and thirtysomethings created an energy here unlike that of any other space at Op-Center and unlike anything Dawson, Williams, or any of the others had experienced in the military. Anne had a thought about that, too, having described the tone here as "cheeky chic." She was right. The Geek Tank belonged in Op-Center, but outsiders didn't really belong here.

The new arrivals made their way to the single glass-enclosed corner office that belonged to Aaron Bleich. He was dressed in Dockers and a *Star Trek* sweatshirt, which set him apart from the other fanboys, who wore *Star Wars* attire—the source of another, lesser skirmish among them. A new sign above his door read Captain Kirk.

In addition to Chase Williams, James Wright, the domestic crisis manager, was present, along with Duncan Sutherland, the logistics director. Dawson and Wright got along like brothers. Wright was just two years older, and, as Mr. Washington Insider, he had the gift of schmooze that Dawson also possessed. Both were former military—though Wright had hung up his suit because of arthritis, not feather-ruffling—and both were divorced and aggressively single. Sutherland was more of a loner, a street kid from

Liverpool who had served in the British Army's Special Air Service and came to the States after marrying a local lady, a wealthy socialite. He and his wife had their own circle of friends—mostly upscale—in Chevy Chase and Georgetown.

Williams stood with his arms crossed imperially, like General MacArthur returning to the Corregidor. He looked over as the new arrivals approached. Bleich did not. He was wearing virtual-reality goggles, his head moving this way and that.

"Sorry about lunch," Williams said.

"That's okay," Dawson said as he retrieved his phone, checking the time and adding bitterly, under his breath, "I got to hear Carolina's latest regurgitation."

Hearing the comment, Williams remained carefully neutral, but Anne responded with an I-am-woman frown.

"What have you got, Brian?" the chief asked.

Dawson checked the time, then brought up the last number. "I've *got* a little over fifteen minutes to call back the former ambassador to Ukraine, Douglas Flannery. He contacted the president's DCOS and asked to get in touch with us."

"Any idea why?" Williams asked, concerned by the sudden proliferation of Ukraine.

Dawson was busy keying the phone back into Op-Center's security system. "No, though he became agitated when the news confirmed a murder in New York."

Williams and Anne exchanged looks.

"A Ukrainian woman?" Anne asked.

"That's right," Dawson replied.

"Call him," Williams said.

The boss's sharp, surprising reaction hurried Dawson along; he redialed the number Flannery had called from and put the call on speaker.

"You've reached the number of Ambassador Douglas Smith. . . ."

Dawson redialed. It went straight to voice mail a second time. He swore.

"Aaron, can you cut into a mobile conversation?" Williams asked.

"I'd need some time," the younger man replied, his head moving this way and that behind the goggles.

"How much time? Minutes?"

"Enough to make at least a half hour," Aaron replied.

"No good," Williams decided. "Brian, is there a receptionist, someone else you can call there?"

"I don't think he wants our involvement known," Dawson replied.

"Anne," Williams said, "let's get everything we can on the ambassador's day and his connections cross-referenced with whatever we can find on Galina Petrenko. And let's get McCord back ASAP. Sutherland, will you—?"

The thirty-six-year-old Sutherland was already calling the intelligence director.

"We should take this to my office," Williams said, uncrossing his arms and moving with a sense of urgency. "Aaron, you keep at it."

"Am."

"Brian, there's more you need to know," Williams said as they shouldered through the Tank.

Dawson nodded as he redialed a third time.

CHAPTER FIVE

Kiev, Ukraine
June 2, 8:45 PM

ABORT MISSION PROTOCOL: B2

The fire of the nine Ukrainian troops was swift and accurate. This drill was judged a failure by their accomplice on the ground, with ordnance not present for the mission. Leaving the compound area without having achieved their goal, they would have been met by enemy troops— shock troops who would have no idea how many of the enemy they were facing. It was difficult to tell how many there were in night-vision mode, with the surprised Russian defense forces falling back behind a new addition: an advancing tank brigade.

"Fall back to the denser tree line!" Major Romanenko shouted. "Team A, cover B."

As the forward four-man unit dug in, allowing the other three to retreat, the Russian tanks moved to within seven thousand meters of their position.

"Sir, I see an opening. I can still make the target—" Zinchenko of Team A said.

"Negative!" the officer shouted. "Withdraw."

This was different from Donbass, where the Ukrainians could hold their positions, hunker down, and wait for their own tanks from other bases in the surrounding area to join the fight.

"Team A, continue firing, maximum rate—don't save any ammo!" the major shouted over the secure radio.

There were two distinctive, blood-red flashes in his goggles. Zinchenko and Tkach went down. This was followed, almost at once, by a tank blast that took all of Team B plus Marchuk of A. The unit vanished in sound and churning olive clouds, but Marchuk died only meters from the major. He was torn nearly in half just below the rib cage, the edges of his Kevlar body armor frayed to tassels. Donbass had a dustoff, too, the capacity to evac by military helicopter. This covert mission had no backup.

It wasn't a fighting withdrawal, it wasn't even an unorderly withdrawal—it was a rout, a slaughter. The Russian shells ripped through the surrounding rocks, trees, and civilian structures without discretion and left them smoking husks on blackened, cratered ground.

Chorna dropped at the hands of a sniper, whom Romanenko placed much closer than he had anticipated, at only sixty-five meters. It was the last calculation the major made before his visor went red and he stopped moving.

He had been struck in the right hip and his view shifted to the horizontal. He had fallen on top of his weapon. Looking out, he saw Chorna move an arm.

Two of them were still alive. The mission was not quite finished. . . .

It was called Bionic Hill, and it was one of the preeminent high-tech centers in Europe. Co-founded by the first U.S. ambassador to Ukraine—whose consulting firm was responsible for developing the dynamic complex—it sprawled across 363 scenic acres in the heart of the great metropolis. Nearly thirty thousand people worked there, developing information and communication technologies, biotech and pharmaceutical innovations, and green, clean energy sources. The facility included a university and tenant space for firms that wished to partner with the Hill.

Buried in the orderly blocks of four-story glass-and-steel buildings was the office of Technological Support Laboratory Global, a vaguely named research division that had once been a part of the Special Operations Forces of the Armed Forces of Ukraine. After forming a secret alliance with the Shemona Group in Israel—a provider of state-of-the-art hi-tech military software and hardware—the TSL was shifted to civilian work.

But only officially.

Apart from the name there was no identification, military or otherwise, on the frosted glass doors. Inside, in seven thousand square feet of clean-lined tables and stools, thirty-seven scientists worked in a fraternal setting, creating state-of-the-art equipment for the SOF.

The only exception was a room, called the Long Barracks, which ran narrowly along the back of the facility. It had been specially selected for its location away from security cameras, away from the main pedestrian walks. It was about as wide and high and long as a pair of railroad cars. Despite the lack of sound-proofing, it was quiet—save for the occasional muted whoop or curse of someone inside.

The Long Barracks was run by a civilian, Havrylo Koval, a thirty-six-year-old who held a doctorate in computer science from Stanford University. Standing in the dark, he and five others were running a beta test on the plan that had been devised by one of the five—Major Josyp Romanenko of the Ukrainian Ground Forces, Operation Command East, and a frontline veteran of the War in Donbass. No one had a better firsthand knowledge of Russian hardware than the man who led the surveillance operations against the "humanitarian convoy" that Putin sent into Ukrainian territory.

Koval was merely an observer, and he had no avatar in the combat simulation. Which was fortunate: unlike the brawny five-foot-seven Romanenko, who had miraculously found places of concealment and narrow venues to advance in areas that weren't designed for those purposes, Koval would simply have stood on a real field of combat in terrified immobility.

In real life, the team was dressed in skintight gray motion-tracking suits that were captured by cameras set around the barracks and fed into the program. What anyone did in reality appeared in virtual reality, and vice versa. The simulation had been designed to accommodate the parameters of the Long Barracks. Whenever Koval noted any kinks or glitches in the program, they would take the new version into the Ready Room. That was in a separate building, a cross between a school gymnasium and an aircraft hangar. The team would spend several days there, cut off from outside communications, so that mission specifics could not be leaked or hacked.

Right now, only Chorna and Romanenko were still moving. Though they were both upright, their avatars in the simulation were lying on the raw, ugly ground. When the digital display in the lower right corner read 1900 hours, Romanenko barked a termination of the simulation. There were deep inhalations to break the tension, a few shallow breaths to relieve the fear. The fog of war had been vivid and shared. The loss had tasted real and crushing.

They were standing in the dark when everyone had removed their goggles. Koval turned the lights on in stages. The simulation was a combination of extremes, from night vision to incoming artillery to the flash-bang explosions the unit had deployed as soon as they got the abort call. Their eyes had been strained in subtle ways to merge the pixel-fine graphics into reality, and that required decompression.

Even after their breathing became regular, no one spoke. No one approached anyone else. This was not the time or place for second-guessing, recriminations, back-slapping, postmortems, or anything other than quiet self-analysis. Given voice, the emotions and adrenaline of combat, real or simulated, inevitably created or enlarged the fractures that come with any team. Romanenko preferred to debrief everyone individually after they'd had time to reflect. In what he stubbornly called "phase one of the war"— instead of the gentler deceptions and euphemisms the politicians and diplomats used to describe the 2014 invasion—Romanenko earned the nickname *niánia*, "the nanny," from his fellow officers for the way he both segregated and coddled his team. They didn't drink or whore with other units. They also weren't exposed to any of the systemic graft that cost the military $450 million that year. That was every dime of the money the United States had given to Kiev for the military. The major couldn't answer for fellow officers or their troops, but he would not tolerate less than one hundred percent mission focus, personal loyalty, devotion to country, and scrupulous honesty in his own team. Built into the virtual-reality program were randomly generated temptations like jewelry, hundreds of *kopiyoks*, pornographic images, and—most desirable of all—pouches of expensive Russian shag tobacco, lying on the ground. If anyone turned to examine them, the program pinged. If anyone stopped to retrieve them, the program stopped and everyone did knuckle push-ups.

Goggles in one hand, his assault rifle in the other, the stocky but thickly muscled Romanenko strode toward the weapons table in the far corner. He moved as if he were a bronze statue come to life—smooth and powerful, no wasted motion. After setting down his weapon and hanging his goggles on an aluminum rack, he went to the personal lockers that lined the far wall on the eastern side of the chamber. He spoke his name, and the sophisticated voice-recognition software popped the lock. The click seemed unnaturally loud in the artificial silence and the semidarkness. The major glanced at his mobile phone.

"Dismissed," he said in a loud, clipped voice. "Not you, Koval."

Without wasted motion, the others finished stowing their gear and left by the front door, the only door. They would do what they always did after a test: go to unit HQ and wait, in silence.

When they had filed out, Romanenko retrieved his cigarettes from the locker, lit one, and turned to the scientist.

"An email from Fedir," he said thickly. "Galina has been murdered. Only her phone was taken."

Koval, who was immune to the virtual violence, felt his legs weaken at the mention of Galina's death. He had never met the woman, but she had been an integral member of the operation since its inception.

"She was supposed to meet with Ambassador Flannery this morning," the major went on. "The timing suggests that she did."

"Then he is exposed," Koval said quietly.

"Galina was a professional, she may not have told him much," Romanenko said as he scrolled down a list of her telephone contacts, thumbed one, put the device on speaker, and handed it to Koval. The scientist would have to translate for the major.

"Who is this?" a man answered in a shaky voice.

The tone itself told both men that dangerous developments were already afoot. Romanenko touched his ear, indicating that he understood, then rolled a finger to indicate that Koval should listen first and translate later.

"Mr. Ambassador, I work—worked—with Galina Petrenko," the scientist said.

"Go on, quickly."

Koval had never met the ambassador, but Flannery was clearly a professional and obviously under pressure. The diplomat did not ask for information that would have been offered if the caller wanted it known, such as "Who is this?" or "Where are you calling from?"

"I am with the contact who is second in the queue in Kiev," Koval said. "He does not speak English—"

"You really weren't expecting to lose her, were you?" Flannery said.

"Mr. Ambassador—"

"No, listen. Whatever you're planning, the other side has turned up the heat. You've got to stand down."

In the growing light, Koval saw the fire in Romanenko's eyes. "That will not happen, sir," the scientist said. "If anything, I believe the schedule has just been accelerated." He waited a moment, then asked, "Was Galina able to secure your assistance?"

"I am uncommitted *and* deeply concerned," Flannery replied. He switched to Ukrainian. "You are on speaker—who else is there?" It was appropriate to ask that now. No one liked to be blindsided.

A cigarette-deepened voice replied, "The commando leader."

"Your name, sir?"

"It is not needed," the major replied. "What is needed, desperately, is the information Galina Petrenko sought."

"Sir . . . what is needed is *patience*," Flannery said. "Diplomacy moves slowly, but, like Galileo's earth, it *does* move. Any action, covert or otherwise, will rightly be perceived as a provocation."

"This matter has been debated and decided."

"By your government?"

"Our government is powerless," Romanenko replied. "They have no motivation to achieve anything of consequence. Not when they are in a position to simply manufacture medals and honors while pressing for foreign aid—which the military will never see."

"Then your plan is not known or sanctioned by the government?" Flannery pressed.

"The prime minister and members of Parliament have not been consulted," the major replied.

"'Members,'" Flannery said, his mind attuned to the use of language. "Were *all* members not consulted?"

"All members . . . have plausible deniability," Romanenko answered.

Flannery's exhalation told the Ukrainians what they already knew: that was not the answer he wanted to hear. The truth was that several militant members of Parliament were aware of *a* plan, but not this plan, and it had their tacit approval. If successful, it would have their vocal support.

"Gentlemen, I am late for a call . . . no, two," Flannery said. "I must speak to you later."

"Only if there is a reason to continue this conversation," Romanenko said. "Otherwise, we thank you for your time and for seeing Galina. We pray that some part of her spirit lives on in you."

The scientist ended the call. The major nodded appreciatively.

"You should have become a diplomat," Koval said.

"I don't have the tongue for it," the major replied. "Or the stomach."

"You have the patience and determination—I've seen you work," Koval said.

The major began walking to the exit.

"Major!"

The officer stopped and turned.

"How should I modify B2?" the scientist asked.

"Add undefused land mines," he said.

"You want it . . . *more* difficult?"

"Absent the ordnance to destroy the pressure plates, we should not assume we got all of the mines going in," Romanenko said. "What if we didn't?"

"But the mission and the retreat both failed without that added challenge."

"When you lift weights competitively, you train with more than you will ever need to press," Romanenko said, exhaling smoke. "When you jog, you run with ankle weights. This is no different."

"I understand the theory—"

"It's more than theory," Romanenko insisted, taking a few steps toward Koval. "Getting all the mines delayed Chorna and threw our timing off by six full minutes. What if he skipped a few outlyers and was then on point for Team B instead of having to fall in, rear guard? Or, even as things were, I could have sent Zinchenko through the opening he saw and ordered Team A forward in support. And two of us were still alive. The mission was not optimal, but it was not over. We will try again in sixty minutes, if you can add the mines by then?"

Koval looked at him a moment longer, then nodded. "Of course."

Alone in the Long Barracks, under full illumination, Koval had to admit that the man had logistical points. As a commander, Romanenko also factored in ephemerals like "will" and "adrenaline" and "camaraderie" and even "competition," elements that did not figure in Koval's work.

The scientist left the room, his eyes happier in the darkness outside the facility. He thought briefly of Galina, of her career, her courage, her patriotism. He felt the stab of the loss but, more important, he felt a flush of inspiration. In the distance, he saw a searchlight stabbing the sky for Russian aircraft. It wasn't much of a deterrent, but it was what the major called a placeholder: it let Putin know that Kiev was not complacent. It was simply in stand-down mode.

For now.

CHAPTER SIX

Op-Center Headquarters, Fort Belvoir North,
Springfield, Virginia
June 2, 1:04 PM

The walk from the Geek Tank to Williams's office took less than a minute, but it was enough time for the director to privately give Anne a quick assignment and then explain to Dawson what Bleich had found.

"A multiplayer game written by a buddy at Stanford, first-person shooter," Williams said. "He's looking for a government job and parts of it ended up on his reel. All of that is common enough, I'm told. What was different is the location of this game. It is built on a basic template that could be one of three Russian bases very close to the Ukrainian border: Voronezh to the southeast, Sudzha to the northeast, or the naval base at Sevastopol—"

Dawson frowned. "The port facility in Crimea that's being expanded even before it's finished?"

Williams nodded.

"I can see where the Ukrainians would want to take that one out," Dawson said. "Putin's thumb squarely in their eye."

"By treaty," Anne pointed out, "signed in 2015 for a twenty-five-year period."

"Where I come from, having a twelve-inch, forty-caliber gun to your head is called extortion," Dawson said.

"Regardless," Williams said, "those three bases are all undergoing a similar and ongoing expansion, which is what caught Aaron's attention. The game includes their standardized expansions."

"Nice to know the kid reads the intel reports I send out," Anne remarked pointedly from behind them.

"Sudzha is on the verge of being operational," Williams went on. "The other two expansions will be ready within a month or two. Those would be perfect targets for Special Ops forces."

"No military advantage other than a blow to Putin's pride," Dawson said. "And it would make tactical sense to take on walls that are not quite ready to be defended."

"A good reason to pick the most difficult of the three," Anne said, looking at images from space. "The trees in the VR don't give us any clues. All the bases have plantings for concealment."

"Is there signage anywhere in the VR?" Dawson asked.

"Nothing," Williams said. "This seems to be an alpha version that was sent somewhere else for completion."

"Right," Dawson said. "The finish would probably have more graphic details about the base as well. I'm assuming the game was commissioned—"

"The RES on Aaron's team tried to find out who, what, where," Williams said as they reached his office. He was referring to the reverse-engineering specialist, Charlene Squires, the daughter of Op-Center's former military leader Charlie Squires. "She said it was an anonymous buyer, cash. But here's the interesting thing: there were obviously no restrictions on the software, no proprietary or confidentiality agreements. That's how it ended up on the reel."

"Restrictions might not have mattered," Dawson said. "I've never known a designer who doesn't like to show off. It's the post-Gates, post-Jobs generation. I see them in bars sometimes, running at the mouth. They're the new jocks, except their secrets can't handle anything harder than Amstel Light."

"*Or* it could be carelessness," Anne suggested, hearing something bitter—about bars, not nerds—creeping into Dawson's voice. "Or an 'If I don't do this, no one will ever know I did it' from the designer."

"Possibly," Williams agreed. "Duncan, you had a thought on that?"

"Yeah." The logistics director, who had been walking behind Anne, shouldered past. "Someone wanted it to be picked up," he said in a Liverpudlian accent that seemed to have been duplicated precisely across an entire population. "Someone wanted to see how the Russians would react to a simulated attack on one of their forward bases."

"Why prod the big bad bear?" Dawson thought aloud, then answered his own question. "To make them drill, see how they would deploy a counterattack?"

"I'd do it to tie up their resources defending three bases and not harassing Ukraine," Duncan told him.

"Damned dangerous brinkmanship," Dawson said. "Putin sees that video, he's likely to use it as a reason to go back to war."

"Sometimes what sounds good in a situation room doesn't jibe with what's real-world smart," Anne pointed out.

Dawson considered this as they filed into the office, Wright giving his close friend a slap on the shoulder, fingers squeezing twice. The gesture was a language unto itself: this one said, "You have the look of a man who's seen a ghost; we'll talk later."

The time to contact the ambassador had come and gone, but Dawson tried one more time.

He got through, and immediately put the phone on speaker.

"Mr. Ambassador," Dawson said with relief.

"You are in a secure area?"

"Yes, sir, with four of our top people, including Director Williams."

"Thank you—thank you very much. I will have to talk quietly. We had a symposium on peace in Crimea. Some of the attendees are still here."

"They have all been vetted, you know them?" Williams asked.

"I do. But I cannot go suspecting my friends and colleagues now, even the ones I dislike."

To everyone who heard it, the man's voice sounded tired, beaten. While the rest of the team sat, Anne and Dawson remained standing.

"You have the floor, sir," Dawson said.

There was a sigh. "It's late. I should be calling—" Flannery stopped, sighed again. "He will have to wait, but I will be brief.

A woman was murdered today. She was a Ukrainian intelligence operative. She came to me, asking for my help. She wanted data on the movement of Russian armored columns toward Ukraine."

Dawson held up three fingers and turned a thumb down. That eliminated the naval base at Sevastopol as a target.

"Did she offer any evidence, details?" Dawson asked.

"All she said was that six armored columns were reportedly going to be involved," Flannery replied. "She said that her people in the Kremlin had 'disappeared'—presumably, those who had acquired this information—and she wanted more information from inside the ground forces of the Russian Federation."

"Wanted it for whom, exactly?" Williams asked.

"She didn't say," Flannery replied.

The ambassador had hesitated almost imperceptibly before answering. Everyone noticed.

"Do you have any thoughts on the ultimate receiver?" Dawson asked.

"I believe it is paramilitary," Flannery said.

"Based on what information?" Dawson asked.

"I just received a call from the commando leader."

Everyone in the room was stunned.

"Go on," Williams said.

"That's all there is, really," Flannery told them. "I talked with two men. One spoke English, neither would provide his name. They only repeated the request Galina had made . . . that I help them. I implored him to give diplomacy a chance. He refused." Flannery drew a long, shaking breath. "He refused with an anger I heard far too often there . . . usually from officers who have been restrained from action."

It took a moment for everyone to process that information.

"No phone number? No location?" Wright asked.

"Blocked," Flannery replied.

"Do you have access to the kind of information they wanted?" Williams asked.

"Not directly, no," Flannery admitted. "Galina Petrenko was relying on an old—let's call it a concern I had for her well-being to motivate me."

Williams couldn't help smiling at that. In some form, that approach was older than Mata Hari. And usually effective.

"After she was murdered," Flannery went on, "before it was on the news, her killer—I assume it was he—called on her phone and wanted to know why she came to me. He threatened my life if I didn't reply . . . seven minutes ago."

"I'm guessing he was Russian?" Dawson said.

"His English was spit-and-polish, Moscow-inflected," Flannery said.

"Do you feel safe now? Are you going to call him?"

"To the former, at the moment I do. To the latter—what do you recommend?"

All eyes shifted to Williams.

"Do you want to have a dog in this fight?" the director asked. "If you tell him what he wants to know, you can probably walk away from this. If you don't—"

"Jim Wright here," the domestic crisis manager interjected. "Mr. Ambassador, you said he's got Galina's phone. If he called you, it's unlocked. That probably gives him access to other members of her unit, here and possibly abroad."

"She said it was a burner—there may not be anything on it," Flannery said.

"Which is why he needs you," Wright said, "which may—with respect, Chase—which may mean he will want you to use your access to get intel for *him*."

"Flip you," Dawson said. "Double agent."

"I'm no one's agent," Flannery said. There was another silence. "I have a missed call," he said suddenly. "From him."

"Mr. Ambassador, we have to believe he will come after you," Dawson said. "Is there anything you can tell him that wouldn't give him too much but would keep you safe?"

Flannery was quiet for a long moment. "He seems a resolute man," the ambassador said. "Mr. Dawson, Matt Berry at the White House speaks very highly of your organization. Is this situation something you can help me with, officially or not?"

"'Or not' is what we do best," Dawson replied, only half in jest.

"Are you asking us to help you?" Williams asked. "Or are you looking for us to help manage this situation?"

"No good diplomat ever thinks of himself," Flannery replied. "Personal risk comes with the job."

Anne applauded silently.

"Mr. Dawson, I'm going to call him," Flannery went on.

"And say what?" Dawson asked.

"What diplomats invariably say," the ambassador replied. "We try to talk nations off the ledge."

"This Russian fellow is probably *not* a statesman," Williams warned.

"What else can I do?" Flannery asked. "This mission—it may be a fiction designed to make the Russians paranoid, and it may never be launched. If I tell him the unadorned truth, more people will die needlessly."

"If you say nothing, they will die the way Galina did while he looks for information," Dawson said.

"Mr. Ambassador," Williams said, "would you allow us to listen to the call?"

"Frankly, I was hoping you'd ask," he said. They heard a chair squeak and roll. "There's a conference phone in the conference room. I'm going to chase out whoever is in there now. I'll call back on Mr. Dawson's phone."

"Call back on mine," Williams said, giving him the number. "If we need to contact you, that will come from Brian."

"Very well," the ambassador said, and clicked off.

"A conference phone in the conference room," Anne said. "The world still has pockets of symmetry."

"You know, there's an ugly fit with the game Aaron found," Wright remarked, scrolling through data on his tablet. "The Fourth Guards Kantemirovskaya Tank Division has just been or is about to be relocated to the base at Sudzha."

"Exactly what Galina wanted to know," Dawson remarked.

"A life sacrificed for a line of data on a tablet," Anne said.

"We need live surveillance of that facility," Williams said. "More important, the area around it."

As if on cue, Paul Bankole entered the office. The forty-

eight-year-old international crisis manager was an imposing figure, standing just over six feet two and walking with a slight limp
that gave him a lopsided but powerful tread.

"Where and when?" he asked.

Williams acknowledged the veteran's can-do attitude with
a little nod. The director brought him up to date, and Bankole
walked to the corner of the room to send a text. As he did, Dawson's phone beeped. The bald-headed, African-American operations
director looked around to make sure everyone was quiet—
Bankole indicating that he understood with a nod. Dawson accepted the call.

". . . had something else that needed to be taken care of,"
Flannery was saying.

"Warning others?" the caller asked.

"I know no others," the ambassador replied.

"Galina thought differently."

Flannery didn't take the bait.

"Very well," the Russian said. "What *do* you know?"

"Only this," Flannery said. "If you don't stand down, if you
don't let me intercede on behalf of *both* sides, a great many
people—"

"Will die, yes," the Russian said. "Sad, but my concern is
much narrower, Mr. Ambassador. What did Galina Petrenko
want from you? This is the last time I will ask . . . over the phone."

While they were speaking, Dawson urgently grabbed a
notepad from Williams's desk and wrote something. The director
looked at the note, then nodded.

Dawson texted the contents to Flannery.

There was a lull in the conversation.

"Ambassador Flannery?" the caller said. "Your answer."

Flannery was silent a moment longer. After what seemed a long, tortured wait that dragged into dinnertime, Dawson heard in a tired, forlorn voice what he had been hoping to hear.

"Galina asked for information about your armored columns by the border."

CHAPTER SEVEN

St. Petersburg, Russia
June 2, 8:15 PM

Sitting behind his desk in the ornately columned General Staff Building, Western Military District Headquarters, Colonel General Anatoly Yershov was gazing at his computer, watching video of a tank engagement. Born in 1963 in Derbent, on the Caspian Sea, Yershov used to watch silent, black-and-white, 8-mm. combat footage on his home projector. His father was a wounded veteran who owned a general store and used to show the two-hundred-foot reels to children on Sundays, along with cartoons. Strife followed by laughter—it was somehow an apt mix.

Yershov preferred the war footage. The jerky moves of the camera, the power of the explosions, the black smoke that seemed to throb, the uniforms as dirty as the men, just like when he played with the other boys in the old quarry—

Of course, death was never shown. Not like the hi-definition video on his computer.

When he graduated from the Krasnoyarsk Polytechnic Institute in 1985, with a degree in civil engineering, Yershov attended the Kazan Higher Tank Command School and was given a battalion of the Far Eastern Military District. The tall gray-eyed man was outwardly steely, like his tanks; only his wife, Lelya, knew that—also like his tanks—there was a man inside.

That man sat in the semidarkness now, and was focused. There was a meeting soon to come, a very special one. He tried not to think of that and paid attention to what he was watching. Though he had seen it many times before, he never knew when he might spot something he had missed, some maneuver, some delay or some small unexpected movement of a tank in the Ukrainian command.

Asymmetrical warfare. The unpredictable nature of those old films was also something that kept him riveted . . . looking for patterns. Even then, he was an engineer seeking order from chaos.

The footage was shot on a spring afternoon in 2014, when a Russian tank column engaged a small division of four T-55s and three T-54s commanded by Captain Taras Klimovich, a young warrior nicknamed the Fox for his swift, unpredictable movements.

Brave but a showoff, Yershov thought, watching the way Klimovich stood in the turret. A *molokosos*, he thought, using his grandmother's term for a youth, a "milk sucker." Although the Ukrainian tanks were old, they were simple and robust—which meant that they were reliable. Their D-10T 100-mm. rifled gun was inferior to most tank guns in the West or in Russia, but it could pump out a half-dozen rounds per minute, and hit a target sixteen thousand meters away.

"There it is," Yershov said, leaning forward slightly as he watched the battle unfold. "The disbursement, like a flower opening."

The most important advantage for Klimovich and his small division had nothing to do with armor or armament. They knew the terrain and had drilled endlessly in war games that anticipated just what was happening right now. While they remained out of range of the Russian tank column, Klimovich had his seven tanks split up and dashed through the foothills west of Labkovicy, hiding from the presumed Russian air cover that they expected would be following the T-90 column. But there was no air cover: the Russians had a rotary-wing Kamov Ka-137 up as a spotter. The unmanned aerial vehicle was also recording the battle.

"Textbook," Yershov said to himself. "Hide if you can. Create multiple targets on terrain familiar to you, not to the enemy."

He saw how the lead Russian tanks didn't move as tentatively as they should have. That was General Novikov's way. *Get there*—reach the target, hammer them hard, burn through your reserves to dispirit, kill, and crush them before they could attack you.

Unfortunately for the Russians, actionable data from their UAV was slowed by the intervening terrain: trees corrupted the signal, and sunlight obscured key portions of the wooded area. Conversely, the Ukrainian tank division had line-of-view contact with their own Altair UAV recently purchased from Germany. Flying fourteen kilometers overhead and two kilometers to the east, well beyond the trees, the Altair—a European version of the American Predator B—had a clear view of the enemy tanks surging west as they emerged from the pine forest on the Russian side of the border.

And then, as the flylike proxies buzzed overhead, the action commenced on the ground: at twelve thousand meters, the T-90s commenced running down an incline with their gun muzzles depressed below an effective firing angle for fully one hundred seconds. He let a half dozen of the enemy start down the hill before opening fire, to devastating effect.

The Russian commander watched the video without feeling the sickness he'd felt the first time, seeing his column stricken along its flank. He watched, as he had many times, the Fox's actions.

"Once revealed, you force the enemy to divide and deploy, but after you hit them with your first salvo," Yershov murmured.

The audio was as distant as the images of destruction. The D-10T rifled gun began spitting out 100-mm. shells that roared toward the Russian tanks at a thousand meters per second. Well within the gun's effective firing range, spear after spear of charcoal-gray smoke flew from the six tanks like noxious demons, rooted to the metal exterior of the tanks by bright red-yellow flashes. The vehicles hopped and swerved like wounded animals, fully half of them coming to a halt, the other half running with treads impaired, steering impossible. Those tanks that could retreat did. Those that could not lost their young crews to long stays in the Zamkova Correctional Colony.

"And that, sadly, is how one man falls and another rises."

It had been three years since Yershov replaced Colonel General Nikolai Novikov as commander of the Western Military District . . . three long years to wait for a chance to avenge the shameful rout of the Russian tank command. He would never forget the look on Novikov's face when he came to assume this post. The general had lost parts of two fingers in the battle when the turret hatch of his tank closed on his hand. He always wore a glove thereafter—though the effect it had was to call attention to the naked hand, the hand that no longer belonged to a warrior.

Yershov would learn now whether he would get the chance that had wormed through his thoughts for those three years.

The video was a forceful reminder of overconfidence and failure, both of which, thus far, were foreign to him. He had worked under Novikov in Tactics and Logistics during the original Crimean incursion, and had written the white papers describing how to fight a modern skirmish—guidelines that Novikov had brashly ignored, woefully underestimating the enemy's resourcefulness.

He would have a chance to right that wrong and also to—

The door of the large office opened quietly and a young senior lieutenant appeared, silhouetted against the darkness.

"General, the motorcade is arriving."

Though the young man spoke quietly, there was palpable excitement in his voice. Yershov acknowledged with a nod and the door was shut. The general rose. He brushed his big hands down the front and sides of the proud olive tunic with red piping. He took his hat from the desk and fixed it under his arm, then walked slowly around the desk. His belly began to burn with uncharacteristic anticipation. This was a moment unlike any other in his life . . . different from moments in most lives.

His boot heels thumped softly on the carpet, then loudly as he entered the bright corridor of the two-century-old neoclassical edifice. The lieutenant was waiting for him and fell in behind the general as they continued across the tiled ground-level hall to the main entrance.

Yershov was at attention, as was the lieutenant behind him, as the Mercedes-Benz S-Class stretch limousine came to a stop between four other vehicles and a noisy police escort. The sedan looked like burnished coal under the bright spotlights of the main entrance. The sleek armored car had solid rubber tires and, above the hood on the passenger side, stood a rigid flag emblazoned with the ancient likeness of a double-headed imperial eagle, the orb and scepter of power in its talons. Unlike many of the older tanks in Yershov's command, this vehicle could withstand a direct hit from a rocket.

Unlike many of those tank crews, millions of people in this region of the world wanted the occupant of the state car dead, the general thought.

Police and men in dark suits leaped from their vehicles and converged on the Mercedes, assault rifles in hand, eyes searching. Most of that was for show—or perhaps for the vanity of the man inside. No one had known about this visit, and very few people would: Yershov only just realized that there was no press, no state photographer. The Kremlin spokesperson, Valentina Zharov, was not present.

From the far door, Yershov saw Maksim Timoshenko, the

Russian Federation's minister of defense, emerge. He looked directly at Yershov without expression—which was his usual expression—then came around the back of the vehicle. At the same time, a familiar figure eased from the door that his security detail had opened for him. He stood five feet seven and was dressed in a tailored suit the color and sheen of gunmetal. There was no jacket against the crisp late-spring air rolling off the Gulf of Finland. The man wore no tie below a face that seemed almost angelic, almost like a painting he had long-admired, *Saint Luke Drawing the Virgin*; his button-down white shirt was open at the top. That was a clear statement saying, "I am here so this visit is important, but my presence is also not official."

Yershov snapped out a strong salute as Vladimir Putin entered, followed by Timoshenko. The men returned it, followed by shakes, the Russian president clasping the elbow of this man he had never met—this general on whom a great honor was about to be bestowed.

For why else come all the way to St. Petersburg, except to endorse—without a written order and with full deniability—the course of action Yershov had been urging. Why else come to St. Petersburg except for security, since Timoshenko was in the process of rehabilitating a ministry that he had described as "perilous with leaks, like the roof of Khrushchev's old country dacha." Only recently, a pair of Ukrainian spies had been working as translators in Counterterrorism Operations.

His arm extending, Putin turned Yershov around with a slap on the much taller man's shoulder, and the minister fell in beside the commander. Then the lieutenant—his presence unacknowledged—guided the men back to Yershov's office, four sets of heels clacking like the military footfalls in Red Square on May Day, echoing through the corridor and across time, the familiar sounds of men prepared to make new war. . . .

CHAPTER EIGHT

Op-Center Headquarters, Fort Belvoir North,
Springfield, Virginia
June 2, 1:22 PM

Douglas Flannery's voice was emotionally charged as he ended the call with the Russian.

"Would someone please explain what you had me do?" the ambassador demanded.

Chase Williams's look told Dawson that he should continue running the conversation. The operations director put the phone on his knee, wiped his sweaty hand with a handkerchief.

"Sir, we've uncovered information here that the Ukrainians may, in fact, have wanted the Russians to know that they have their eye on the armored column—and, in particular, one of the three expanded bases where they're stationed."

"Why would anyone do something so *obviously* dangerous?" Flannery asked.

"That's what we're trying to figure out, sir," Williams said.

"What—what kind of information?" Flannery asked.

"A software program, Mr. Ambassador. I can't say more than

that right now," the director said. It was his call, no one else's, whether to release secret information.

"What if you're wrong?" Flannery said.

"We found it," Dawson said. "They surely did. They killed once for more information . . . they won't stop there."

"They killed Galina for intelligence they think they gleaned . . . from a computer game?" Flannery said with disbelief.

"It's possible," Dawson said. "Unless they tortured the spies Ms. Petrenko said they uncovered in the Kremlin."

"Two pieces of information leading to the same place," Williams said.

"Galina . . . she mentioned that the spies in New York were usually—well, she made it sound as if they were actually cooperative," Flannery said. "You must be right."

"I think our intelligence director could explain Russian cells and their relation to Ukrainian cells better than I could." Dawson looked over at Paul Bankole. "For our benefit, if nothing else."

Bankole wasn't entirely sure what was going on, but Dawson had given him enough to tee off. "Intelligence cells are like organized crime—sometimes they feel the need to thin the ranks of the opposition. Unless there is a specific trajectory to the assassinations—for instance, to eliminate what we call the 'bloodline,' every member of a specific team—this goes back and forth randomly until both sides have had enough."

"This certainly smells like bloodline," Dawson confirmed.

"Then if we have favorites up or down that particular ladder, they should be alerted," Bankole said. "Quickly."

"Ambassador Flannery?" Williams said. "Do you know others?"

"I do not," he said. "My God, all Galina had to do was tell them what I just told them and she would still be alive. Such a waste."

"Mr. Ambassador, we don't know what the big picture is and what else the Russians may be looking for," Dawson said. "It may also have been a long-simmering turf battle, as Paul indicated."

"I don't mean to sound cold, but that's in the past," Williams said. "We have to talk about what happens next. Mr. Ambassador, would you mind staying on the line?"

"If I can help," Flannery said flatly.

"I'm sure you can, thank you," Williams replied.

The ambassador's low, sad monotone threw the room into its own mild depression. Williams leaned over and grabbed a bottle of water, unscrewed the cap, and took a long swallow. His palms were wet but his mouth was dry. Anne was wrong: the world was still off balance.

"Chase," Anne said, her tablet cradled in one forearm, "are we opening a general file or adding this to Aaron's work?"

"New," he said.

That nudged everyone into a higher level of alertness. Williams clearly thought there was a growing threat here. They all did. Only now it was official.

"There are suddenly a lot of moving parts," Wright said, looking down at his smartphone. "More than we've said." He waggled the phone and looked at Williams. "I just got an NYPD counterterrorism alert. The wound on the dead woman matches the way an Estonian diplomat was killed last year in Chinatown."

While everyone was processing that information, the ambassador spoke.

"That was Maarten Laht," Flannery said. "Very outspoken, virulently anti-Putin."

"Was that a lone-wolf hit or is there a connection?" Williams asked.

"The killer was never found," said the domestic crisis manager. "But—hold on." Wright was typing on his phone. "Mr. Laht was not a contract killing, as far as we could determine. None of our for-hire sources had heard of it. Forensics on that killing," he continued typing, reading, "showed traces of—oh boy, what they described as plastic with 'lacing,' a substance used to create a brushed-metal appearance on credit cards. One of our contacts in the Ukraine Security Service *heard* of a Russian who killed, presumably, with a sharpened credit card after a man was found dead in the Nikitsky Botanical Garden in Crimea. Flecks of gold paint were found in the wound. The dead man was a journalist, Stanislav Vovk."

"Who, I'm guessing, opposed the Russian invasion," Dawson said.

Bankole nodded.

"So, an assassin, loyal to Putin, killed Laht and now most likely Galina," Williams said. "What does that get us?"

"A starting point," Bankole said. "Our killer is an *institutional* assassin, someone who watches only certain groups, probably one at a time—so he can also watch his own back against retaliation—and has a great deal of latitude for independent action."

"A license to kill," Dawson said.

"In a way, yes," Bankole said. "If this individual has been charged with eliminating Ukrainian assets or impediments—" He paused. "I'm sorry, Mr. Ambassador. I didn't mean to be impersonal there."

"I understand," Flannery said.

"My point is, this killer clearly moves around and is probably very knowledgeable about other Russian agents working around the globe," Bankole said. "He's going to be like a dog with a bone on this one, looking for anyone who can tell him more. And, once again—quickly."

"I want this," Dawson said suddenly.

Williams regarded him. "Want what?"

"New York, the assassin," Dawson said. "I want to find him."

"Why?"

"Why? As a primary conduit for international or domestic crisis response—"

"Brian, I wrote that job description," Williams said, cutting him off.

Anne scowled at Dawson, who should have known better than to quote the regulations to Williams.

"Okay," Dawson said. This time he thought for a moment before speaking. The truth was, this command center was closing in. He didn't want to sit here and think, he wanted to go to New York and *act*. Carolina—she'd made him want to run anywhere,

and that would pass, but he was eager to be in the field again—
any field.

"Okay . . . ?" Williams pressed.

"We have to find the point of origin here," Dawson said,
this time more thoughtfully. "We have to see what, if any, American interests beyond our diplomat may be at risk. This killer
probably knows every move in the NYPD and FBI playbooks.
Let me see if I can surprise him. We may only get RUMINT, but
even rumors and gossip will give us something."

Williams took only a moment to decide. He could tell that
the former Fifth Special Forces Group commander was restlessly
eager, but Dawson was also a good man in the field. And Williams would still have Anne and the rest of the team. Op-Center
didn't have many redundancies, but it had great people capable of
multitasking.

"Take Mike," Williams said.

Dawson frowned. "We need subtle. Even in civvies, the guy
screams 'soldier on leave.'"

"Which is exactly what you'll need in case you find what
you're looking for," Williams said with a take-it-or-leave-it expression. "And you two have a history."

"So does Ukraine and Russia," Dawson said.

"I'll alert him," Anne said before Dawson could protest further.

Based at Fort Bragg, North Carolina, Mike Volner was the
Joint Special Operations Command leader for Op-Center, responsible for organizing and deploying all military operations
ordered by Williams.

Before terminating the connection with Flannery, Dawson asked the ambassador how much longer he would be in his office.

"I usually leave around six," he replied.

"Would you mind, sir, waiting until I contact you?" Dawson asked. He looked at his watch. "I should actually be in your neighborhood about that time."

"I'll do that," the ambassador replied. "Thank you."

Dawson thanked him and killed the connection.

The operations director left with Anne while Williams reviewed departmental matters and general housekeeping with staff members. As Dawson himself had once put it, "Even in a crisis, the bureaucracy soldiers on."

Anne turned to him when they were in the corridor. "Whatever is on your mind, it's scrambled eggs," she said.

"Yeah, there's a lot going on, but that doesn't mean I can't do this without a twenty-nine-year-old 40 Mike-Mike," the operations director complained.

The play on Volner's name was a reference to an M-16 mounted M203 grenade launcher—a slam at the young veteran's penchant for blunt, some would say, action.

"Did it occur to you that Chase was doing you a favor?" Anne asked.

"How?"

"After we left the Tank, he told me to put Mike and another JSOC team member on standby."

"For New York?"

She nodded. "You bumped Sergeant Moore. He has family in Brooklyn. He won't be happy."

Dawson scowled. "Okay. So I put my foot in that one."

"You did," she agreed. She pointed a finger at her tablet. "Was there anything else? I've got to arrange for transportation with the travel office."

"No, sorry, thanks," Dawson said as if they were a compound word. It was a bad habit of his, becoming flustered whenever women were incontrovertibly right. Again.

"I'll text you your departure information," she said.

Dawson smiled awkwardly and left, just as the others were filing out of Williams's office. The men were all engaged in pockets of conversation except for his buddy Wright, who was on the phone. He shut the door behind him and gave Dawson a thumbs-up. It was the crisis manager's usual hail-fellow-well-met departing gesture—but right now it was a lifeline.

Feeling settled suddenly, Dawson turned and headed for the elevator.

CHAPTER NINE

St. Petersburg, Russia
June 2, 8:33 PM

The large conference room was wood paneling and marble, oil paintings and vintage globes, overhead lighting that bordered on candlit-amber—a respect for the past without the particular heritage represented by the czars and their abuses.

The president encouraged Yershov to enter before him, with the defense minister bringing up the rear and shutting the door behind him. Water glasses and crystal decanters had been set before three places at the rectangular burl conference table. Here Vladimir Putin went directly to the head of the table. He extended his arms to both sides and the men all sat in unison. It was a silent display of respect by the officers and of silent command by the leader.

It gave Yershov an unprecedented thrill. This general who had walked down the aisle at a very young and uncertain age, who had been in combat, who had seen a Soyuz-FG booster rip from its moorings and carry a crew into space—this unsheltered witness to history suddenly felt as if the world revolved around this place, this moment. He had listened over and over to the speech the president had given before Parliament a year earlier, on the seventy-fifth anniversary of Nazi Germany's military aggression against the Soviet Union. Putin had been speaking for men like Yershov when he said, "NATO is strengthening its aggressive rhetoric and its aggressive actions near our borders. In these conditions, we are duty-bound to pay special attention to solving the task of strengthening the combat readiness of our country."

But it was more than Putin's nationalism, more than his charisma, more than his attitude. Power was not an incident; it was a physical and spiritual *quality* unlike anything Yershov had ever experienced.

There were notepads at each seat but no electronics. There were no security cameras in the room. This meeting was not only off the record; it was off the radar. It was a place where concepts like "law-abiding" and "villainous" didn't exist. There was only "policy," and that was in the hands of one man.

The president settled his arms on the table and folded those hands. He looked down at them. "It is good to be home," he said softly. A slight turn of his head indicated that he was addressing Yershov. "I was born here, you know."

"Yes, Mr. President."

Putin looked down at his hands, then flattened them on the table. "General, I have read all your white papers on Operation Gray Wolf, and I have discussed them with my top advisers. I have decided to postpone the assault phase in favor of a strategically enhanced buildup."

The jowly expression of Defense Minister Timoshenko did not change. Yershov stiffened visibly but remained silent.

Putin continued to stare. He permitted a moment to pass for his order to sink in before continuing.

"During World War Two, my father was stationed near Leningrad, on the Neva—Maksim, you know he was wounded there."

"A very, very brave man, sir," the defense minister said gravely. "As was your brother, in Leningrad, rest his heroic soul."

Putin acknowledged the comment with a barely audible "Thank you," then turned to Yershov. "My father used to tell a story of how the patrols would march in a circle, within the concealment of trees and boulders, to convince the enemy that the Nevsky Pyatachok region was more heavily defended than it was." He circled his index finger, pointing down at the tabletop, then grinned. "It's an old tactic used in Greece, Rome, Persia—but an effective way of avoiding needless conflict." Putin looked at Yershov with steady eyes. "Needless," he repeated. "There must be no hesitation, no backing down when combat is necessary."

Putin sat back as if he were relaxing, though there was a stiffness to his movements, like a coiled snake on a cold night.

"I want to enter a Ukraine that is free of resistance," he went on. "I want the Russian presence in Sudzha to appear so overwhelming that there will be no need to fight. Yes, yes, we have the tanks, we have the personnel, we have the artillery to go in. But *psychology* is the war of the future. Through ingenious deployment, around-the-clock activity, visible high spirits among the troops, I want Sudzha to cast a shadow, a dark zone, so absolute that no one would dare to challenge us. *Then* we move without hindrance. This is not the mutual assured destruction that guided the nuclear age. It is an enemy living with the fear of *assured* destruction so absolute that our very presence will cause capitulation. War without war, conquest without loss." He tapped his right temple. "A siege of the mind."

"It is a difficult concept for old warriors like us to embrace," Timoshenko said, speaking directly to Yershov. "But there is wisdom in this approach. Courage."

"And éclat," Putin said with a flourish. "Victory through reputation through intimidation."

Yershov understood: that was how Putin had gained power, through daunting object lessons. When the man became president in 1999, foes of every stripe were hammered flat. Imprisoned, murdered. Militarily, he showed no mercy in Syria, in Crimea. Yershov knew that those adventures had come at a heavy cost—national pensions pilfered for funds, foreign sanctions endured—but Russians had suffered many times for the state. He assumed they would do so again.

Was he wrong?

"General," Putin went on—paternally, now—"I need for *you* to go to Sudzha and make this happen. Keep morale high, eyes on the western horizon. Training must continue as if war were to come at any moment. And, of course, if it does we will be ready to fight it." Putin looked at the defense minister. "Maksim, have you anything to add?"

"You've covered it very well." Timoshenko's dark eyes fixed on Yershov. "Though I would add that we are taking very strong, assertive steps to blind the enemy as to our actions and intentions."

"Yes," Putin said, as though glad to be reminded. "Our agents abroad are shutting down key sources of intelligence."

"There is good reason for this," the defense minister went on when he was certain Putin had finished. "The Cyber-Surveillance Directorate of the GRU has uncovered what we believe is a plot against one of our bases—most likely Sudzha, given what the spies in the Kremlin learned about our armored deployment."

The Glavnoye Razvedyvatel'noye Upravleniye was the nation's main intelligence agency. The CSD was comprised primarily of old bureaucrats running teams of young men and women whose college education had been paid for in exchange for a minimum of ten years of service. As with so many military conscripts, enthusiasm for the job was low: fully eighty percent of Russian troops were indifferent to their work, and on remote bases like the Balkhash Radar Station or the 7018th Base for Storage of Rocket and Artillery Equipment, performance was flatly unreliable.

"One of the young veterans was conducting due diligence on online employment applications for the FBI and the CIA when he uncovered a video embedded in one submission," the defense minister said. "It depicted an assault on a base and our armored vehicles and tanks were delineated." The big man shrugged. "Most technologists would have thought nothing of it, would perhaps only have filed the video, but our man checked the background of its creator. His name is Chingis Altankhuyag, and he is newly graduated from Stanford University in America. He is from Ulaanbaatar. His father is a high official in the Energy Ministry."

"Not a friend of Moscow," Putin added.

"To be sure," Timoshenko agreed. "We are investigating further, but our immediate need is to have someone in place who is prepared to manage whatever might arise." The defense minister nodded respectfully toward Yershov.

The general dipped his forehead in acknowledgment of the compliment. Until that moment, he had not been entirely sure this wasn't a demotion. The military had a way of cleaning house that defied understanding. Perhaps the ministry had decided it missed the bold if ultimately foolhardy way that General Novikov had acted. The Putin regime was fickle that way: sometimes the president favored the brash, sometimes the steady, sometimes both within the same week.

Timoshenko regarded the general. "Do you have any questions, Anatoly?"

"As you said," he replied, his voice hollow, "you and his excellency have covered it."

"Then—walk me around?" Putin said to the general. "We have a dinner at ten, but I have not been in this building for many years."

The men rose and Yershov motioned toward the door, Putin and Timoshenko leaving in that order. The lieutenant was waiting outside and hovered behind them as they walked, the general talking knowledgeably about the tripartite triumphal arch, with its epic sculptures depicting the Russian victory over Napoleon in the War of 1812.

But his voice, like his manner, was suddenly reserved. Yershov could bring himself to say nothing about what he considered to be a recklessly dangerous gamble. In an age of satellites and drones, of cyberhacking and cell-phone cameras, what the president was proposing was logistically impossible. And, uncovered, maneuvers designed to create an impression of power would expose what had been rumored for years: that Russia could no longer afford to maintain its wars. Timoshenko was a capable man but a bureaucrat; his reaction was expected. And even though Putin, in person, seemed no less dynamic, no less confident than he had appeared on television or in public, Yershov couldn't tell whether the president himself believed what he was saying or whether he was spinning a bad—perhaps dire—situation.

The motorcade departed nearly an hour after it had arrived. Putin had left the general with a warm handshake and a cocksure smile, both of which had an unexpected effect on Yershov: they made him *want* to succeed. But there was something else on his mind as he returned to his office to phone his wife and tell her that he was coming home and that they were going to Sudzha.

The general realized that he was about to become the face of the *new* military in Crimea. If this modified Operation Gray Wolf failed, if the mood of the Ukrainians remained defiant, it was his reputation, his career that were at risk.

Thinking of Putin, and then of his disgraced predecessor, Yershov found himself possessed of a sudden demon. He would not share General Novikov's fate. Fueled by his own strong natural resolve, enriched like uranium by some residue of Putin's charm, magic, charisma—whatever it was—the general was determined to succeed.

No guns would be turned toward the enemy. No Special

Operations units would parachute behind the lines. Not even drones would cross the border, since those were all tied up in Crimea. And Colonel General Anatoly Yershov would mount war games in that frontier the likes of which would define psychological warfare for generations to come.

CHAPTER TEN

The location had not been chosen at random.

When it was established in the sixteenth century, the town of Semenivka, in the Poltava province of Ukraine, had been little more than a rest stop for horses and riders. The way station was a sad, muddy, lonely reminder that the Golden Age of Kiev and Vladimir the Great had come and gone.

Vladimir was a scion of the fabled Rurik Dynasty. A Slavic Rus who had fled fratricidal conflict in his native Russia, he established a new, increasingly powerful empire in Kiev. The glory that began in AD 980 lasted for four centuries, after which members of the Polish-Lithuanian Commonwealth warred on Kiev and carved Ukraine into pieces that were constantly being shuffled from one foreign dynasty to another.

In the itinerant roots of the legendary king and the subsequent carving up of his realm, possessory claims were created that persist to the modern day.

But the way station persisted and a town was founded

around it, and it has remained an agricultural town known for its grain, sugar refinery, and flour mill. The coat of arms consists of abundant wheat and rich cherries, and the air is wholesome with the smell of what the town proudly produces. The sixty-two hundred citizens are industrious, and, for the most part, they are Ukrainian loyalists—many fiercely so—who often wear the blue and yellow of the flag in their daily dress.

At the heart of Semenivka is a boxy three-story building made of peach-colored brick with rust-colored brick between the windows. A central section was four stories high, made of the same pale brick, with a double row of azure brick between each floor. At the top of the central tower was a mosaic of a shield with an upright sword behind it and a bold red star on the face, the emblem of the local police.

A spotlight shining down from the roof, and the hooded glow of a nearby streetlight, were the only nighttime illumination. Apart from public drunkenness and an occasional anti-Russian protest, the police did not have to respond to many emergencies day or night. The one-time castaway location was now a hamlet largely shut off from the chaos centered in Russia to the east and Kiev to the west. But the isolation was not absolute.

On the third floor of the police station was an office that overlooked the main street. It was painted a faded forest green and the linoleum was water-stained. There was an old, heavily scuffed and chipped dark-brown wooden desk that had been taken from a schoolroom in a schoolhouse that had been destroyed during the Second World War. On top of it was a clunky black dial telephone, an ashtray, a smartphone, and a MacBook. Tucked in the corner, under a window, was a working stereo record player with speakers dangling wires from the wall and an old brass rack filled with LPs—Sinatra, Aznavour, as well as local Ukrainian artists of the 1970s. It was playing now, the A side of the debut album of the seminal folk group Kobza.

At this moment, nothing else seemed appropriate.

Sitting rigidly in a stiff wooden chair behind the desk was a man dressed in a long-sleeved, mottled blue camouflage uniform—his customary attire. It was a half size too small, intentionally hugging the thirty-three-year-old officer's lean, athletic form, though the breast was flecked with ash. Above it was a dark round face with a long, traditional Cossack mustache and close-cropped salt-and-pepper hair. The eyes were brown . . . and damp with tears.

The man refused to look in the direction of the smartphone. Tonight, it was an enemy, a devil, something evil. It had informed Captain Taras Klimovich of the bloody murder of his friend and loyal colleague Galina Petrenko, who had just completed what she assured him was a carefully planned liaison with her former employer, Ambassador Douglas Flannery. The dire report from Fedir had been confirmed by a glance at the news on the computer.

"You know this from years of struggle," Klimovich told himself over and over. "Nothing is guaranteed."

But the loss was bitter and incalculable just the same. And unexpected. It was like his little sister, the wife of a commercial jet pilot, who accepted that her husband would be coming home after work . . . until the day he didn't. Years of borrowed time in an inherently dangerous profession suddenly flood your soul until it is immobilized by the weight, numb to the reality.

And then, slowly, the truth takes hold.

Captain Klimovich had lost people before—in tank battles, on surveillance missions, but never to an assassin. What made this worse was that, unlike warfare, there was time to move with caution, safeguards that could be put in place. Unless you become complacent.

That's when a predator strikes you or your team, he thought.

Vigilance was the reason he was stationed here instead of with his command. They communicated by courier, not by phone, radio, or email. It wasn't because he was fearful, and he certainly wouldn't want to suggest to his men that he was more important than any one of them. Rather, the cost in time and manpower of having to watch his back against just such an assassination would have been prohibitive. That was why his office was here, with two floors of police below, his back to a brick wall, and a Fort-224 carbine in the top drawer of his desk. The fast, compact Israeli-built bullpup assault rifle was a favorite of the Israel Defense Forces and Ukraine's many special operations detachments.

A cigar he had lit when he returned from dinner lay cold in the ashtray. Klimovich knew that he must allow his anger to cool as well: the mission would continue after this brief, brief period of mourning, and revenge would be taken on the savages who had ordered this murder. The same savages who had invaded his country. The same savages he had defeated before and would defeat again.

Only this time it would be different. He would undermine everything the Russian people held dear in coordinated moves so unexpected, and a show so dramatic, that every corner of the world would take note. When he took charge of his command once more, it would create a visual and psychological impression so strong that Moscow would never be the same. Literally overnight, Ukraine would become the voice of oppressed citizenry everywhere on earth.

Slowly, with effort, he reached into his shirt pocket and withdrew his lighter. With the other hand, he raised the cigar. He lit it again—not because he needed the smoke but because life must continue, fire must not be extinguished.

The captain took no joy in the familiar aroma. He had started smoking them because virtually every adult male who smoked, smoked cigarettes. Klimovich disliked the smell, and the cigar was a way of dispersing it while remaining sociable. That was, in fact, how he got his nickname. He had been with a group of officers who teased him about how they had nobility in their midst, someone who could afford the more expensive extravagance.

Klimovich had replied, "How better to put a fox amid the hounds than by distracting them with a smoke."

As his feint-and-concealment tank tactics proved triumphant in drills and in combat, the name had fallen into general usage.

Hiding in a glen, behind a tree, in a long shadow. The Fox.

Drawing on the cigar, Klimovich had to prioritize. Galina's colleague in New York, Fedir Lytvyn—the man who had called to inform him of the murder—had been ordered to go to ground at the embassy. He hadn't wanted to; Fedir was eager to go out and find her killer, but Klimovich had told him to stay where he was, at least for the present. He needed time to think. The New York Police Department and the FBI would be pursuing the murderer, and he couldn't afford to risk the life of his only other New York agent. Although the captain had no legal authority over the Sluzhba Zovnishn'oyi Rozvidky Ukrayiny—indeed, he had no official sanction for this operation whatsoever, other than the quiet approval of certain of his superiors who had given him an invaluable associate, a hawk circling the bear—everyone involved in the multidivisional action was fully committed to the captain's vision.

The captain had to remain sharply zeroed in on that mission: to strike the Russian aggressor hard, fast, first, and in a way that he would never expect.

The captain looked at the landline. That was the last place he had spoken with Galina. He spent another moment of reflective respect, then considered his next move before picking up the receiver to dial Fedir's number.

The twenty-eight-year-old Fedir was a tech-savvy young man who had come to the attention of the SZRU when he was a student at Cherkasy State Technological University. He was also a black belt in the native Ukrainian form of karate, Simmey-do, which made him an essential hire. In one of her daily eyes-only intelligence reports from the start of this project seven months before, Galina had indicated that she suspected Fedir had a very strong crush on her. She had found that flattering, not threatening, and had mentioned it only "in the event harm should befall me and drive him to a rash reaction."

The young man answered with a snap in his voice. "Is there news, Captain?"

"I have spoken to no one other than you," Klimovich replied

with characteristic calm. He did not feel the need to explain that he had been sorting through his own thoughts and feelings.

"Sir, I can't just sit here," the young man said. "I cannot."

"It's difficult, I know," the captain replied. "But I want you to continue doing just that. We lost a valuable asset and a treasured friend."

"Which is why you must tell me her assignment, let me complete it."

"Special Agent Lytvyn, the news report I read said that the Russian dog took her phone," Klimovich told him. "Her contact is the only name on it. They will certainly be watching this individual in New York."

"Then I will scout the source patiently," Lytvyn replied. "Spiral approach, around the target and then in. I'm not afraid!"

"If I thought you were, you wouldn't be a cornerstone to our intelligence gathering," the captain remarked. "That's why I must continue to insist that you wait."

"Captain!"

"They will watch the embassy as well," Klimovich said. "You know that!"

"Then I am perfect bait," he said.

"Fedir," he said, shucking the formality he had employed earlier. "Have you ever known bait to survive a fishing trip?"

"The fish dies, too," Lytvyn said manfully.

"True enough," Klimovich agreed. "But I want to make sure we get the right one—Vlaidimir Putin."

Lytvyn fell silent.

"I know I cannot order it," Klimovich went on, "but let's see what law enforcement might learn. The embassy will follow up. Stay inside. There is still time, and we must know more."

"For the operation, yes," Lytvyn replied. "Every minute that passes, the killer himself gets further undercover."

"I say again, the objective is *Russia*," the captain said emphatically. "The goal is the heart of the bear, not an eye or a fang. Strike that and we have inflicted a mortal wound."

Klimovich could hear Lytvyn breathing heavily at the other end of the phone. He remembered what it was like to want vengeance so acutely that it eclipsed other thought, larger goals, rational behavior. Klimovich had spent a great deal of time in Russia, when it and Ukraine were still part of the Soviet Union. He graduated from the Leningrad Higher Military Command School in 1983 and commanded a motorized infantry division in the Transcaucasian Military District. In 1996, the young man graduated from the Academy of the Armed Forces of Ukraine. There his best friend—Jakiv Antonyuk—was badly beaten by Russian troops who found out that the boy was gay. He died in the infirmary. Klimovich's first thought was to kill the Russians one by one, assuming—correctly, as it turned out—that justice would not be served in a court martial. There was no way the death of a soldier who was both homosexual *and* a Ukrainian would put Russians in front of a firing squad. On the contrary. They didn't even go to prison, the verdict being that Jakiv had provoked them, sexually. Jakiv was retroactively discharged. In the ensuing twenty-plus years, that hatred had metastasized into governmentally sanctioned gangs that roamed the breadth of Russia attacking gays.

At that time, Lieutenant Klimovich had requested, and was

granted, permission to resign his command under the assumption that he, too, was gay. Returning to his homeland in 2002, he joined the Academy of the Armed Forces of Ukraine. Fueled by his hatred for Russia, he rose quickly to his present command. He resolved that there was no reason to kill those men, though he would welcome the opportunity to kill them honorably if it arose in combat. It was enough to shame them and those who supported their actions. A mission, any mission, is not nurtured solely by rage but by patience—"the long journey," as he had come to describe it.

"Commander, this is . . . sir, I am trying, but it is *impossible*." This was the only word the young man could think of.

"Special Agent, we will get him, I promise you," Klimovich said, his voice showing steel now.

"How, if he dissolves in the shadows?"

"We will dissolve the shadows," Klimovich said, even though he knew that Lytvyn was right. Chances were good the killer would never be caught.

Another silence, more heavy breaths, and finally Lytvyn replied, "I have never put faith in platitutdes, sir."

"Then . . . put it in me."

"I will try. I will . . . *try*."

The captain thanked him and ended the call. Sometimes, more than an order, the compassion of a respected superior was enough to temper rash behavior. Klimovich hoped that was the case now. But he wasn't sure. The same ungovernable impulses were also what made Lytvyn such an effective agent. Youth, the desire for instant gratification, and the lack of immediate oversight were a dangerous combination. For most soldiers, that meant nothing more impulsive than a visit to a tavern or a brothel. But a confident—bordering on cocky—field agent was not most soldiers.

Klimovich set his cigar in the ashtray and went to the computer. He opened a file called "Long Journey" to continue reviewing what intelligence they had, whether they could launch their ambitious attack against the Russians with a delayed or an attenuated data flow.

Of course we could, Klimovich thought. Of course we will.

He decided to go to a subfile and bring up the virtual-reality program for the attack, see where additional modifications might be needed. Watching the computer-generated figures, he took heart. This was the basic program, not interactive. These were cyphers facing Russian conscripts; they were not Ukrainian patriots. That reality would represent an undefinable quality of courage that no computer program could capture.

Watching the battle play out, Klimovich thought of his own hatred of the Russians, felt his own fighting spirit rise. He thought of the real endgame, the one no one knew. The one he and Admiral Volodymyr Berezovsky had conceived.

Patience, Lytvyn, he thought. The ultimate victory will be ours.

CHAPTER ELEVEN

New York, New York
June 2, 2:46 PM

Off busy Third Avenue, Forty-ninth Street was an eclectic street in a most eclectic city.

Three consulates anchored by the iconic Manhattan eatery Smith & Wollensky. It was a street of banners. The flags of three nations are suspended above the street, along with the flag of the quaint Amster Yard, a hidden courtyard garden, and the flag of a Spanish restaurant beside it; farther east, an apartment terrace flew the rainbow colors of the LGBT community.

The consulate general of Ukraine in New York was located midway between Third and Second Avenues on the south side of the street. It was just a short walk from the United Nations and the East River, where joggers, dogs, and tourists mingled and flowed like the waters of the tidal estuary itself. A black iron gate fronted the pale stone façade that perpetually looked as if it were in need of a good hosing down. One had to walk down a short flight of steps to enter. The consulate was neither as warm nor as welcoming as the shade-tree-fronted Consulado General del

Perú, the leaves throwing a changing set of masks as the sun moved quickly and with an ascending staircase that seemed proudly above, not below, the traffic both vehicular and human.

The pedestrians were as eclectic as the structures. The majority were people headed to the embassies for work or assistance. The rest were mostly upscale residents walking their dogs or headed to offices. A few were delivery people, mail carriers, and sanitation workers.

One was none of those.

Fedir Lytvyn noticed him standing to the west, toward Third Avenue, when he went outside for a smoke. He didn't really need the smoke; he needed a reason to disobey the Fox and go outside. He needed to see who was watching the embassy and from where.

The man—older, it seemed, wearing a pale-blue windbreaker against an unseasonable chill—was standing in front of the low fawn-colored metal fence of the Consulate General of Nepal. He was looking at a map of the city. Lytvyn didn't have to see the details to know that's what it was; glossy maps were always being unfolded around the U.N.

Lytvyn stood behind the fence, facing the Peruvian Consulate, though he kept his eyes shifted to the left, toward the man. The man who didn't flip the map or move from that spot.

Because he isn't a tourist, Lytvyn thought. He is watching us.

He was watching from well beyond where the security cameras of the Ukrainian Consulate could see him. Had he been there that morning? Had he been a spotter who informed someone that Galina was leaving?

The Russians didn't usually have observers like that. All of their meetings with Ukrainians were in coffee shops or parks, street corners or buses. Very little actual, constructive work was done at the U.N.

Lytvyn flicked his cigarette to the street and stood a moment longer. He had let Klimovich believe that he wouldn't go out. He had not actually *committed* to following that course of action. There could be no harm in taking a walk around the block on a sunlit spring day. Buy more cigarettes, see who this man was.

Taking out his cell phone, pretending to check messages, Lytvyn passed through the gate and crossed the street. Still studying the screen but, in fact, watching the man—who still hadn't moved—the young man walked toward the Mexican restaurant. He intended to take the man's photograph, see if their facial-recognition database had anything on him.

As Lytvyn reached an angle where he could swing the cell phone around and snap a flurry of shots, the man finally moved. He turned suddenly and walked quickly to Third Avenue, arriving as the walk sign turned green, and hurried crossing the street. The Ukrainian assumed that the man was hurrying to the Permanent Mission of the Russian Federation to the United Nations, which was located on Sixty-seventh Street. If so, he would have sought a cab or even entered a waiting car on the corner. He had done neither. That actually seemed to reinforce his guilt: the spotter didn't want to implicate his countrymen.

Without seeming to run, Lytvyn hastened across Third Avenue while he still had the light. He remained across the street as the man walked quickly toward Lexington. Dodging pedestrians, both men were doing a strange, synchronized dance that was apparent only to them—and, Lytvyn hoped, would mean nothing to the NYPD when he caught up to this man and forced him to give any information he had about the murder of Galina Petrenko. Lytvyn didn't have a weapon and wouldn't need one; there were locks in martial arts that were easily applied, caused unimaginable pain—wrist and elbow joints forced to work in ways they weren't designed to—and obtained information quickly and without attracting attention.

What bullshit story will you give me? Lytvyn wondered, with rising determination to find out. He stuffed his cell phone into the back pocket of his jeans, out of harm's way, and kept his hands open, moving, *preparing*, as he power-walked ahead. A cautionary part of him—a cautionary *particle* of him—knew that he could be taking bait that would lead him into a trap. A larger part of him didn't care. A still larger part was confident that he would be all right regardless: he was in public, and he would remain in public. And he knew how to stop a man—hard, fast, and permanently if he was accosted with fists, knife, or gun. It was all second nature to him.

The man turned down Lexington on the east side of the street. Now he was on the same side as Lytvyn. The Ukrainian couldn't figure out where the man was headed—until, at the corner of Forty-sixth Street, when the light turned, he hurried across the avenue. Grand Central Terminal, Lytvyn thought. The man wouldn't be going for a train to Connecticut or upstate New York; he'd want something to get him away fast, and the maze of subway lines that intersected here was extensive.

Lytvyn followed, watching the crosstown traffic to make

sure no one swung onto Lexington and suddenly, accidentally, overshot the grid and struck him. The young man began to jog as his quarry reached the side entrance between Forty-fourth and Forty-third Streets. That wing of the terminal wasn't heavily traveled, but if he made his way to the main concourse and ditched his windbreaker it would be difficult to find the man again. He could go straight through and out the other side, turn left onto busy Forty-second Street, or go right into the Metropolitan Life Tower and head north along Park Avenue. Apart from the man's options, the cluster of police and National Guard troops gathered there, protecting the terminal, would make it impossible for Lytvyn to accost him.

You will not get that far, the Ukrainian screamed inside.

The man stopped long enough to yank open one of the heavy brass-framed glass doors that opened into the terminal. Now Lytvyn ran. He had tracked people before, as far back as his university days, when he suspected that his girlfriend, Halyna, was seeing another student, the footballer Stepan. His craft had evolved naturally over those few days. It ended when he found them together at the Olimpiyskiy National Sports Complex, going to a Dynamo Kiev match. There it wasn't the crowd outside the park that had stopped Lytvyn from doing more than confronting Halyna and Stepan. It was the emotional stab of the two of them noticing him in unison, with uncaring eyes, that pierced his heart and made him turn him away.

That ache, that loss, had lain dormant for years, and Lytvyn knew damn well it was back and helping to drive him now. He didn't care. *This* man would be stopped.

Lytvyn stepped wide around a homeless man sitting in the

street, staring ahead vacantly; he could be an accomplice. He reached the northernmost door and thought that he saw the target only a few meters ahead; it was difficult to see inside because of the way the light struck the glass door, reflecting the street and obscuring the inside. He reached for the handle. The big brass bar was on the right side, swinging the door to the left.

There was a two-meter-wide space between the entrance and the wall to the right. Lytvyn smelled, then saw, the woman standing there, an unlit cigarette in her mouth. She was rummaging through a red handbag, apparently looking for a lighter. She stood a few inches taller than he and was dressed in a red pantsuit, a floral-pattern head scarf, and large oval sunglasses. As he had been trained to do, Lytvyn took in all the details in less than a single stride, with a single mental snapshot.

She looked up and her red mouth pulled into a big, welcoming smile.

"Fedir!"

That held his attention an instant longer. Long enough for her to jump toward him, throw one hand behind his neck, kiss him . . . and, with the hand that had been in her bag, withdraw a nondescript six-inch blade from between his ribs and jam it straight into his heart.

If the young man had been less focused on pursuit, his martial-arts training would have kicked in. Lytvyn would have turned ninety degrees toward the aggressor, brought his arms up—elbow to elbow, bent in front of him—creating an intervening wall of bone and flesh. He would have relaxed his knees, dropped his center of gravity, assumed a powerful stance to stop the attacker cold. He could have pressed her back to the wall, rotated his arms to pin and disarm her.

Instead, Lytvyn felt the wickedly sharp pain on the left side of his chest, was aware of his heart momentarily going a little mad, felt his breath stop, and lost strength in his legs. His arms moved toward the pain but drooped; she had him, holding him, pinning him, still kissing him. He tasted her lipstick, smelled her strong perfume, did not see, only felt, a second terrible pain in an exposed portion under his throat as someone else joined the embrace. A man with one strong arm around his back, the other up against his jaw. The newcomer, too, cheered the young man's name.

"Fedir!"

To passersby, they were family or friends reunited. Absorbed in cell phones or music, or rushing to catch a train; no one would think anything of the three bobbing up and down in celebration. No one would notice the blood being absorbed by the close proximity of the killers.

Lytvyn felt himself fall. He did not feel himself hit the rust-colored tile that was speckled with white. By the time a pool of red began seeping from under his dead body, the killers were already gone, covered with loose-fitting New York Mets shirts the woman pulled from the handbag. It covered their bloody clothes down below the waist.

The man turned left and headed back up Lexington. Before the woman left the shadowy overhang of the terminal awning, she paused to give the homeless man money. As she did, she used tissues to wipe off her lipstick, folded the sunglasses into her bag, and yanked off her head covering. Then she turned right, headed toward the subway entrance at Lexington Avenue and Forty-second Street.

They would meet again late that night for one more preemptive strike, to remove the ambassador, who was still a potential liaison with the enemy.

CHAPTER TWELVE

Op-Center Headquarters, Fort Belvoir North,
Springfield, Virginia
June 2, 3:40 PM

Chase Williams was huddled with Roger McCord, his intelligence
director, reviewing the latest data pertaining to the western Russian frontier. It had come from a variety of electronic intercepts,
satellite data, and open-source media collected by the NSA, the
CIA, and the National Reconnaissance Office. Brian Dawson
had been there for the first few minutes of the meeting before
grabbing a go-bag from his office and leaving by helicopter for
Fort Bragg. There he would link up with Mike Volner; the two
would be in New York in time for dinner—which would be a
couple of street-vendor hot dogs near the place where Galina Petrenko was murdered.

Williams was leaning back in his chair, looking at the new
wall monitor that was wirelessly linked to every tablet and computer in Op-Center. Smartphones were excluded from the mix
since, by charter, private calls could not be subjected to potential
scrutiny.

"So there is absolutely nothing to support the Ukrainian plan, as Ambassador Flannery understands it," Williams said, looking at the multiple windows that included images, data, and transcribed HUMINT reports from frontline observers.

"Nothing as yet," McCord replied.

McCord, a former marine, was sitting in an armchair that was too soft to suit his six-foot-two-inch frame. But he had come back from lunch to find the team chin-deep in this matter and had gone to work with Paul Bankole to grab as much as they could, quickly, from as many sources as possible. The international crisis manager had continued to dig while McCord presented what they had to Williams. The forty-four-year-old embodied the saying "Once a marine, always a marine." Though he held a PhD in international affairs from Princeton, his bearing was no different from when he had been a battalion exec in Iraq: outwardly calm, inwardly alert for any and every kind of incoming. He watched people with eyes that were like little machines, missing nothing; when he listened, it was not just for words but for inflections. He was single, a difficult man to get close to, and Williams was the only one who had made inroads.

"The Russians may only be chest-thumping," Williams said. "They do that more often than they invade."

Before McCord could reply, Anne Sullivan walked through the open door.

"They're also killing," she said. "There's been a second murder in Manhattan."

Williams sat up. McCord didn't seem to react, though Anne knew they were both crunching the news. She always felt conflicted delivering reports like that to her boss. On the one hand, someone had died. But, on the other hand, Op-Center consumed information the way her Land Rover guzzled gas. Even bad news was information, another tessera in the mosaic.

"The victim was also attached to the Ukrainian Consulate—Fedir Lytvyn, twenty-nine," she went on. "He was stabbed in the heart and also had his throat cut, probably with a finer weapon."

"Like a credit card," Williams said.

"Exactly like that," Anne said. "The NYPD is looking into it, saying there are 'earmarks of a calling card' in both killings. Nothing was taken, but that may have been a matter of haste: the man was killed in the Lexington Avenue side vestibule of Grand Central Terminal. No security cameras inside; the police are collecting footage from other sites two blocks in either direction. They're also asking for anyone who may have seen Lytvyn and whoever he was with to come forward."

McCord flipped through material on his tablet. On the way back from lunch, he had been briefed by Bankole on everything that had taken place in the earlier meeting.

"Galina Petrenko and Fedir Lytvyn are the only known operatives attached to that mission," McCord said. "But."

"But?" Williams pressed.

"It's like fighting a brushfire," McCord said. "You cut a much wider firebreak than you actually need."

"Meaning?" Williams asked, then answered his own question. "The ambassador?"

McCord replied, "If I were the Russians, I'd go after him. There's no telling what he might do now that one, possibly two acquaintances, friends—whatever they are—have been butchered."

Anne and Williams exchanged a look. Williams nodded.

"I'll let Brian and Mike know," she said, then left the room.

"Let's go back for a second," Williams said, swiveling toward the other man. "If the Ukrainians *aren't* up to something, why provoke Moscow and get knocked around like this? It's not like these deaths benefit Ukraine in any way. It'll be a blip in a pair of news cycles."

"Which lends support to what Galina told Flannery—that an attack on Russia, in Russia, is imminent," McCord said.

"Right."

"But here's a—well, let's call it a more elusive idea," McCord said. "What if Moscow wants this Ukrainian business shut down because they're not planning to do a damn thing with these armored assets except put them on the border. Maybe Russia doesn't want to be attacked, provoked, and forced to respond."

"Since when?" Williams asked.

"Since Crimea, then the military support of Assad in Syria," McCord said. "Putin's ability to borrow money is nonexistent. He's started tapping household savings in Russian banks—and that's just to maintain their current level of activity. They're already covering Crimea's annual budget deficit of nearly two billion dollars. Take more territory, you take on more debt."

"But, knowing this, Kiev—or someone in a position of power—is obviously worried about *something*," Williams said.

"Yes," McCord agreed. "Peace through intimidation."

An occupation force that doesn't destroy infrastructure isn't

compelled to put down resistance—in effect, a Vichy arrangement. When the Germans occupied northern France in 1940—
by armistice, not warfare—the French were required to pay for
the three hundred thousand German troops. That came to twenty
million Reichsmarks a day, more than fifty times the real cost."
McCord leaned forward, his blue eyes fixed on his superior. "Since
the Russian treasury does not possess the resources to finish the
job they started, the last thing they would want is people checking up on their very specific, very particular capabilities on the
ground."

Williams shook his head. "Political games," he said. "Christ,
they're more dangerous than war games."

The blond-haired intelligence director cleared the screen.
"Soldiers are soldiers, but politicians are an amalgam," McCord
said. "Soldiers have one goal, to survive a winning battle. Politicians bring too many disciplines, too many objectives, and too
many advisers to the table."

Williams was listening, but he was also thinking. "Roger,
should we talk directly to someone in Kiev or at the SZRU about
this?"

"Two of their embassy employees were just killed," McCord
said. "We probably know way more than they do at this point.
They're probably finding out everything they can from their han-
dlers, and then they're going to want to hit back somehow. Is
Op-Center prepared to help? They'll press for that."

"Of course not," Williams said. "But that's not what I was
thinking."

"What, then?"

"During the call before, I asked the ambassador if he knew who Galina wanted the intel for," Williams said. "He said he assumed it was paramilitary. There was some sketchy logic attached, but if it *was* regulars why wouldn't the Ukrainian armed forces have gotten in touch with their own contacts in Washington to ask about this? We've got private cooperative agreements that everyone knows about."

McCord thought for a moment. "Because it's black ops. Possibly rogue ops." The intelligence director took a moment to chew over what he had just said. "No, definitely the latter," he decided. "Operating outside known channels."

"Why do you say that?"

"Because it's been how many hours since the first murder?"

"Nearly four," Williams said.

"Right," McCord went on, having checked the time himself. "And there hasn't been an RFA from the SZRU. Meaning Ukrainian intelligence may not be sure what *they're* dealing with. Black ops would be on their radar, at the very least."

An RFA was a request for assistance. That was a pro-forma, almost involuntary request from allied intelligence services when they had any kind of "unfolding situation." If none of the U.S. intelligence services had heard from the SZRU—and McCord had already checked the in-box they all shared via the Homeland Security National Network of Fusion Centers—it was because the Ukrainian agency wasn't sure what to ask. This latest killing wasn't likely to clarify anything.

"Recommendations?" Williams asked.

"I want to go over that virtual-reality program with Aaron," he said, rising. "It was created to reflect a very specific target. The Russians wouldn't have posted images of an under-construction base online but, obviously, they had to come from somewhere."

"I like it," Williams said as McCord turned to go. "Thanks, Richard," the director said as he departed.

McCord half turned and nodded as he left.

Williams opened their online channels to the NYPD and the FBI in New York to see if there was any additional information in real time. He found McCord a tough man to know, a challenge even to like, but something about the man's analytical style seemed to force the others to up their own games.

Anne sent him a text:

```
I've given Brian the ambassador's home
and office info. He says to tell you
"the garlic's on the window." I don't
see it in the code list.
```

Williams chuckled and wrote back:

```
You won't. Private. Thanks.
```

It was a joke that dated back several years, when a new team, with a fresh global outlook and a powerfully diverse skill set, took over the dormant Op-Center. Every boutique government agency had a high incidence of burnout and attrition, and former director Paul Hood and his number two, Mike Rodgers, had experienced theirs. When Williams came aboard—hired by Hood himself—he sought to change the role the Critical Incident Response Group and SWAT element played in overall operations. The original military component, code-named Striker, was a dedicated arm of Op-Center. For the new incarnation, the CIRG/SWAT team was seconded to Op-Center. That meant the transfer was for temporary duty, and it gave the military leader—Mike Volner—greater leeway in go/no-go decisions. That wasn't an easy partnership for Williams, which was where the garlic reference came in. It came after Dawson's first long, boozy meeting with the twenty-nine-year-old at a sports bar in Richmond. Impressing the kid with his fluency in Arabic, Dari, Pashto, and other Middle Eastern tongues, Dawson had effectively convinced him that his rise through the ranks would be a "sure thing," with high-profile Op-Center assignments instead of the pick-a-number promotions at the Department of Defense. Volner seemed to agree, which prompted Dawson to send Williams the text:

```
Garlic's on the window, DOD vampires
kept at bay!
```

While there had been trying times when Volner felt the pull of the big, institutional family at the Pentagon versus the cadre of retired brass at Op-Center, if nothing else the phrase had stuck.

Noticing the apple that remained untouched on his desk, Williams picked it up and took a bite just as an alert came through from the NYPD. He punched a number on the office phone and hit speaker.

"Yes, boss?" Aaron Bleich replied after a brief delay.

"Got a project for you and your biometrics people, top priority," Williams said. "I'm sending it over—will be there in a minute."

"At the ready," Bleich said, even as Williams finished typing and ran from his office, the apple left doing a lonely dance on the desk.

CHAPTER THIRTEEN

Fort Bragg, North Carolina
June 2, 3:55 PM

It had made real-world sense—not, as is frequently the case, backward military logic—for Brian Dawson to take the circuitous route that Anne Sullivan had laid out for him.

It began with an hour-and-forty-five-minute helicopter flight south to Fort Bragg before heading north. His ride was a UH-72A Lakota, a helicopter with aerodynamic skin like molten copper, a hingeless main rotor system, and composite rotor blades. It always gave Dawson a smooth, quiet ride conducive to work—in this case, reading up on Ambassador Flannery and studying a map of Manhattan. Dawson knew every street in Washington, D.C., many in Philadelphia, but New York was relatively new to him. His experiences there had primarily been at meetings and in hotel rooms. The hotel visits weren't always for work.

Volner was waiting on the tarmac when Dawson arrived. The men were scheduled to board a C-17 that was headed to Stewart Air Force Base in Newburgh, New York. From there it would be a quick helicopter ride to Manhattan. The skies were dark and menacing. A storm was coming, and departure status was SONG: soon or no go.

Coordinating a commercial departure from the D.C. region would have saved some time . . . but then there would be no way to bring even a Swiss Army knife for protection.

Volner looked like a man who was less bothered by long flights than by rules he knew should never be applied to him, especially by the TSA. Standing five feet ten inches tall and weighing a deceptively lean 160 pounds—all of it sinew, no body fat—Volner had short-cropped brown hair, brown eyes, and a look of serenity that came from his strong Lutheran faith. He was dressed in civvies: jeans and a short-sleeved button-down white shirt. He looked like a soldier on leave, but there was no getting around that.

"Hello, Mike," Dawson said, his grip thrown over his left shoulder, his right hand extended. He looked the man over as he approached. "Where's your pacifier?"

He was referring to the slim Smith & Wesson M&P Shield 9 mm. the officer carried when he was off duty. The slim-cut clothes didn't allow for either a shoulder or an ankle holster.

Volner patted the laptop case he carried. It was made entirely of Kevlar and doubled as body armor in a pinch; it, too, would never have made it through airport screening.

Only now did Dawson notice the slight bulge created by the handgun. It had a one-inch profile, but its light weight allowed for swift tracking and consistent multiple-round placement. Dawson had fired the weapon and was envious of its proficiency. At the same time, though, he was sorry for Volner: he would never know the challenge of having to choose between power and low profile in concealed carry weapons. The only two guns Dawson owned were a fairly nonlethal 22 Derringer, which he could keep in his pants pocket, and a blow-your-head-off .38 snub nose that he wore in a shoulder holster. For the past seven or eight years, they had been in a safe in his bedroom closet; there were too many traffic checkpoints, too many metal detectors, too much scrutiny of good and honest citizens to make it convenient to bear private arms.

"By the way, Moore has sworn to kill you," Volner said, cracking the barest hint of a smile as he shook the other man's hand.

"I'll buy him a beer when we get back," Dawson replied.

"I think a round-trip plane ticket may settle him," Volner countered as they ran up the forward stairs of the massive 174-foot-long aircraft. "Nothing less. He has a new niece."

"That's why FaceTime was invented," Dawson said, aware that he had sounded crankier than he intended.

Volner's already tentative smile vanished. Old sewage rose to take its place, all of it pinned to one event—

The two men sat side by side in one of the narrow black fold-down seats that lined the aircraft's cavernous interior. They were surrounded by ninety-eight troops of the XVIII Airborne, who were headed north for a joint training operation with the Royal Canadian Air Force.

Dawson shut his eyes and sat back as the rumbling, screaming giant rose into a clear sky. It was always white daylight inside, as rows of fluorescent lights provided unchanging illumination in the windowless interior. It was really the first chance he'd had to catch his breath, and take a step back from the mood that had prompted a bank shot at Moore and compelled him to request this mission. It wasn't just feeling trapped behind a desk, though God knows that was a big part of it. When Chase Williams recruited him, the deal was to "try Op-Center out for size." That trial period was past its one-year expiration date, and Dawson had gotten—itchy? Bored?

No, it's full-on cabin fever, he decided.

He liked and admired the Op-Center team, and he never felt underutilized. But everyone had a function, and while job descriptions were never strictly enforced, everyone was careful not to bump shoulders. Dawson preferred a strict chain of command . . . where he was on top.

It also wasn't just Carolina who had fired up his need to *go*, even though he'd plugged back into her like a phone charger the moment he saw her. And the attraction—at least from where he sat, as lunch rolled on—was still strong. But she had moved on. Though she hadn't said much about her new man, his stink was all over her in a way that only a former lover could detect: checking for *his* texts and smiling, smiling differently from the way she did with him; wearing a new scent that *he* must have bought her—

"Stop!" he told himself. He didn't have time to nurse a new hate. Not now.

All of that was a trial. Not quite Tajikistan's Pamir Mountains in the winter but, in its own way, worse: he had no real training for the dynamics and realities of Op-Center . . . or for Carolina's moving on.

Yet, as he thought about it, neither of those was the outstanding reason he had wanted to make this trip. This was—and he knew it now, as he elbowed those other two things out of the way—this was goodbye. This was the vacation you take before you quit. This was the perspective you take to make a major change. The fact that he didn't know what that next step would be was the reason he had to get away.

Shit! Dawson thought. He hadn't realized his mood was that sour until he let it out to breathe. They were at thirty thousand feet and beginning to level off before he opened his eyes.

"Headache?" Volner asked, speaking louder than normal to be heard above the four roaring Pratt & Whitney F117-PW-100 turbofan engines.

"Huh? No," Dawson replied. "Why?"

"You were wincing."

"I was thinking," he said. "Tougher to push that boulder up the slope these days."

"Prayer," Volner said. "I know you don't put much faith in it, so to speak, but you should try it now and then for what ails you."

"Yeah," Dawson said—though, by inflection, he meant "No."

Volner shook his head slightly—not where Dawson could see—and dug for the tablet he carried in a shoulder bag. Dawson retrieved his own iPad and the men began reviewing what they knew and didn't know and how they should deploy at Flannery's building. They had decided not to let him know they were there, not at first. Volner suggested that Dawson watch the ambassador while he did recon of the perimeter.

"Chances are we won't be facing a sniper but a close-proximity assailant," the JSOC commander said. "Someone is autographing these kills for a reason, and isn't likely to stop now."

"Not until the cease-and-desist message is acknowledged," Dawson agreed.

"We working line-of-sight?"

"I think that's best."

That meant neither would ever go anywhere the other couldn't see him. They brought up a map of the area around Flannery's office and overlaid the NYPD "ring of steel" graphic: the location of every public and privately operated surveillance camera in the region, which were indicated in blue, and both permanent and mobile radiation detectors. There was barely a square foot of ground space that wasn't covered.

"I told the ambassador we'd make contact when we got to the city," Dawson said.

"Right. We'll do a perimeter sweep before we bring him out," Volner said. He reviewed the data on the Lytvyn murder. "We're dealing with at least two assassins, possibly a spotter."

Dawson nodded. "Doubles or triples our chances of seeing someone who doesn't belong."

"The enemy has that advantage, too," Volner pointed out.

"The enemy," Dawson repeated. "I think I'm tired of having enemies."

"I'll stop fighting if they will," Volner said.

"Maybe that's not what I mean, then," Dawson said,

reconsidering. "I'm thinking—my folks grew up afraid of the Russians. Then we had Reagan, Gorbachev, détente. After that— Putin, and we're back passing 'Go' again. Maybe I'm tired of the merry-go-round that doesn't seem to get anywhere."

"There's a simple solution to that," Volner said.

"I know. Get off. How's the line go? 'What, and give up show business?'"

Volner regarded his companion. "Sir—I do my duty and save the thinking for downtime and God," he said. "If I drilled down like you're doing, I think I'd never get out of bed."

"You want to talk about the eight-hundred-pound gorilla?" Dawson asked.

"Not particularly, sir," Volner replied. "I wrote a report that was solely factual. We made a mistake, a man died."

"Op-Center made a mistake, you mean," Dawson said.

"I never said that anywhere," Volner said.

"No," Dawson told him. "But there is a fine line between 'accident' and 'mistake,' and, in my judgment, you crossed it."

"There was no fallout that I'm aware of," Volner replied.

"The thin blue line," Dawson said. "We defend each other because those like us is all that stands between civilization and anarchy. Politicians don't need to know every detail as long as we do."

Volner fell silent, not in acquiescence but in recognition of the fact that the ammunition on both sides had been spent without a victory.

Dawson envied the ability of the JSOC cell leader to seg- regate like that. Dawson could do that, too, when there was something urgent—but then he would slip back into trying to comprehend the plate tectonics behind and below it.

The forced air of the cavernous interior, and the subtle vibrations of the cabin, caused Dawson to grow drowsy and fall asleep. The white noise of the engines helped keep him there. He didn't wake until they were wheels down in Newburgh. A Bell 412 was waiting to fly them to the Downtown Manhattan Heliport, a sixty-three-mile trip that set them down on Pier 6 in the Battery at precisely at 5:57. The men walked separately to the faux Art Deco terminal, where Volner went to the counter to ask questions about schedules—and to keep an eye on the six people waiting for flights—while Dawson phoned Flannery. They weren't expecting anyone to be here, watching for them, but they also didn't know if Flannery's communications devices had been compromised in any way.

When Flannery didn't answer his cell phone, Dawson called the main number of the York Organization for Peace. He used his private phone, not one that would show the Op-Center connection.

A male answered the phone. Dawson asked to be connected with the ambassador.

"I'm sorry," the man informed Dawson, "but Mr. Flannery has left for the day."

Before Dawson could ask anything more, an icon signaled that he had an incoming call. He ended the conversation with the York office and took it.

CHAPTER FOURTEEN

One of the great skills of Chase Williams—which was the primary reason Paul Hood had hired him—was the man's ability to *not* compartmentalize. Most military, active and former, were like university PhDs: they knew what they knew exceptionally well within a narrow field. His old friend Chuck Bridger, commander of U.S. AFRICOM in Stuttgart, Germany, wasn't expected to be knowledgeable about activities overseen by Colonel Eugenie Bundy in the Defense Information Systems Agency in D.C. There was no crossover connecting of dots. Information went vertically up and down the chains of command, not horizontally, across strictly defined lines. The bridges between them were few.

That had never been how Williams's brain worked. Threads of information twisted through his brain like DNA strands, looking for points of overlap, the foundation for a plausible scenario to begin to emerge.

It was still too early to find a structure built on two dead Ukrainian spies, a former American ambassador, a virtual-reality training program from Stanford, a new Russian outpost, and Vladimir Putin's designs beyond Crimea. And that was assuming they were all interconnected. Williams's instincts told him they were, and his job now was to determine whether that was true . . . and figure out the next steps. As a result, his mind was a place of unrest, part of it chewing and processing, another part seeking more information—any scrap, any shadow, any anything. It wasn't a panicked reaction any more than a marathon was a panicked run. The process just burned through a lot of internal resources.

As a result of external input and internal data-crunching, revising and refining his thoughts, it had been a bear of an afternoon for Chase Williams—beginning with the summons to the Geek Tank and Aaron Bleich's excited words: "New York doesn't have this yet."

Williams had gone over to see what New York didn't have. Aaron was like that; a lot of twentysomethings were: *"You have to see this!"* Williams wondered what elementary-school classrooms were like at a time when it was all about "show" and rarely about "tell." He adjusted to the Millennial way of doing things better than most forty-and-overs; he had to. It was also exciting, in its own way, to see the next generation of intelligence worker being crafted less by need than by tools. The United States had made a mistake in the 1980s, when it began dropping human assets in favor of electronic spyware—when even *that* word had a different meaning. A friend at NASA said the same thing about space exploration: when you send robots instead of people to Mars, it takes billions of dollars more, years longer, and a limited ability to correct mishaps to get the same result. In Williams's line of work, that kind of delay cost lives. The intelligence communities got back into the game of having eyes on by paying foreign nationals and dropping Special Ops teams into L&S—locations and situations—that required judgment rather than data.

Now we're going in the other direction again, he thought as he reached the Tank. He called it CPI: couch-potato intelligence. After putting his operations director through a little bit of a wringer about going to New York, Williams quickly understood why: he was jealous that Brian Dawson was on his way to do fieldwork, legwork, to get his hands dirty with reality instead of pixels, to improvise rather than calculate. As director, that was an indulgence Williams couldn't really allow himself.

Arriving at the Tank, Williams discovered that the brilliant but often jovially vague Aaron had been referring to two things New York didn't have: the technology and the particular results it had achieved.

Chase Williams followed the young man to the station where the thirty-four-year-old Tankster Kathleen Hays worked. Beside her, young meteorologist Gary Gold remained slumped in his seat, though he did brush the crumbs of peanut shells from his lap.

Hays was a short raven-haired woman with a pale complexion who lacked the tools of social interaction with outsiders, as did most of her colleagues. She was a former computer-graphics artist for DreamWorks specializing in quadrupeds. Aaron had recruited her after meeting her at New York Comic Con the previous October.

For Op-Center, she created a matrix that she called 4DT: four-dimensional triangulation.

"We got all the footage NYPD Counterterrorism has of Fedir Lytvyn's run from the Ukrainian Consulate to Grand Central Terminal," Aaron said as he and Williams walked to Hays's station. "So, all the intelligence agencies have these bits of video, and pretty much the same facial-recognition software, but the program that Kathleen wrote allows us to study all these images of Lytvyn in *four* dimensions: length, breadth, width, and, most important, time. Using those measurements, and applying them to the position of the man's head relative to impediments like people and cars and lamp posts in front of him—watching how his head moves and weaves while his body charges ahead—we can tell exactly where he was looking. In every frame, at every angle."

"So within each view you can also tell who he was looking *at*," Williams said almost reverently. "Brilliant."

"It is, and we got him," Aaron said. "We got the bad guy."

The young man pointed at the screen. In seven different views of the thirteen on hand—those that featured Lytvyn *and* his target—she had constructed eye-line contact with a figure in a blue windbreaker whom Lytvyn was undoubtedly following.

"Incredible," Williams said again. "Any idea—"

"Chief," Aaron interrupted, repeating excitedly, "We *got* the bad guy!"

Hays played the file that contained the FRA—facial-recognition analysis. There were six relatively clear images of the man in question, and they matched a black-and-white passport photograph taken in South Africa in 1988, as well as a color image snapped by routine surveillance of the Russian Embassy in London in 1990.

"His name is Andrei Cherkassov," Aaron said, limning a bad Russian accent. "Well, I guess you got that from the passport. The guy was Spetsnaz in Afghanistan—nasty dude, if the number of citations and complaints he received from fellow soldiers is any indication." The documents gathered on the screen. "They're in Russian, obviously, but blue with an eagle is probably good, and I'm guessing that red with no eagle or flag isn't so good."

Kathleen brought up a CIA dossier. No one there, or at the FBI, had logged in to look at the very slim Cherkassov file since May of 2012.

"But wait, there's more," Aaron said. He jerked a thumb over his shoulder at a station where a tall, cherub-faced man sat wearing earphones and a look of intense concentration. "Dick Levey there checked plane reservations on all the computerized systems. Our man Cherkassov frequently traveled with a lady named Olga Iudov, a human-resources director at large for the Moscow diplomatic corps, who *also* traveled separately with a guy named Dimitriy Arsky. His passport was scanned by MI6 in London, which reveals him to be—"

An already familiar, scowling face appeared on the monitor.

"Andrei Cherkassov," Williams said.

"Correct. And Arsky was in Crimea when a journalist was killed there a couple of years back. Not just killed: his throat was cut with an MO that exactly matches what happened to Ms. Petrenko."

Williams rose slowly as his phone pinged. An update from Anne contained a first filing of raw eyewitness accounts from Grand Central Terminal. Seven people had come forward so far. Five recalled seeing the dead man hugging a woman. One said a man had joined them. There was not yet a statement from the young couple who had found the body; the men had been taken to Bellevue Hospital for sedation and were presently at the Midtown South precinct being interviewed. The NYPD's preliminary situation assessment was that the victim had been "directed to that specific location for that specific result."

"Chief?" Aaron said, his voice a respectful nudge.

"I'm with you," Williams replied, and his eyes shifted back to the monitor.

"Here's Olga's picture," Aaron said.

It showed a middle-aged woman jogging by the Pearl Street Playground in Lower Manhattan. The time stamp was 11:55 that morning. That was roughly where and when Galina was killed.

"Has either of them shown up anywhere else on the grid?" Williams asked.

"We only have access to what the NYPD has pulled from surveillance," Aaron replied. "We can't just go hacking them like they do on TV."

"No, but can't the NYPD do live looks using facial recognition?"

"It would have to be a pretty narrow area unless you have a few thousand eyeballs, but yeah."

Williams clapped Aaron on the shoulder. "Thanks," he said. "Fine work, Kathleen."

"Thank you, Director Williams," she replied, turning and flushing.

Williams hurried back to his office, swinging through Anne's door on the way. "Would you please get me the counterterrorism bureau chief in New York. Iris . . . ?"

"Irene Young," she said affirmatively.

"Right," he said. "And stay on the call," he added as he continued to his office. He closed the door and dropped behind his desk.

"She's in with the mayor and the police commissioner," Anne said via the intercom on the landline. "Do you want to talk to the chief of department?"

"I don't," Williams said.

"Should we try to get word to her?"

"Can you text her directly?" he asked.

"I can."

"Good," he said. "Ask her to call back as soon as she can."

There had been a very public outcry when veteran Alphonse Spigoni and several other chiefs had been leapfrogged over by the commanding officer of Patrol Borough Manhattan South, a junior female who had distinguished herself during the World Trade Center attacks. Most of the complaining had come from

Spigoni and his staff, including the chief of Citywide Operations, who would have risen had Spigoni been promoted. Williams didn't know Irene Young well—couldn't exactly remember
her name—but he had met her at a symposium on international
counterterrorism and she had impressed him. Ambassador Flannery was safe for the moment, and his own team was working
the problem and also en route to the scene; he was comfortable
waiting. More comfortable than trusting an untrustworthy lieutenant.

Williams listened as Anne relayed the message. She requested,
strongly, a priority return call as soon as possible.

The audio channel was always open to the deputy director.
Those were the rules, that she be fully informed in the event that
Williams was gone from the office or incapacitated. Placing calls
for him wasn't in her job description, but that was the beauty of
being under the radar: they had fallen into the relationship they
had, where Anne took care of the vertical details while Williams played with his tic-tac-toe board of information. Any
kind of oversight from any form of human resources would
have pointed out—in the form of a reprimand—that Anne was
not a secretary. Williams would have been the first to agree. The
truth was, she really ran the place. In effect, he just played in
her sandbox.

Williams eyed the still uneaten apple and hesitated to take a
bite; that's when she would jump on the call.

She didn't. He had over an hour to work on the daily business of Op-Center: reviewing Anne's alerts, returning calls and
emails, discussing other operational, budgetary, and personnel

matters. He didn't feel the need to dive back into the Ukrainian matter at any point: time away brought clarity, which itself was often the best way to serve an active investigation.

Williams had just begun to clear through the backlog when he turned back to the apple . . . and Irene Young phoned.

"Director Williams, sorry to keep you waiting," she said in a voice that was smooth as poured milk. "The Ukrainian ambassador was Skyped into the meeting, and then there was the press—who are still waiting."

"I know that drill," Williams said sympathetically.

"Tell me you've got something."

"We do," Williams replied. "We think we know who killed the Ukrainians."

Instead of asking who, Young's first question was: "Threatcon?"

"Alpha, as far as New York is concerned," he said, referring to the lowest of the four levels.

There was an audible sigh. It meant there was a general threat against personnel, institutions, and/or installations, the nature and extent of which was unpredictable but apparently limited.

"Thank you, Mr. Director," Irene said. "Please—go on."

Williams explained what the team had uncovered, though he declined to say how. A very real and unfortunate area of responsibility for the director was making sure that Op-Center had enough funding to keep the lights on. That meant holding tight to proprietary technology, as long as the findings themselves were made available to other services. He also went back and forth on whether to tell her that Dawson and Volner were headed to her city. He decided against it; he didn't want any jurisdictional bad feelings, and he didn't want to lose eyes-on in the arena.

"Is there anything you can share?" Williams asked when he was finished.

"Something that actually got me out of the press conference early," she said. "We had the Flannery connection through Galina Petrenko, and we also had repeat business in the area around his place of employment."

"Repeat business" was when an individual kept showing up at or around a crime scene. Williams was suddenly very alert, since that was where his team was headed.

"We had a fuzzy image of a man at the intersection of Water Street and Maiden Lane ten minutes after the Petrenko murder. The same face showed up in the Lytvyn pursuit. And now he's been spotted by camera in Bowling Green, a two-minute walk from where the ambassador works, and moving in that direction. We're in the process of extricating Mr. Flannery."

"You're escorting him out?"

"Two members of my personal detail are taking care of it," she said. "They're going straight from Police HQ a few blocks southeast, then back again. Low-profile operation. Given the narrow, twisting streets around the ambassador's office, we don't want to risk remaining blocked or static."

Williams didn't know how he felt about the plan. A line of black SUVs, patrol cars, and a phalanx of no-nonsense cops might be enough to stop Cherkassov and Olga—but two officers alone? A classic quick extraction if no one expected it. But so far the Russian seemed to be on top of everyone.

Thanking the deputy commissioner and agreeing to exchange whatever new information he had, Williams hung up and immediately called Brian Dawson.

CHAPTER FIFTEEN

New York, New York
June 2, 6:03 PM

The York Organization's offices were on the quiet side of 77 Pearl Street. That was the side that actually overlooked the street, a very thin, elongated crescent that, before landfill, was once the eastern coastline of Manhattan. The odd angle of the door—facing slightly west where the rest of the building faced southeast—was an effort to thwart the sustained winds that still blew in from the harbor. Dormer windows circled the building, the back of which was on the noisy side of the block: Coenties Alley was filled with tables and covered with a festive array of restless banners. For nine or ten months of the year, it was alive virtually around the clock with clients of the many eateries that occupied the ground floor of the old structure. When the new owners first brought Flannery to the offices, he responded enthusiastically to the site. On most days, it was the yin and yang of diplomacy—soft and loud, a perfect place to do the Jekyll-and-Hyde work of gentle coercion and unyielding stubbornness.

But this had not been most days.

Rattled by the events of the past six hours—had it *only* been that?—Douglas Flannery had tried to concentrate on the handful of guests who lingered after the symposium—those few scholars, journalists, and diplomats who had not come for lunch, as Galina had insisted. Though shaken inside, outwardly he'd been able to maintain a calm, attentive manner as he chatted with the last of the guests. With an eye on his watch, he made sure all of them were gone well before Brian Dawson was due to arrive.

The call from the office of the police commissioner, and the subsequent arrival of her two-man detail, happened so suddenly that Flannery had no time to think or to prepare. He did not mention that Op-Center had a representative en route—a seasoned diplomat, he had a sense of what would cause conflict and what would create calm. Introducing the fact of outside conversations, which he would be asked to divulge, would be clumsy statesmanship. It might also create intermural problems for Dawson and Chase Williams. He would have called Dawson but for the sudden arrival of the two officers.

The officers were in uniform and on alert. The receptionist, Irina, had called Flannery to her desk to look at them on the security camera. The Pearl Street entrance was the only way in from the street, and the ambassador could see the NYPD squad car parked behind them. One man was facing the door, the other looking around behind them. They weren't carrying assault rifles and their weapons weren't drawn; they could have been stopping at the corner pizza shop for dinner to go.

"All right," Flannery instructed Irina.

She buzzed the two men in. They heard the buzzer and the

distinctive, hollow click of the awkwardly positioned door echoing up the staircase. It was followed by the tromp of shoes on the old wooden steps, the sound of big men weighted down by Kevlar tactical body armor.

One man appeared at the frosted glass door and Flannery walked over to admit him, placing himself between the entrance and Irina.

"Ambassador Douglas Flannery?" said a man whose blue eyes were made paler by the dark blue of his uniform. His badge was colored in gold-and-blue enamel.

"I am he," the man said, nodding.

"I'm Captain Jacoby, this is Lieutenant Foster." He indicated a man who was still at ground level, watching the street. The man raised a hand in acknowledgment but didn't turn around. "We're here to escort you to One Police Plaza."

There was no room on the tight staircase to step aside, so the captain entered the office to let Flannery pass. Foster didn't exit; the ambassador realized, with sudden horror, that if these men were killers there was nowhere for him to run. His heart began to slam against his ribs on all four sides.

It seemed to take forever for Foster to crack the front door. Flannery exhaled loudly when he did so.

And then he heard two things that caused him to freeze on the bottom step.

Andrei Cherkassov had been at this business long enough to know that espionage and assassination were games of odds.

Two assassinations in one day, and a scattered history of

global, unsolved crimes—all of that was sure to narrow law enforcement's search. And, as he neared the end of a storied career, the man actually welcomed that. Otherwise, he would not have left his singular calling card at every scene. Murder would otherwise be technocratic, like the work of a sniper. Such kills were no less decisive, but they induced boredom. And one must never become bored, distracted. It wasn't about giving an adversary a chance; this wasn't sport, it was war. But for many in his line of work, it wasn't enough to succeed; one must also baffle and taunt. Absent that, each mission became the same, the killer lost his edge, and that was more dangerous than dropping clues. The card he carried was for easy concealment, but it was also a constant reminder to remain sharp.

It was a different world today than when he had started, with surveillance everywhere and ordinary citizens with cell-phone cameras. It was like Nazi neighbors reporting on people stashed in attics, only more so. Everyone was a snitch, an informant, a narcissist looking for media or Internet attention.

Look what I saw! or *I almost died!*

Cherkassov was glad to be getting out, but only after he finished this one last assignment.

Halfway between Pearl Street and Coenties Alley were plexiglass rectangles set in the street, revealing intact old foundations and wells found in the area during construction. The Russian pretended to look at them while watching both the front and the back of 77 Pearl. In the front, he could see Flannery as he exited. In the back, he could watch anyone who was watching the front. There was nothing behind him but a modern office tower, and he had already checked that for spotters. They were always easy to see: whatever they were looking at they studied in slow motion, turning book pages, unfolding maps, or texting with an absentmindedness that indicated their attention was elsewhere. Even the best watchers slipped up. He had also scanned the surrounding windows, and was positioned in a shadow that would provide murky surveillance images in the slanting sun of dusk. He smoked a cigarette as he stood there—in New York, a way to not only justify standing outside but guarantee that people walked wide of him.

The squad car pulled up with the out-of-place quality of a snake in a swimming pool. Cherkassov had to admire the simplicity of the strategy: after his conversations with Flannery, plainclothes officers might not convince the ambassador they were authentic; shields and an official vehicle would. At the same time, those same symbols might discourage an assassin from attacking.

Or they might just cause his adrenaline to jump and his senses to heighten, Charkassov thought. He had already cased the building and knew the stupidly easiest way to get inside, something the NYPD hadn't bothered to check because they were running an on-the-clock drill: arrive on scene and get away as fast as possible. And with only two officers, so as not to risk collateral damage or casualties by friendly fire if a wasp drifted into their midst, moving in and around and forcing them to shoot randomly.

"Simplicity, but at the cost of leaving an enormous security hole," Cherkassov told himself. Crushing his cigarette, he moved toward the alley, through the tightly packed dinnertime crowd of

Wall Streeters, tourists, and students. Cell phones were a potential enemy, but they were also his greatest friend: at least half of
the people he saw were looking down at them, not noticing the
lithe figure moving toward the back entrance of 77 Pearl. Though
the windows back here were barred, the door to the basement of
the hamburger restaurant was open. A chef stood beside it, smoking. Cherkassov chucked a fresh cigarette from the pack and
poked it between his lips. He walked toward the man, waved to
an imaginary someone down the stairs, and asked for a light.

The young Asian man with a hoop earring was happy to
oblige.

"Hold on—this is dumb!" Cherkassov said, stopping him.
"I'll wait till I come back *out*!"

"Yeah, Sarah'll have your head, bro!"

"Sarah has had my head before." He grinned, clapping the
man knowingly on the shoulder and walking in.

Cherkassov hurried down the utilitarian metal stairs, making his way through shelves loaded with nonperishables. This was
all one building, one structure; there had to be a way into the
York section above.

A young man wringing out a mop stood between a stairway
that led to the kitchen and two doors. One was wood, and it was
open; it was a closet with a sink and cleaning supplies. The other,
steel-reinforced, had to be a fire exit.

Cherkassov smiled at the kid, who had the guarded, skittish
look of an illegal worker. The Russian raised a finger and *shhed*
him as he pushed the pressure bar on the door. He didn't really
care if an alarm went off; alarms went off all the time in New

York, and it was still far enough from the front of the building that the police might not be too concerned.

Even if they are, what can they do? he thought. *Flannery can be removed only so fast.*

There was no alarm, but there was the smell of old smoke.

Cigarettes in the winter, he thought. *That's why the alarm had been disabled.* He raced up the metal stairs. They turned at a landing and headed up to both a skylight and a fire door on the third floor. The smell of cigarette smoke was fresh here. Someone, possibly several someones, had used it recently. He opened the door. Again, there was no alarm.

Cherkassov found himself in a long, dark, narrow corridor lined with shelves full of books, magazines, and pamphlets. He turned sideways and hurried toward the end, one ear outward, listening to a voice—

" . . . here to escort you to One Police Plaza."

Cherkassov withdrew his cell phone, typed a word, but didn't yet send. He didn't know if anyone else was on the premises. He assumed so, though there wouldn't be many. It was past midnight in Eastern Europe, so there was no one to hector at journals, news outlets, or in government, and intellectuals in think tanks liked to intellectualize over libations, such as those being served in Coenties Alley.

The bookshelves ended in a common corridor that opened onto offices and ran the length of the top floor. At the far end, he saw a receptionist behind a desk and, beyond her, a police officer standing inside as Flannery moved past him.

Cherkassov crouched as he neared the receptionist's station.

He pressed Send on his cell phone and then vaulted onto and over the desk.

The receptionist turned toward him and screamed. The policeman on the steps stopped and spun, his hand on his weapon. He was unable to draw it before Cherkassov crashed into him, sending the captain and Flannery both down the stairs. Cherkassov had grabbed the jambs on either side to steady himself, and scurried after them. As he did, he palmed his sharpened credit card, holding it now so that the sharp edge jutted between his index and third fingers. That would enable him to slash with a backhand sweep, but also to stab with a lunge.

The lieutenant at the bottom looked back and drew his weapon, but wasn't watching the street as Olga stepped into view, yanked open the door, and stuck a six-inch blade into the side of his throat. He fell in a spray of blood, and she stepped over his body as the captain and Flannery landed at the foot of the stairs.

Flannery was groaning from the impact, and Captain Jacoby tried to both shield him and draw his weapon. Cherkassov was on him with a deep, severing slash to his carotid artery before the firearm could clear the holster. The officer continued to make the effort but, holding the handrail, Cherkassov brought his heel down hard on the man's wrist, snapping bone.

Olga pulled the quailing Flannery out from under the dying officer and laid him on top of the lieutenant like a virgin sacrifice. Cherkassov straddled the captain and crouched beside Flannery.

"You are my last," he said in English as he moved the edge of the card toward the man's throat, savoring this last kill.

"Cherkassov!"

The Russian snapped around involuntarily, surprised to hear his name, his real name, from the top of the stairs. There was a man in office attire rushing toward him. Maybe he worked here; most likely he didn't. The assassin didn't know who he was, how he knew what he knew, and didn't care. The man couldn't stop him in time, and he would not leave behind a blemished record. Cherkassov turned back toward Flannery and, with an uncharacteristically feral expression, shot his hand forward—

A crack sounded from the street as a thin man with a thin gun holding a thin laptop case put a single bullet into the Russian's forehead. Cherkassov flopped back as, above him, Brian Dawson used the handrail to swing over his body. He came down between Flannery and Olga. The woman raised her knife to finish the mission, but the combat veteran grabbed her wrist in two powerful hands. He forced her to her knees and twisted until she dropped the weapon. Mike Volner assumed a wide stance, pressed the muzzle of his still-smoking handgun to her temple, and made sure she didn't get up again.

Dawson recovered the knife and handed it to Irina, who had come down behind him. He motioned for her to stay where she was and knelt beside Flannery.

"I'm Brian Dawson from Op-Center," he said. "Don't try to move, Mr. Ambassador. That was quite a fall."

The man looked up at Dawson with terrified eyes, but in them was still the intrepid diplomat who said, "That . . . was quite . . . an introduction."

CHAPTER SIXTEEN

Kiev, Ukraine
June 3, 12:10 AM

ASSAULT MISSION PROTOCOL: AI

It was another drill that presumed the hidden ordnance was not where it should be. With it, damage was assured. Without it, damage would have to be inflicted in close quarters.

The Ukrainian Special Forces team was crouched within the high grasses outside the Russian complex. In most forest regions, the Russian military permitted the grasses to remain high. While it offered concealment to potential attackers, it also provided cover for nocturnal predators like the Eurasian wolf or the brown bear, animals that would be afoot during nighttime assaults. Their howls from the field were the best early-warning system the Russians could want. The only animals represented in the program were Vesper bats, there to prevent the soldiers from crying out when the creatures flew low overhead.

The brush served another purpose, too, one that Major Josyp Romanenko hoped to use to his advantage.

A ten-foot-high chain-link fence surrounded the base, with another four feet of razor wire strung along the top between each of the *fifty-three steel fence posts. Beyond it was an above-ground bunker that served as a sentry post; beyond that were a dozen canvas-topped military trucks; and beyond those was a four-story cinder-block complex painted gray that consisted of an armory, an administration and command structure, and barracks. In the distance was an airfield. Between the barracks and the airfield—invisible from their current position—were state-of-the-art Russian armored vehicles. Chief among these was the T-72B1 main battle tank, equipped with a 2A46M main gun, thick composite armor, and the capacity to fire anti-tank missiles. These had been added as a result of the humiliating defeat they had suffered in a tank battle with Ukraine's Captain Taras Klimovich. Also in the Russian arsenal were BTR-82A BTR-82 armored personnel carriers, with greater speed and more efficient plating to protect the troops. Searchlights mounted on top of a pair of fifty-foot towers scanned the ground in lazy circles. There were wide, heavily fortified TASs over each—tactical avoidance shields, which were elaborate umbrellas to help protect the towers from precise targeting by unmanned aircraft. The Russians didn't expect a squadron of bombers, even from NATO.*

The arms carried by the team preparing to attack the base were the same that they had used earlier in the day, Vepr assault rifles. The word meant "wild boar," and it was a 5.45 × 39-mm., gas-operated, rotating-bolt weapon capable of firing 600–650 rounds per minute, with a magazine capacity of thirty rounds. The difference between earlier and now was that the men had spent one hour in the real-world shooting range built beneath one of Bionic Hill's weapons-research labs. The power of the weapon—and the confidence it bestowed—was still very much in their minds and in their hands.

Crouched on one knee before his team, Major Romanenko looked as if he were in prayer. In a sense, he was. He prayed for victory and, to that end, his instructions were simple: "Concentrate your fire on the targets marked 'X,' and do not retreat."

The stocky officer rose and turned while, at one end of the Long Barracks, Havrylo Koval used a virtual drop-down screen to drag the markings to areas on the perimeter of the complex that Romanenko had identified earlier. It troubled him more than a little that details of the new Russian base were still extremely sketchy. With the loss of now two of their operatives in New York, the opportunity of getting accurate data via American intelligence channels was problematic. They could not count on the Kiev-Washington connection for help in an off-the-books operation like this.

Romanenko raised a hand. "On my signal, Team A go! Team B will cover until positions are secured!"

The hand came down and the four men moved as they had drilled. Belly-walking was a skill they had acquired during night training in a dry, cool 8.2 hectares of barley just outside the city; they had also become accustomed, there, to the night-vision goggles: the unfamiliar presence of the awkward, forward-weighted units; the ability to discern targets, especially moving targets, in the slightly fuzzy, monochromatic image; and the lack of extreme peripheral vision, which forced the head to turn frequently.

The chain link parted audibly as one of the avatars cut a vertical opening. In the Long Barracks, that man was on his belly, limning the actions of the computer-generated image. Another man came forward, and the two held the flaps open while the other troops wriggled through on their bellies, Romanenko leading the way. The men waiting their turns stood ready behind their Veprs. Each man who went through rolled left or right to make way for Team B, and also to train his weapon ahead. They formed two forward-facing columns, one for each team. The men would not break ranks unless in retreat. Sweeping, side-to-side fire might be necessary at times, and the visual restrictions imposed by the goggles could result in friendly-fire casualties.

When everyone was through, they made their way to where the "X"s were clustered. Computer-generated troops ran out and were savagely cut down. Team A would lay down cover fire by lying on their bellies, shooting, pencil-rolling to a new position, and resuming fire. Team B would advance, then perform the same covering action as Team A came forward. The only time the entire unit stopped moving was when one of the searchlights passed close by. Their movements had been timed and coordinated to avoid any direct crisscrossing of movement.

No one spoke. Everyone moved according to Romanenko's hand signals, and the sergeant himself moved according to the plan that was branded in his brain.

There were unexpected gopher holes, generated by the program— mole hills—and the bats. The men adjusted ably, as they had practiced. They were now close enough to see men in the nearer of the two towers, roughly three hundred meters away. At this distance, the Ukrainians could also be seen.

Koval heard several men inhale, sucking in their bellies as if deflating a few millimeters would help. Perhaps it did, though; the actions of troops under duress were outside his purview, but he had heard Romanenko's admonition: "Be very present in your body, and your mind will not wander."

A sentry came from the bunker, which was at a two o'clock position from the team. He emerged to relieve himself under the moonless sky.

Romanenko's team stopped moving . . . and breathing. That was a new, randomly generated addition to the program. So was the wind that stirred the grasses. The sentry looked out across the field.

Koval had never seen men lying so still. They were not like mannequins that possessed the veneer of life but like the stone figures from Pompeii, all animation suddenly stopped.

The sentry finished his business, sauntered back to the bunker— and sounded an alarm. The pitch and cadence of the claxon told the tower just where to turn their lights.

"Attack!" Romanenko cried, bolting upright and charging forward in the same move.

The seven men moved forward in two columns, with the major on point. They ran toward the cover of the sentry post, firing to keep the men inside. Two men in Team B dropped under fire, peppering the field from twin RPK light machine guns in the tower. They were not seen to, not now; if possible, they would be recovered on the way out.

Romanenko reached the bunker and flipped an anti-personnel, fragmentation hand grenade into the concrete structure. Everyone inside died. He did not motion the men inside: regrouping would only give the enemy more time to marshal a defense. He simply didn't want Russians at his back.

Motioning the remaining members of Team B to use the bunker to keep the tower occupied, Romanenko led Team A toward their target, the structure whose ground-floor doors and windows were marked with "X"s: the command center. He wanted the blood of Russian leadership.

There was no time now for belly movement. At his sign, the men had jumped forward in straight-line formation. One man fell, hit in the leg. The shots had come from a window, and he returned fire, driving the shooter back. Romanenko continued ahead, his men trailing like a mechanical thing, a torpedo, their constant fire targeting the windows and doors—which would not have been possible in a safer, zigzagging serpentine approach.

The armory and the command center were some five hundred meters distant. Romanenko snarled without meaning to, wanting to be there now, wanting to pounce. They were going to make it—

An explosion nearer to them than the structures rocked the Ukrainians back. There had been a low whumping sound and a faint whistle, so it wasn't a land mine.

Romanenko was done, along with all but two of his men. The real sergeant, not his avatar, continued to look ahead.

Tanks. There were two coming from behind the command center, like Hannibal's elephants descending upon Italy. A second burst, and the last two men were torn to pieces.

"Over," Romanenko said.

The others rose and removed their goggles, silent reflection replacing the oaths they'd uttered weeks before, when this was still a game.

"We'll run it again in ten," the sergeant said, lighting a cigarette and grabbing his cell phone from the locker. "No tanks," he told Koval over his shoulder.

"Shouldn't we be thinking of—?"

"No," Romananko cut him off. "I am assured they will be taken care of. Did you reserve the rooms and truck?"

"I did," Koval assured him. "I'd do more if you'd let me."

"That's enough," Romanenko said sharply, adding, "The commander has other plans for you, and I can make any additional arrangements, thank you." He made what passed for a grin. "I *had* a private life once."

"Of course."

The major relaxed slightly. "I'm sorry for snapping. There's a lot to do. I'm going to the shed."

Koval knew what that meant. "It has arrived," he said.

Romanenko didn't answer. That was an answer.

"You know what you're doing, yes?" Koval asked. "I don't mean operationally, I mean—this will start the clock. Are we ready?"

"We could wait another month to no purpose," Romanenko said. "No one is ever truly ready for a mission like this. But with what has happened in New York we run the risk of being discovered abroad *and* at home. We must move."

The computer engineer went to his laptop and made the adjustments while Romanenko left the Long Barracks to make a call. Koval glanced at the clock on his screen.

Romanenko was right. It was time to move.

For the first time, Koval was scared. But he knew his own next part in the operation, and he looked forward to the challenge . . . and, with luck, an event such as the nation—and the world—had never seen.

CHAPTER SEVENTEEN

Op-Center Headquarters, Fort Belvoir North,
Springfield, Virginia
June 2, 7:46 PM

When he first joined Op-Center, Chase Williams was immediately impressed with one thing about Fort Belvoir: the food court at the Post Exchange. The presence of so many fast-food places and coffee shops wasn't just a convenience but a safeguard: when there were just mess halls and menus that hadn't changed since the 1940s—in some cases, the condiments may also have been that old—agents of foreign nations tended to watch off-base pizza parlors, Chinese restaurants, hamburger joints, taco huts, and similar places. For planned gatherings, federal agencies tended to have them catered, lavishly, on the government's dime. But if any command HQ or federal agency placed a substantial order at a place like that, chances were good that personnel were involved in a significant crisis that required all hands on deck.

So dinner was ordered from Anthony's Pizza No. 1, Taco Bell, and Charley's Steakery. The deal was, when people had to stay, Williams had to pay, and he did so gladly. These were the people who made him look good.

The food arrived shortly before the antiterrorism bureau chief, Irene Young, held a press conference about the shooting in Lower Manhattan. The team ate while they watched.

Williams had already spoken with Brian Dawson and Matt Volner, neither of whom had been charged with any crime. On the contrary.

"They're talking about us like those three American guys who helped foil a shooting attack on a Paris-bound train in 2015," Dawson said. "Megyn Kelly asked us to come on her new show."

"Which, sadly, you cannot do," Williams had told him.

All Op-Center employees were bound by a document that prohibited them from discussing operational matters until their comments had been cleared by their superior—in this case, Williams or Anne. That would require questions being submitted in advance, which would reveal the nature of their highly secretive employment.

"I know, *technically*," Dawson replied. "But, hey, it was worth running up the flagpole."

Williams hadn't been sure whether his operations director was more disappointed about not being on TV or not being around a woman who might boost his Carolina-trampled ego.

Volner was somewhat more taciturn, seeing as how he was the one who had killed Cherkassov. Williams knew from experience that it wasn't the shooting itself but the instantaneous decision to do it that tended to affect service personnel and law enforcement the most.

Williams had also spoken with Young, who was still dealing with the deaths of her officers but was grateful to Op-Center for the actions of its men. She was still formulating her response but assured him that the men would not face charges, nor would their affiliation with Op-Center be mentioned.

Anne, Paul Bankole, Roger McCord, and James Wright were watching on the big screen as the press conference began at 8:00 PM. They were joined on video by Meagan Bruner, the on-call psychologist at the Navy's Bethesda Medical Center.

In addition to Young at the podium of the One Police Plaza press room were the police commissioner and the mayor on her right, Dawson and Volner on her left. Flannery wasn't present; he was under police guard at Bellevue, where he was being treated for cuts and sprains sustained in the fall.

After thanking the reporters, the petite, silver-haired bureau chief eulogized the two officers who had died in the line of duty and offered condolences and prayers to their grieving families. Then she introduced the "American heroes" to her left and explained how, after receiving an intelligence tip that the life of former ambassador Douglas Flannery was in jeopardy, it was decided to immediately place him in protective custody in a way that was designed not to attract too much attention.

"Covering her ass because the escort was too small," Bankole suggested.

"Not necessarily," said Wright. "It's easier to peel off a single squad car than to mobilize and coordinate a convoy. Quick extraction was the right call, especially in a building like the one they were in."

"Brian said the attack came from inside," Williams said. "More personnel wouldn't have helped."

"And they had 40 Mike-Mike on site," McCord remarked.

Volner was introduced as a Special Forces operative on leave; Dawson was described as a friend of the ambassador's who had flown in that day to talk about a consultancy with York. Other questions about their backgrounds were deflected. Little was said about Cherkassov, other than that he was a Russian-born assassin whose affiliation was "unknown," and that the NYPD and the FBI hoped to learn more when his unidentified companion came out of surgery.

"They're trying to keep Moscow out of this," McCord said, though everyone knew the backdoor conversations that were certainly taking place between the State Department and the Kremlin. Killers running loose in New York, murdering foreign nationals and NYPD officers, was a serious matter.

Williams killed the video as everyone finished eating and picked up tablets or—in the case of McCord—a yellow legal pad whose pages could be shredded, with no electronic footprint.

"Roger, did you come up with anything else on the video?" Williams asked.

"I sent frame grabs of the terrain, sans soldiers, to a friend at the U.S. Geological Survey," he said. "Those graphics are based on a 2008 survey conducted by the International Monetary Fund, which did a land evaluation as part of a proposed economic-assistance program. While they were there, the Kursk Oblast Duma—the legislative body of the Russian province—asked them to look at Sudzha and several other towns as locations for cooperative ventures. The computer graphics match that survey, which was publicly available."

"What do we have of the Russian base?" Williams asked.

"You mean the data that cost two agents their lives?" McCord said. He put satellite images on the screen. They refreshed every few seconds and showed a sprawling complex of fences, buildings, four guard towers, an airfield, and row after row of tanks and armored personnel carriers.

"What the hell?" Wright said, leaning forward as one image flashed.

"Those BTR-82 armored vehicles by the fence?" McCord said, pausing the image. "They aren't on drills. They're the sentries."

The team took a moment to study the eight-by-eight low-lying vehicles. They looked like squared-off cammy-colored beetles with a humped shell.

"I saw one of those in action when I was at MARSOC," McCord said, referring to his tenure as commander of the Intelligence Battalion at the Marine Corps Forces Special Operations Command. "That turret is equipped with a pair of 14.5-mm. KPTV machine guns, and one 7.62-mm. PKT. The guns aren't fixed, so the vehicle isn't accurate on the go. But when they sit down in defense mode, forget it. There are also six 81-mm. smoke grenade launchers that will literally create a fog of war."

"I didn't see those on the video," Williams said.

"Hence the request for help from the ambassador," Bankole said gravely. "The Ukrainians probably have no idea what's out there."

Williams broke the ensuing, pensive silence.

"We were talking earlier about Putin's response if he saw the virtual-reality prototype," Williams said. "Maybe these killings *are* his response? A warning."

"To whom, Kiev or Washington?" McCord said ominously. "He has to know we've got eyes on Sudzha and he doesn't want us sharing."

"Wouldn't sending his thugs after our former ambassador have the opposite effect?" Anne asked.

"Any thoughts, Meagan?" Williams asked, switching her image from his computer to the big screen.

"Mr. Putin is a compulsive risk-taker, short and sweet," she said. "There was a DOD profile early in 2001, during his first presidency, that said we can count on him to act out the dangers his father and his brother faced but he hadn't. At the very least, he does what he needs to do and cares very little for the consequences to the nation."

"Or to himself?" Anne asked.

"That's where the braggadocio and the swagger come in," Meagan said. "He acts invincible, and every time he gets away with something he feels more invincible."

"Until he ends up in a bunker with a gun barrel in his mouth," McCord said.

"But Hitler wasn't a Russian despot," Meagan pointed out. "Look at Lenin, Stalin, Khrushchev. They imprisoned or murdered millions to expand the circle of safety around them. Putin began that process two years ago, and he doesn't care that it's gone public."

She was referring to the killing of opposition leader Boris Nemtsov in 2015. He and his girlfriend had left a Red Square restaurant to go to her apartment. As they crossed a bridge, a white car drove by and put four shots into the fifty-five-year-old Nemtsov.

The team considered the information.

"Paul, this is your bailiwick," Williams said.

The international crisis manager exhaled. "Let's assume the virtual-reality program has two purposes," Bankole said. "First, to train for an assault. Why else render it in VR instead of in an easier, less elaborate computer graphic?"

"The DOD has both," McCord noted. "One is for boots-in-the-mud drilling; the other is simply instructional."

"Right," Bankole said. "So, second, the VR alpha was leaked to provoke Putin into fortifying the frontier—one, two, or three bases, or all of the above. Why?"

"To see how he would deploy or, if the gnats are bothering him, to get him to strike first," Williams said.

"Exactly." Bankole looked at the screen. "Meagan? Which does he do?"

"Obviously, he wants to attack," she said. "That's in his DNA. If he had the wherewithal, he'd want to roll right through Eastern Europe, put the Soviet Union back on its feet. He's never made a secret of that."

"But he can't do that," McCord said. "And I don't think it's just because of NATO."

"No," Wright agreed. "He's like the guy who puts an arm over a girl's shoulder and works his way to where he wants to go in stages."

Anne shot him a disapproving look. He shrugged back.

"I may not like the analogy," Williams said disapprovingly, "but Jim's right. He'll challenge NATO in slow, irregular stages, like a poker player who thinks he knows the outcome and savors the slow build. Roger, *if* he goes in, he's at war with Ukraine . . . again. He's already stretched thin. Question: What happens if he goes in and *loses?*"

"I think that's what has me most concerned, given what Meagan just said," McCord replied. "Vladimir Putin does not lose. If he goes down, he'll take everyone with him."

"Chase, you asked me what we should do?" Bankole said.

Williams nodded once.

"As *The Diamond Sutra* teaches, you control cause and effect by removing the precipitating condition," he said. "We don't know where this is going, but we know how it must not end up."

CHAPTER EIGHTEEN

Santa Barbara, California
June 2, 5:16 PM

Chingis Altankhuyag had arrived in the Santa Ynez Mountains overlooking Santa Barbara just after dawn. Following six years of intense study—which included summer breaks, which were anything but—the computer-science student had been determined to take his first real vacation.

With his girlfriend, Pride Mahelona-Dembélé, a climatology major from San Francisco, the twenty-five-year-old had loaded her Prius and driven south. They had wanted to see the dawn as the Native Americans of the region would have seen it, from amid the splendor of the mystical painted caves they had left behind.

After a long, leisurely drive in the darkness, they left U.S. 101 and headed up Foothill Road through Mission Canyon. There had been a mist on the crags when they passed three thousand feet elevation, and the couple got out and sat on a ledge, lost in the fine, cool clouds. Occasionally, they would hear a *whooshing* sound pass closer overhead; too large for a bird of prey, they thought, but they got a blanket from the car and covered their heads just the same. Later, as the sun burned through, they saw that their companions were early-morning hang gliders hoping to catch the morning thermals and ride out over the Pacific.

The colors of nature were still muted that early, and the bright blues and reds of the great wings were oddly jarring; Pride resented the unnatural intrusion, although Chingis pointed out that their Prius, though environmentally sound, was no less an outsider.

"You are truly an attorney's son," Pride said. "You find loopholes in everything."

"My mother is a botanist," he replied sweetly. "I also see beauty in everything."

Chingis distracted her with a kaleidoscope of monarch butterflies that had settled on a field just above them. She took out her cell phone and sent video to her mother, and then they ate breakfast and hiked and explored until late in the afternoon. A private loving nap under the blanket that had sheltered them earlier in the day ended as the sun was beginning to sink over the ocean, a burning wick atop a pale red-orange candle that sank toward the horizon.

They were about to head to the town for dinner when the young man's cell phone played an atonal theme created by his favorite composer, Béla Bartók.

"My mom," he said with a crooked smile as he stepped outside the car for better reception.

"*Baina uu*, Mother," he answered.

"Chingis, *help us!*" she screamed in Mongolian.

The boy had been leaning against the hood. "Mom?" he said as he frowned and stood upright.

"H-here . . . talk . . . to—"

Another voice cut his mother off. "I have a question for you," a man said in a careful Mongolian accent—not native, Chingis knew at once. "You created a virtual-reality program. Tell me who it was for or you can listen to your father scream as your mother's bedclothes are torn away."

The words failed to register at first. Chingis stood there in dumb silence. A shredding sound and his parents' screams snapped him back to the moment.

"Mother!" he cried.

Pride left the car and came around to him. Chingis moved away. His father had continued to scream as his mother sobbed.

"Mother!" Chingis shouted again.

The caller returned. "She is unmolested," the cool voice assured him. "For the moment. Your father is handcuffed beside her. He wriggles quite energetically for a man of his age."

"Who are you?" Chingis demanded.

"Answer my question, boy, or your mother will be shamed."

Chingis looked out at the ocean and the crisp blue and purpling sky, his mind still trying to reconcile the calm he saw with the violence he heard. Pride's touch on his arm caused him to start. He took a step away.

The young man had expected his work to be seen, had been encouraged to use that program when he looked for a job. But he had not been warned about a possibility like *this*.

"It was commissioned by a former assistant professor at Stanford, a graduate student named Havrylo Koval."

"Ukrainian?"

"Y-yes."

"Where is he?"

"In Kiev," Chingis replied stupidly.

"*Where* in Kiev?"

"He has an office at Bionic Hill," the young man said.

"How was it paid for? By whom?"

"Wire transfer . . . it was . . . something called TSL," Chingis sputtered. "I don't know anything else!"

"I am going to check on this," the caller said. "If you have lied to me, or withheld information, I will be back."

"I haven't—I swear it!"

The man turned slightly from the phone. "If any of you say anything to anyone about my visit, Chingis will die in California. Do you all understand?"

Chingis heard his parents respond in the affirmative, then said in a trembling voice that he understood as well.

There was a faint thump and then indistinct sounds.

"Mother? Father?" Chingis said into the phone.

"I am here," his mother said.

"Is he *gone*?"

"Yes," the woman replied.

Chingis heard clicking—the handcuffs being undone, he presumed—and then both of his parents sobbing. He turned to Pride, who was standing several feet away, her beautiful face glowing red in the sinking sun. She wore a look of deep concern . . . and compassion.

He tried to force even a weak, reassuring smile, but it wouldn't come.

"My son?"

It was his father. Chingis turned back to the phone. "Sir?"

"This man—he wore a mask, came in as I was about to leave for court," the man said. "He struck me . . . there was nothing I could do."

"No one is blaming you," Chingis heard his mother say.

"Son, say nothing of this for now," his father cautioned. "Not even to your friends, to Pride. No one."

"I understand," he said.

"I'm going now . . . I will call later."

The call ended, and Chingis stood there. Pride took a step forward, but no more.

"What happened?" she asked with quiet concern.

Chingis turned to her. "I mustn't say," he told her. "We should leave, go back north. I'm sorry."

Pride touched his arm as he walked past, to the car, to a once ordered world and a promising future that had suddenly been turned chaotic.

CHAPTER NINETEEN

Op-Center Headquarters, Fort Belvoir North,
Springfield, Virginia
June 2, 8:44 PM

Chase Williams sent everyone home, though Anne stayed. She usually did, except when she went to Tai Chi, even when Williams left. Keeping track of incoming intelligence from all the other agencies—not just U.S. but around the globe—was not a nine-to-five occupation. And this was the only secure location where she could do that.

They were together so much, in fact, that it surprised those around him that they seemed to have no sexual chemistry. Part of that was Anne's own business-only approach to everyone at Op-Center, along with her very private personal life. But that had always been true for Williams, here and in the military. He had been long and, as he put it, "rapturously" married to a woman who died young. He suspected that his subsequent mourning and immersion in work had calcified into a kind of permanent withdrawal from dating. He was sociable at parties, pleasant to women, and interested and charmed by them. But he didn't seek more, and his reserve was clearly palpable. Women certainly didn't gravitate to him the way they did to Dawson and Wright. To hear them talk when they occasionally went out for drinks, every military unit or workplace they had ever been in was a potential smorgasbord of not so innocent nights, broken hearts, and women requesting transfers. Listening to his co-workers, Williams was amazed that the world functioned at all.

As soon as the rest of the team had gone home—Aaron was still playing with the virtual program in the Geek Tank, looking for more of its secrets—Williams poured himself an orange juice and phoned the president's deputy chief of staff, Matt Berry, on his mobile phone.

"Chase!" the Houston native drawled. "How about our hero!"

"We should buy him a white hat," Williams suggested.

"Whoa, is that cynicism?"

"No," Williams said. "Exhaustion."

"Hold on—I'm at a bar. Let me go outside."

And there, to Williams's point, some natural, communal gene was obviously dormant in him but was alive and active in others.

"Sorry about that," Berry said. "Spring in the nation's capital. So, anything POTUS needs to know about now?"

Both men were aware that they were on an open line.

"Not right this minute, but it could get very hot very quickly," Williams answered. "And it's too much to text."

"Okay. I'll make a call and get back to you," Berry said. "Office?"

"Office," Williams replied.

He hung up and sipped the orange juice he'd already forgotten about.

"Maybe you should go home, too?"

Williams looked over, saw Anne in the doorway.

"I will," he said. "Just waiting to hear back about whether I'm briefing Midkiff."

"Your idea, or did someone else get wind of this?"

Williams pointed a thumb at himself.

"What do you hope he says?" Anne asked.

"Good question," he replied. "Every time one of these pops up—it's always an inner conflict, too, isn't it? Do I want another big challenge on the international stage, something that's going to test every part of me—or do I want to go home and watch TV?"

"No conflict here," she said. "I like managing peace more than war. That's probably why I was drawn to General Services Administration for a career. When we left Belfast, I was old enough to remember the tension that filled the streets and shops and schools. I feel it here now, too, despite Midkiff's big, bold war."

She was referring to a string of domestic terror attacks at football stadiums and malls, all of which were linked to Tehran. That triggered a brief but effective war with Iran that knocked the hostile state back on its heels. The price tag also set back President Midkiff's expansive domestic agenda, something that had discouraged him from taking on other costly foreign adventures. That had benefitted Op-Center directly, if having more work managing international and domestic crises could be described as a benefit.

Williams sipped more juice. "The world is mad, yet here we are, an Irish Protestant working side by side with a California-born Catholic."

"We are not full of hate," she said, "but we are also Americans first. I don't think of myself as any of the hyphenates that could apply to me, like Irish-American. As soon as you start identifying by clan, taking on their vitriol, that's when things go south. Which is why I prefer managing peace."

"I should feel like you do," Williams said thoughtfully. "I do, about the tribal stuff. But the truth is, I miss the Navy. I miss the four stars, the big combat command. I even look back fondly, if you can believe it, on the long climb up that ladder. The missteps, the learning curve, the superior officers who had too much politician, too little patriot in their bones. Do you know that earlier today, when I had to decide whether to withhold information until I could talk to Irene Young or give it to her grabby subordinate, I chose not to tell him?"

"That doesn't surprise me." She smiled. "This job is about judgment and intuition as much as it's about rules, which is why you're so good at it."

"Thanks, but my point is I liked making that call. I liked crunching down someone with rotten morality. There aren't enough of those crossroad moments. I like this job. I like knowing everyone I work with. I like *liking* everyone I work with. But I actually wish this thing were my call. Ultimately, we end up enacting policy, for the most part. A crisis happens, we manage it to fit the vision of the administration."

Anne shrugged. "Then run for president."

Williams smiled crookedly. "Do you know how many problems that would create right out of the gate?"

She gave him a puzzled look.

"Just handling the Joint Chiefs would be hell," he said. "The Navy would expect me to favor them and the Army, Air Force, and Marines would join forces to make sure that didn't happen. I appoint a chairman who isn't Navy? The Navy thinks I'm a traitor. I appoint one who is? The others plot like something out of Shakespeare."

"You seem to have actively thought about this," Anne said, grinning.

"One can only watch so much TV," he replied as his private line trumpeted "Anchors Aweigh." He glanced at the caller ID. "Good evening, Mr. President."

"Twice in one day," Midkiff said. "Either the world is in trouble or you're the guy keeping it safe."

"Once every year or so I win the lottery, too, sir," he said.

Anne entered quietly and shut the door behind her. Williams put the call on speaker.

"Is this about Ukraine?" Midkiff asked.

Williams was impressed.

"Yes, sir. Have any other channels been in—"

"Not yet," the president interrupted. "Abe sent me a link to your men in New York with the former ambassador. They weren't there by accident?"

Abe was Secretary Abraham Hewlett of Homeland Security. He was a vigilante official, though Wright said that his endless updates to the president were in large part "his brown nose sniffing for power."

"No, sir," Williams admitted. "We have a possible rogue military operation being planned against Russia, probably a ground-forces attack on the new base in Sudzha, near the border."

"Do we know who's running it?"

"Not yet, sir."

"Does Kiev know?"

"There has been no indication of that," Williams informed him. "But Moscow seems to be up to something as well. Those killings in New York were all against Ukrainian agents."

"Bloody Putin," Midkiff said. "Does he know about the plot?"

"Possibly," Williams said. "A training video was made, leaked."

"By?"

"Apparently, whoever is behind this operation," Williams told him.

"Jesus," Midkiff said. "There are a half-dozen ways this can ignite. What's your recommendation?"

"I would have to defer to you and State on that, sir. We have to decide whether or not to go to Kiev with this."

The president's response was immediate. "No. Boyko's

government is too volatile. This could cause it to become even more partisan. It's also damned porous. We help, Putin hears it. He turns that into 'NATO helped' and uses that as an excuse to lob shells into another former Soviet Republic. Then NATO's forced to reply."

"In which case, sir, there's only one course of action," Williams told him. "The plot has to be undone."

Even as he said it, the director knew where this was headed. So did Anne, from her grim expression.

"We need HUMINT," Midkiff said. "I know what that means—"

"It's all right, sir," Williams said. "That's why we're here."

The president was referring to the fact that Op-Center was still mourning the loss of Hector Rodriguez, command sergeant major at Third Group and the Joint Special Operations command, who had been killed in an assault on an ISIS compound in Mosul.

"I'm giving this one to Matt Berry, so he's your point man," the president said. "Good night, and good luck."

"Thank you, sir."

Williams ended the call and looked at Anne. Her expression had softened just a little.

"What are you thinking?" he asked.

"I didn't know you won the lottery."

He smiled. "DC 3, never the big money."

"I suggest you take his advice and go home," Anne said. She nodded toward the phone. "Matt won't call with 'vision of the administration' guidelines until morning, and Michael won't be back until early morning. He and Mike are flying back commercial, five-forty-five AM departure."

"Who okayed the hotel?"

"Irene Young, actually," she said. "Brian says it will be good to network with her and her people."

Williams *hmmed*, aware that by "people" he meant women, probably under thirty, especially those excited by his celebrity. He couldn't begrudge Dawson that; at the moment, he envied the man's ability to unwind.

The director thanked Anne. She said she wouldn't leave until he did, and, raising his hands in surrender, he pocketed his cell phone, finished his juice, and followed her out.

As he left, Williams mentally tried to enumerate the ramifications of having put just a two-man team on the ground in New York. The benefits had been enormous. The gains from human intelligence gathering, from boots on the ground, were always considerable.

You've got the authority, he thought. Use it.

They knew a fair amount about this situation, but not enough. The region was a tinderbox, but so was the location of every military incursion he'd ever made.

You lost a man last time. . . .

That happens sometimes. It became the headline. But the main body of the story was: the mission was a success.

"You need eyes-on at ground level," he told himself. "You need ears-on, too."

He had already decided by the time he reached his car: he had the assets, he had what the military called "reasonable concern" about enemy action, and he had just enough time, he believed, to put his people in place.

Volner and JSOC—along with the untested Paul Bankole— had to go to the region.

CHAPTER TWENTY

St. Petersburg, Russia
June 3, 4:33 AM

If Colonel General Anatoly Yershov had been asleep, the phone call would have awakened him.

Yershov had grown up in Derbent, on the Caspian Sea. Not only was the city among the most ancient in Russia—over fifty-five hundred years old—it had what his Derbent-born wife jokingly referred to as "normal hours."

In June, the sun rose at around 3:30 AM and set shortly before 11:00 PM. The blackout shade on the bedroom window of their charming dacha at 12 Bolshaya Alleya kept out the sun . . . but it didn't keep out that ineffable feeling that the day was begun. Birds came to life in the surrounding trees, the tall green grasses of the lawn blew with the wakening breeze, the dew that collected on the window began to heat and spread its warmth before evaporating.

Yershov had adjusted better than his wife, Lelya, who was a painter and felt that she *must* be in the atelier to use the morning light. In the winter, of course, she was depressed that she had to wait hours for the sun to arrive. She was good-natured enough about it all, but she always hoped that "our friend Maksim," as she called him—less good-naturedly—would see fit to transfer them somewhere else.

She got her wish, though Yershov had told her the night before that he didn't want her to join him in Sudzha.

"You know that Russian bases aren't built for comfort," he had said as he packed a trunk for the journey.

To which she had replied, trying to pull a suitcase from a packed closet, "But I am an officer's wife."

To which he had answered, "One whom I will not have in a potential war zone."

And then she had stopped tugging the handle and grew very quiet as the reality of the danger he'd be in took hold.

They spoke little before retiring, holding each other in a way they had done not for many years.

Yershov spent most of the rest of the night thinking. The afterglow of Putin was still upon him, despite his wish that it weren't. It had been so long since he had been impressed with one of his superiors that he couldn't think clearly. His joy over late-night coffee had actually encompassed Lelya—until he brought up the transfer.

He lay there, looking into the absolute darkness, feeling the gentle brush of a fan they kept running when the window was closed. He wrestled with the challenge the post presented: not tactically—he could handle that—but politically. That region, and one skirmish in it, had been the downfall of General Novikov. A wrong move—either heeding Putin's admonition not to fight but to preen or shaming Putin by preening when judgment told him to fight—could cost them everything. For himself, Yershov could bear that. But not for Lelya.

So he had held her close, as if in that proximity he would find a gentler energy, an artist's soul instead of that of a warrior, an empathic mind instead of a logical, tactical brain. The melding did not happen. This was war, not a walk through the Hermitage.

And then Maksim called.

"Anatoly, I have news," he said, sounding groggy or drunk—probably both. "We have confirmation of a plot. I will tell you more when you are en route, on a secure line, but an attack of some kind is apparently being readied."

"Are there new orders?" he asked carefully. Both men knew what he meant: did Putin's mandate stand or had the president himself changed it.

"No," the minister replied. "But I wanted you to know that drills must be conducted as if you were on a war footing. Make sure everyone knows what they are doing before they go out."

"Understood," Yershov replied.

What he meant was that any spotters in the sky or on the ground must see something precise, large, and threatening. Second thoughts must be given before going in.

"Was that Maksim?" Lelya asked from under his arm.

"Yes," her husband said. "Go back to sleep."

"He is very loud when he has been drinking."

"Most officials are," Yershov replied.

"Not you," she said. "You get quiet."

"I am like the Caspian," he joked.

"Big and deep and ready to bear whatever man or the elements places upon you," she teased.

Lelya snuggled deeper, and as he lay there Yershov saw the vast blue expanse of his youth, the largest enclosed body of water on the planet. He smiled as he pictured the majestic gulls and terns, the turtles, the large sturgeon. Vivid, variegated life, coexisting. Maybe that, and not just the balance between night and day, was why he found himself romanticizing more and more the days of his youth.

But this is now, and "now" must be addressed, he thought with fresh resolve. If it was a show Minister Timoshenko wanted, then he would have one.

CHAPTER TWENTY-ONE

Washington, D.C.
June 3, 5:35 AM

Brian Dawson slept on the Delta flight that left New York's La-Guardia Airport promptly at 5:45 AM. It wasn't a long nap—the plane touched down at Reagan National a little over an hour later—but it was irresistible and it took the edge off.

While Mike Volner had gone over to the W Hotel on Albany Street, Dawson ended up there only after accepting an invitation to drinks from a deputy mayor, who wound up leaving the hotel only after Volner called to tell Dawson that the NYPD escort to the airport was already downstairs. He had just enough time to shower and throw on fresh clothes from his go-bag.

Volner was quiet as Dawson got into the sedan provided by the mayor's office. He immediately recognized his companion's expression. He'd seen it dozens of times.

"You did the only thing you could have," Dawson told him.

"Sure, same as other times," Volner said. "I've never liked it, though. It never bothered you?"

"Of course," Dawson said, then flopped back in the seat.

"'It,'" he went on. "Neutral word for a shitty but necessary act. You know what I really hated about it, Major? The fact that there was never any time to think. That, not the deed itself, is what leaves you second-guessing every time you remember it."

"I can't disagree," Volner admitted. "Killing that reflex to hesitate was the toughest thing I had to overcome. I was always fast. I was always accurate. But I wasn't always sure."

"That there was no other way?" Dawson said. "That guy, every guy we've faced, was in a business where they knew that call might one day be made against them. They'd have made it against us. I look at this as you saved a man's life. I'm not saying you have to smile about it, but one of our guys is alive and one of their guys isn't. A man, might I remind you, who had already killed two people for breakfast and lunch."

"Like I said, I'm not lamenting the *kill*," he told Dawson, pointedly avoiding the euphemism. "I just get stuck in that microsecond." He shrugged. "It comes with the uniform and the oath."

Dawson nodded, then frowned as he remembered something he'd half noticed getting into the car. He sat up and looked over his shoulder, out the smoky black rear window. "Who's in the other car? Those are federal plates."

"Ambassador Flannery," Volner replied without turning.

Dawson looked at him. "What did I miss?"

"Chief called last night, didn't want to leave a message on your phone," Volner said. "He spoke with his boss and we're amping up involvement. We'll need someone who speaks the language."

Dawson shook his head. "Guess I'm not the only one who didn't sleep last night."

Volner gave him a look. "I was up, too, taking the calls you didn't, working out a report."

"Mike, I'm not going to apologize for that," Dawson said. "We earned our pay *and* a little R and R yesterday. I'll sleep on the way, be fresh as a newborn when we arrive." He regarded the major. "There something else?"

"Camp Lejeune took some bad weather last night, waiting to hear from buddies there."

Dawson nodded and kept his mouth shut. He knew that several of the JSOC team hailed from there.

Dawson greeted a wan-looking Flannery when they got to the airport. The NYPD had taken charge of Volner's weapon and said that it would be returned to him at Bragg when the investigation had been completed. The major thanked them, and they went inside. He took a separate flight from the others, headed back to his command.

Dawson had napped at the gate, napped on the flight, and napped in the car-service sedan that took them out to Fort Belvoir. It was a skill he had acquired early in his military career: grab what you can when you could. That philosophy had applied to the night before as well.

Dawson and Flannery entered the National Geospatial-Intelligence Agency. After a thumb-scan background check—it matched the one Williams had forwarded—they took the elevator down. Williams and Anne were waiting for them. Flannery walked slowly, favoring his left side, a virtue of broken ribs and tight bandages.

"Thank you for coming," Williams said after introducing himself and his deputy. "It's an honor."

Flannery complimented him warmly on the heroic actions of his team—and, by inference, their leadership—after which Anne fell in beside Flannery and led the way. Williams walked beside Dawson.

"Hello, Brian."

"Hello, Chase."

The smiles were pursed, but the handshake was sincere. The ensuing silence between them was pregnant but well shy of awkward. As former military, both men understood that the needs of those in combat and the requirements of those in command didn't always mesh. In a situation like this, where a battle had been exemplary, the war was permitted—though not encouraged—to go briefly on hiatus. That would end in about two minutes.

Williams offered Flannery coffee, which the ambassador gratefully accepted, along with an everything bagel.

"One gets spoiled by the meals on international flights," he said.

The ambassador's voice was strong—a diplomat's voice tended to rise above all challenges—but, in addition to his pallor, the man's eyes looked beat. He sat erect in the armchair beside the table, a napkin on his lap, but Williams knew that the past twenty-four hours had taken a lot out of him.

"Other members of the team will join us later," Williams said as he shut the door and perched on the corner of his desk. "I wanted to have this chance to bring you up to date on what we know, what we think, and what—well, frankly, what we're worried about."

"War," Flannery said. "That's the concern. Too many people over there are *itching* for it."

"Explain, sir," Williams said.

"These are all old schisms that Moscow *and* Kiev have inflamed," he said. "I can put it simply. Citizens in the western and central oblasts—the provinces—are mostly pro-Western. Ukrainians in the southern and eastern oblasts are pro-Russian. Those boundaries used to be pretty clear, geographically speaking, especially when everyone had to pull together to survive economic hardships. Those difficulties were Ukrainian problems. But now, with constant news coverage, social media, bloggers, agitators of all ages, and Putin promising help and prosperity—well, you know the rest. Moscow takes territory *in* Ukraine, supported by those traditional Soviet-longing oblasts, and the disenchanted on both sides become more entrenched."

"Galina Petrenko and Fedir Lytvyn were working for people who apparently want to attack a base inside Russia," Anne said. "Some of our people have been reviewing dossiers, trying to figure out who in the military, in government, would be part of such a group. Do you have any thoughts on that?"

"Ms. Sullivan, it is almost impossible to speculate," Flannery said. "Those motivated by patriotism oppose Moscow. Those who are greedy welcome Russian support. Sometimes people are both. There is very little clarity among the leaders of either side. And I would include NATO in that mix. They don't want Putin to push them, which is why they've been staging these massive joint military exercises in Ukraine, more than two thousand troops in each, war games that simulate attacks from across the border."

"Which is one possible flash point," Williams said, putting an image up on the big screen. "Given the buildup we've seen in Sudzha, in particular, we're expecting Moscow to respond in kind," he said, changing images. "You can see in these pictures, taken just hours apart, dozens of vehicles and hundreds of personnel have been off-loaded from Antonov An-70s and other cargo vehicles on the airstrip."

"The Battle of Camlann," Flannery said sadly.

"Sir?" Williams asked.

"King Arthur's final battle—right, sir?" Anne said.

The ambassador nodded. Williams and Dawson were both visibly impressed and simultaneously perplexed.

"Troops were massed on two sides of a line," Flannery said. "One army for the king and the other for his rival, Mordred. A knight was bitten by an adder and drew his sword to kill the snake. Others took the drawn sword to mean the battle had been joined. There's no record of how many warriors were lost—just the two leaders."

"Mutual assured destruction," Williams muttered.

"And that was an accident," Dawson said, thinking aloud. "Imagine if something like that was triggered with careful calculation, with a social-media campaign in place and ready to be fired up—#PutinisHitler or #WelcometoBlitzkrieg."

Williams closed the pictures, regarded Flannery. "Mr. Ambassador, what I'm about to tell you must remain confidential, of course."

The diplomat nodded.

"First, I am about to issue an order to insert a Special Ops team into the eastern border region of Ukraine," Williams said.

Everyone but Anne seemed to jerk to stillness. Extraneous sounds vanished.

"Their mission will be to collect intelligence on movements and, more important, attitudes and aberrations on both sides," Williams said. "What's happening, that's not business as usual. I'll need your help establishing mission goals. Second, neither Kiev nor Moscow will be informed."

Williams was expecting a protest from the ambassador. He received none.

"You agree with both propositions?" Anne asked, moderately surprised.

Flannery's gangly shoulders sagged slightly. "I agree that HUMINT would be helpful if a conflagration is to be prevented, and I agree that neither government would approve of your plan. What choice is there?"

"A diplomatic solution?" Dawson suggested. "That's been your life."

"I'm not sure there is such a solution in this case," Flannery said. "I tried to reason with two of them and failed. And they weren't the leaders, who are invariably more determined to seize moments in time, acquire power." The room went quiet, and then Williams resumed the briefing.

"I spoke with our military liaison, Major Volner, while he was on his way back to Fort Bragg," Williams said. "He's working out the details." Williams stopped when he saw Flannery looking down at the gold carpet. "Sir?"

"It's an insane world, isn't it? I, who have always worked for peace, have just endorsed a military action and—I tell you this, I will *never* forget Major Volner's face yesterday evening after he killed that Russian agent." Flannery's eyes were moist as they rose to meet those of the others. "Nothing in diplomacy is so resolute as what I saw in his expression. '*Veni, vidi, vici*.' Excuse me, but—"

"It's all right," Anne said with a smile.

The ambassador smiled back at her. "'I came, I saw, I conquered,'" he said, picking up his last thought. "I am alive because he had a touch of Caesar in him—God bless that quality which I have *fought* my entire career. I would never have thought that a man with eyes of steel, with a pistol firing in my direction, with a stance as fixed as some ancient Celtic statue could look so beautiful. But he did." He turned to Dawson. "I couldn't see you, Mr. Dawson, but I could see him. I have to thank you again for what you did."

Dawson had to clear his throat to find his voice. "You should tell him that," the operations director remarked. "I know it would mean a lot."

"I will be sure to do that," Flannery said.

There was nothing uncomfortable about the ensuing silence. On the contrary, it brought everyone in the room closer together.

"Mr. Ambassador," Williams continued carefully, "while we make plans for the team, there is one thing we don't have. I assume you have been to the border region in Ukraine?"

"I vacationed in the Kharkivs'ka and Luhans'ka administra-

tive divisions," Flannery said. "It is lovely there, mostly mountains, with wooded foothills and expansive coastal plains."

There was a knock at the door. It was Roger McCord. Williams told him to come in and introduced the ambassador before
continuing.

"Mr. Ambassador," Williams said, "would you consider
going to that region again—virtually?"

"I don't understand."

"If you would consider staying at Op-Center, we would like
to link you via body cameras when our people go into the field,"
Williams said. "It would also, frankly, keep you safe while we
make sure there are no other Russian agents out there."

"There very well may be," McCord said. "We picked up an
alert from the General Intelligence Agency of Mongolia that a
tax attorney under wiretap in an ongoing corruption investigation was interrogated by a home invader about—of all things—our
virtual-reality program."

"How freakin' global *is* this thing?" Dawson asked.

"Apparently, the program was created by the lawyer's son,"
McCord said.

"Was the intruder Russian?" Williams asked.

"That's what the GIA is trying to find out," McCord said.
"But the kid gave up a name and location: Havrylo Koval, a computer scientist who works at Bionic Hill."

"Kiev's Silicon Valley," Flannery said.

Anne had already brought up Koval's biography on her tablet. "Ukrainian, no known political affiliations," she said. "He
taught at Stanford—which is where Chingis Altankhuyag, the

job seeker who attached the computer graphic to his reel, just graduated from. Koval was recruited to work for the Technological Support Laboratory Global, which we"— she switched screens—"believe is a research front for the Ukrainian military, though it receives its funding from an American group, International Scientific Solutions. ISS was founded by—"

"My predecessor as ambassador to Ukraine," Flannery said. "He reportedly made a great deal of money in the deal, which he set up during his last year in the diplomatic corps. Very shady stuff."

"What does ISS get out of spending a fortune in Kiev?" Dawson asked.

"A seat at the table," Flannery said. "Access to some of the twenty billion dollars the IMF has already loaned Kiev, and the more than two billion dollars we've loaned them, a great deal of which goes to energy industry subsidies—"

"Which forms the backbone of the ISS subdivision ClimateKind," Anne said, reading their latest security filings.

"Sounds like a detergent," Dawson said.

"Before we go rooting in all that, back to this voice on the wiretap," Williams said. "Roger, is the GIA tracking the guy?"

"Lost him," McCord said. "He apparently left by a basement door, no security cameras. A custodian saw someone in a black ski mask. We don't know if he's Russian, Mongolian, or Other, only that he's interested in this and he's off the radar."

Williams looked at Flannery. "All the more reason to watch your back, sir. He could be sent to any of the consulates in the U.S."

The phone on Williams's desk performed its naval anthem. It was Matt Berry.

"Hi, Matt, I'm here with Brian—"

"Chase," Berry cut him off, "turn on Fox News."

Williams grabbed the remote from his desk, punched the monitor back on, and changed channels.

"My dear God," Flannery said as he gazed up at the screen.

CHAPTER TWENTY-TWO

Kiev, Ukraine
June 3, 3:00 PM

The large U-Haul International van was parked on Akademika Vernadskoho Boulevard, not far from the main artery of Peremohy Avenue. The vehicle sat heavy on its tires and the driver seemed to have the weight of the sky on his back.

Ivan Glinko rolled a thick cigarette and poked it between his lips. He flicked a match with his thumb, lit it, and tried to relax. It had been a long night without sleep, a long drive with no breaks except to fill the tank, and he was exhausted. Yet, even sitting back, the older man's watery eyes could not help but be active behind his prescription sunglasses, shifting restlessly from the rearview mirrors to the side-view mirrors—waiting and watching. There would be time enough for sleep later, when the assignment had been completed.

A tall, relatively new residential complex was set back from the curb; it was a place where a moving van would not raise suspicion. It was also a place where he could see a particular swath of sky along the wide road.

You won't be here much longer, the driver thought, looking at the digital clock on the dashboard.

He hadn't been there long as it was, only fifteen minutes, though the gravity of the operation made it seem interminable. Everything had been loaded a half hour before. Every*one*—he did not know about them. He did not know where they were going or who, exactly, they were. All he was told, by his former tank commander, was to be *there* at two-thirty to collect military gear—but to remain in the cab while it was loaded—and then to be *here* at three. He was told what to watch for, and who.

Glinko could certainly use the forty 500 hryvnia notes, there was no doubt of that. The conflict with Russia, the chaos in the European Union, the enduringly weak global economy—none of these had worked in favor of a cab driver with a stubbornly aging taxi. Before setting out to deliver a crate to Bionic Hill the night before, he had been instructed not to deposit so large a sum in the bank at once, and he was just as happy to put the currency safely in a box containing his son's military honors, including the gold-and-blue Hero of Ukraine medal.

But there was also the matter of the man he honored, the officer his late son had served: Captain Taras Klimovich. When Lavro was killed in the heroic skirmish at Labkovicy, Klimovich came to Kiev to attend the memorial and the funeral. A patriot and a widower, Glinko had nonetheless struggled terribly with the loss of his only child. With proud, smiling eyes perched on that distinctive mustache, Klimovich not only spoke at the interment but remained behind to sit with the inconsolable father and a grieving aunt to explain the importance of the young man's sacrifice.

"A nation does not always remember the individual lives lost in combat, for the carnage of war is invariably vast," the captain had said. *"But* this *sacrifice in* this *battle will never be forgotten. It was a blow to the enemy, a blow to his pride, a blow to his leader. It will never be forgotten by me, nor by those who were there, and not by the foe crippled by this loss. I promise you—his family, his friends, his fellow corpsmen—the demon Putin will remember Lavro."*

The captain had then pulled the cloth from a framed photograph standing on the podium. It showed a tank—Klimovich's own—with the boy's name painted on its side. It was a theatrical gesture but no less heartfelt, and practically every one of the three dozen or so attendees had wept openly.

Three days before, when Klimovich had called, Glinko had agreed to rent this moving van and be at the two places he was told. He was instructed not to write anything down and to tell no one. Glinko had not pressed for details. A plainclothes courier had arrived with the banknotes before two hours had passed.

The cab driver pulled on the cigarette as if it were oxygen. He had been fine until now. He had taken fares to and from Bionic Hill—he knew the roads—but this was the first time he had been to the unofficial military quarter. The animated figures and the chatter on the sidewalks of the other blocks died there, as if he'd entered a library. Heads leaned toward heads to whisper. Hands clasped tablets or laptops. There was a noticeable uptick of smokers. And no one sat on benches eating lunch. Even the sun was dimmer there, though that was an effect of the trees that had been planted when that section was completed early in the construction of the complex.

There was a very loud bang from somewhere behind the van, as if someone had tossed a firecracker in a metal trash can.

Glinko's eyes shot to the mirror. Even with the window half-open, the air was very still and the cabin of the U-Haul was full of smoke. He had to squint to see what he thought he saw. He saw pedestrians in front of the U-Haul stop, look, and point. He had to turn and stick his head out the open window to make sure he was seeing what he thought he saw.

He had. Smoke was rising from the area of Bionic Hill. Not just smoke but peaks of flame licking through the budding trees along the promenade. The smoke darkened, thickened, over the clearing. He heard sirens not so far away.

There had been no mention of this; perhaps it had nothing to do with him. He was told to wait for a man who would identify himself as "a patriot."

Police cars sped by. Ambulances raced after them. Glinko drummed the steering wheel with increasing anxiety. It couldn't be a coincidence. He had just been there, he had come away with military supplies, there was a fire after what sounded like an explosion—

And his employer was a military hero. A patriot.

He didn't think that Captain Klimovich was coming. And why would a Ukrainian hero attack a complex in Kiev? It made no sense. . . .

A tallish, slender man walked briskly toward the passenger side of the U-Haul. He was the only pedestrian actually moving now. He carried two shoulder bags and wore a determined look. One bag was for a laptop; the other was like a military grip, stuffed quite full.

He opened the door without hesitation.

"I am a patriot," he said.

Glinko had no response. He left the cigarette on his lip and started the engine as his companion squirmed from the bags, put them on the floor, pulled the door shut, and settled into the seat. The man stared straight ahead. It wasn't hot, but he was perspiring.

"There is water in the—"

"I'm fine, thank you," the new arrival said breathlessly.

"Sandwiches, too, in the glove compartment," Glinko went on, trying to make at least a superficial connection.

"Thank you, I . . . I'm fine," the man repeated unconvincingly after a long, deep breath.

"Okay," Glinko said.

He had picked up enough fares in his life to know which ones were open to conversation and which weren't. This man was not. This man was like a bank robber he had once inadvertently picked up, an innocent act that had nearly cost him his license. If it weren't for Lavro's being a tank commander, and the police detective being from western Ukraine, it could easily have gone the other way.

Glinko guided the van into the moderate late-afternoon traffic, which was lighter than usual as people pulled over to record the distant flames on their cell phones.

They had a considerable drive ahead of them. All Glinko knew was that he was to take the patriot to Kharkiv, in the Kharkivis'ka district, a distance of about 350 kilometers. He would be instructed where to go when they arrived.

"Would you like music?" he could not help asking his passenger.

"As long as it isn't Tchaikovsky or Stravinsky," the patriot replied.

The driver grinned. "No Russian composers here," he said. "Tiomkin?"

The passenger nodded, and Glinko turned on his cell phone, which was jacked into the dashboard. A lively, folk-inspired fox trot filled the cabin.

"Nice?"

"Very," the passenger replied.

Like a fever breaking, the mood in the cabin brightened. As they left the golden domes of the capital behind, Glinko looked over the tops of his sunglasses as he drove.

A devout, lifelong member of the Autocephalous Orthodox Church, he had held tight to his faith even when it had been suppressed by the Russian Orthodox Church during the Soviet years. When the church was reestablished in 1990, Glinko had helped raise funds by overcharging on fares to and from Boryspil International Airport and donating the overage to the church.

The sky was hazy, giving the sparse clouds a diffuse, celestial glow. He imagined his boy above, smiling down on him. If not for fate, he would have remained in the military, his lifelong dream, and this mission perhaps would be for *him*.

It still is, Glinko thought, his eyes returning to the road. This drive is, I suspect, for the ideals you held so dear.

CHAPTER TWENTY-THREE

Washington, D.C.
June 3, 8:30 AM

When President Wyatt Midkiff arrived at the Oval Office, Trevor Harward, the national-security adviser was waiting just outside the doorway, along with Deputy Chief of Staff Matt Berry. The president's chief of staff, Evelyn Graves, was in Beijing planning an upcoming summit with his ceremonial counterpart, the vice premier of the State Council of the People's Republic of China.

It was Harward who had called Midkiff in the upstairs family quarters to alert him to the explosion in Kiev.

Seeing the president's two-person Secret Service detail coming down the stairs, Berry quickly terminated his call with Op-Center. Harward was not a fan of the agency, which he considered to be "reckless and potentially rogue," as he had said when the unit was revived. But Berry knew that Williams and his team were working on a related matter, and he wanted to know whatever they knew. Still, he had made a point of turning away when he placed the call.

Berry followed Harward, who had shouldered first into the

sun-splashed office. Seniority trumped politeness, especially when one player felt that his fiefdom and his access to the president were being threatened by the other.

"Who did this?" the president asked as he sat behind his desk. By a slight turn of the head, he had directed his question at Harward.

"The Kiev Department of Internal Affairs says there is indirect surveillance video, but we haven't seen it yet," Harward replied.

"What the hell is 'indirect'?" the president demanded.

"Nothing of the attack itself," Harward said. "Meaning the spot was chosen so only the results could be viewed."

"Chase Williams and his people were working on that VR training video," the president said to Berry. "Have you been in touch?"

Harward didn't react to the mention of Op-Center. He would already have seen the call on the president's phone log.

"They haven't called, Mr. President," Berry answered truthfully.

"We need some context here," Midkiff said, his tan, leathery seaman's face shifting from man to man. His eyes had a natural squint, earned on deck in the Navy as a surface combatant. "Get Williams on the line."

"Yes, Mr. President," Berry replied.

Berry didn't look at Harward, but he could feel the man's furnace eyes on him. The DCS didn't immediately put the call on speaker; he didn't want Williams to answer and pick up where the conversation had left off.

"Good morning, Chase," he said. "It's Matt Berry, with the president and Trevor Harward."

There was only the slightest hesitation. Williams got it. Berry relaxed.

"Good morning, Matt," Williams said, Berry thumbing the speaker function so the others could hear. He flipped off the ringer and set the phone on the glass coffee table that separated him from Harward like a DMZ.

"I assume you've seen the feed from Kiev?"

"Watching it now," Williams said.

"Chase," the president said, taking over, "it's Wyatt."

"Good morning, Mr. President."

"What are your thoughts on Kiev?"

"Sir, we're waiting for the satellites to report in, but our tech team just informed me that the cell-phone video we saw on TV is from a position at the south side of Bionic University, which just opened there—sorry, I'm reading the email—and the explosion looks to have originated at or near the location of a military research station."

"Accidental?" the president asked. "It *is* a research facility."

"Unknown," Williams said. "The video shows a lot of people in white coats running toward the camera—most likely from that building, which is the only lab in that area. We're not seeing mass casualties, just coughing, which suggests that ground zero wasn't in their midst. That lends support to a rear impact."

"Trevor Harward here. What's back there?"

"Before she was murdered yesterday morning, the Ukrainian national Galina Petrenko informed former Ambassador

Douglas Flannery that military drills were being conducted in a secret facility, which could be that complex."

"What leads you to that conclusion?" the president asked.

"The main lab isn't a secret room, its employees are listed— yes, Aaron?"

There was a muted voice, as though from another speaker-phone.

"My tech chief says that the personnel list of TSL Global— Technological Support Laboratory Global—has a Facebook page for members of the scientific community there. So that section isn't a secret. However, our techies have pulled electrical blue-prints from last year that suggest there is an add-on room *inside*. In the back."

"So that facility behind the laboratory may have been the target?" the president asked.

"If this was an attack, not an accident, that would be my guess."

"It *could* have been an accident," Harward said.

"Of course," Williams agreed. "If they were reckless enough to handle dynamite or some other high explosive among twenty-nine civilian employees."

"A transformer fire?" Harward persisted.

"There is no indication of wiring for a large generator of any kind on these blueprints," Williams said.

The exchange was a rebuke, though a mild one.

"Is there any indication *who* was inside—" the president began.

"Hold on, sir," Williams interrupted. "Sorry, I'm just looking

at an overlay of winds my meteorologist pulled from NOAA . . .
I'm reading his analysis: 'The smoke is being blown east to west
and rising at roughly one mile an hour . . . shadows on the adjoining structure puts the origin at the north end of the facility, the
location of the hypothetical secret room.'" Chase paused. "Analysis of the cell-phone video says that there are no sparks evident
that would suggest an electrical condition. And—people at the
facility are reporting a strong smell of burning plastic behind the
building."

"Computers, wiring melting," Harward said.

"There is that," Williams agreed, "but it's blowing one way—
this smell is being detected well back. My demolitions guy says
the smoke profile is identical to an exploding mortar. My chemist
says that if it *is* an artillery shell, the description of the smell
matches a burning polystyrene or related plastic, or else a butadi-
ene rubber. That's how the propellants ammonium perchlorate and
potassium perchlorate are stored, inside a polymer matrix."

"So you're saying, I think, that this looks like an RPG attack?" the president said.

"The evidence seems to be converging in that direction,"
Williams said.

Berry's eyes scrupulously avoided Harward.

The president sat back in his chair. "Trevor, let's see what
satellite overheads the NRO has."

Harward speed-dialed the head of the National Reconnaissance Office, the government's eyes-in-the-skies agency.

"Gentlemen, we've just received confirmation from Lackland," Williams said, referring to the Texas base that was the

headquarters of Air Force Intelligence. "The X-37B was in position over Crimea and got the shot. Sending now, Mr. President."

An image from the Air Force's secretive robot plane appeared on the president's computer. It showed a remarkably sharp overhead view of the eastern section of Bionic Hill. Though the entire rear of the science center was on fire, the thickest smoke was uncoiling like a black snake from a hole in the back.

"As you can see, there is no debris field on the courtyard back there," Williams said.

"Meaning nothing was blown *out*," the president said.

"No, sir. This looks like an entry wound. Lackland says they're going back through the imaging to see if anything suspicious shows up."

"Thank you, Chase," the president said. "Is there anything else?"

"Yes, sir," Williams said. "I'm putting a recon team on the ground there."

Midkiff made a face. Technically, he could stop Williams . . . by firing him. But the president wasn't convinced it was a bad idea.

"We'll talk later," Midkiff replied.

Berry killed the connection. Williams had killed the discussion.

"The NRO is already going through their imaging," Harward said, somewhat sheepishly.

The president heard without reacting. "Matt, get out to Belvoir now and liaise with Op-Center," Midkiff said. "I want to know everything they're planning with the JSOC team. Give Trevor any updates."

"Absolutely, sir," Berry said with a soupçon more enthusiasm than the assignment required. He nodded at Harward and redialed Williams as he was leaving the office.

"Mr. President, do we want to talk to Kiev or Moscow?" he asked. "Or NATO," he added. "If Moscow is organizing attacks—in addition to the murders we know they've committed—command may want to raise their alert status to DEFCON 4."

Harward was careful not to commit himself to any of these suggestions in case they differed from the president's view.

"Not yet," Midkiff replied. He pulled over the typed folder containing his daily national-security briefings. "If we see any drift in that direction, or in the Russian maneuvers we expect at Sudzha, we'll let them know."

Harward clearly didn't agree, but he said nothing except that he would keep the president informed.

The NSA hurried to catch up to Berry, who was walking through the west wing to the exit.

"I'm obviously concerned about this Special Ops action," he said when they met in front of the vice president's office.

"Chase and his team have a lot of brass between them—and they've done it before."

"They've been lucky before."

Berry stopped. "I wouldn't describe the death of Hector Rodriquez in Mosul as 'lucky.'"

"You *know* what I mean," Harward snapped. "Williams, McCord, and your friend Dawson are all cowboys."

"Cowboys tamed the West."

"And left a lot of ruin in their wake," Harward said. "I read the report from Major Michael Volner on that action. He urged greater caution in the future. Is sending a U.S. military team into that region 'greater caution'?"

"Why don't you go back and ask the president?"

Harward faced Berry unflinchingly. "He was on the fence and you know it. With those Op-Center guys, the line between 'observe and report' and 'shoot to kill' is written in smoke. Look at New York!"

"They saved the ambassador and took one prisoner."

"They shot up a building in Lower Manhattan and killed a man attached to the Russian Embassy," Harward replied.

"Look," Berry said, "I hear that, and I'll make sure Williams and Major Volner are very aware of the parameters *and* of your concerns. Hey, I've got them, too, which is why I want to get out there." Berry waited another moment. "We good?"

"Yeah," Harward answered. "Perfect."

Berry smiled broadly. "Then . . . great!" he said as he continued to the lobby and out the side door.

CHAPTER TWENTY-FOUR

Kiev, Ukraine
June 3, 3:42 PM

Parking his hornet-like LF250-19P motorcycle in the public lot adjoining the old Kyiv-Passazhyrskiy Railway Station, Major Josyp Romanenko joined his team under the awning outside the magnificent central arch. The vehicle was legally purchased under a false name two weeks before, in the event that plates were checked. As he headed toward the front of the station, he looked behind him. The curls of smoke marked a distant event, the sirens faint, none of it causing officials to suspend service.

The men were all dressed in civilian clothes, and as Romanenko arrived, wearing jeans and a blue polo shirt, he pretended to check an itinerary tucked into a travel envelope as he visually accounted for every man. None of them acknowledged one another; in the days ahead, all surveillance footage of the station, the bus terminals, and the airports would be carefully reviewed to find the perpetrator of today's actions . . . and the actions to come. Individuals leaving the city at this time would be scrutinized; that was why they all wore something on their heads, from baseball caps to woollen caps and a wig for bald Marchuk. Zinchenko actually wore a military cap he'd bought at a pawnshop. It featured the red-and-black emblem of the Ukrainian Insurgent Army from World War II. He felt naked in civvies and thought that no one could object to the partisans who had bravely fought the Nazis.

To further conceal their facial features they all looked down—at electronic devices, at newspapers or magazines, at trinkets for sale at an outdoor stand. They all carried backpacks and canvas grips filled with street clothes, toiletries, and train schedules with the wrong routes identified in the event their bags were searched. The only one who carried a weapon was Zinchenko, a Swiss Army knife. That vulnerability had not gone over well, but Romanenko had insisted.

"If stopped, you might be tempted to use it instead of your cover story or your wits," he had said.

Romanenko had been here to check out surveillance cameras, and the men had all scrupulously avoided them when they returned to buy their tickets in the preceding days—lest the train be sold out—and again, now. Each man had a reason for being on the train headed east. Student returning home at the close of the semester, a job interview, a family visit. Romanenko had papers indicating that he was reporting for duty as a police officer in Semenivka, Poltava Oblast.

Despite the aggressive anonymity manifested by the dozen men, when Romanenko arrived the eyes of each of them complimented the officer on a job perfectly executed. After he entered the station, they all purchased tickets to Sumy separately. Some waited in a coffee shop, some shopped aimlessly, one pretended to nap, others texted messages to false family members that matched their fake identification cards.

Before the Russian invasion, the number of trains headed east had been well run and numerous. Tourism was high. Since 2014, many lines had been cut back and services to cities like Novooleksiyvka and Kherson had been eliminated entirely. The fact that ordinary citizens could not get there, that routine business could not be conducted with the rest of Ukraine, did as much to cede the territory as the presence of Russian and loyalist troops.

There were only two trains to Sumy, one at 5:00 PM and the other at 10:00 PM. The trip was seven hours, and while Romanenko would have preferred the quieter, darker overnighter, it was too risky for them to remain in Kiev.

When their train was announced, each man boarded separately, though they converged in the same car, evenly divided near both exits. In the event of trouble for one man, the others would know it at once. A few sat together, ignoring one another. As they'd planned, Zinchenko sat next to a young woman. It was a tactical move; if necessary, she would be a hostage.

Romanenko and Tkach, the youngest member of the group, sat together, the leader at the window. He wanted to be able to see the train stations as they passed, watch for any law enforcement that might be waiting. It wouldn't be long before the fire was out and forensic specialists from the Department of Internal Affairs were able to go through the wreckage. They would not find much, but they would certainly reverse-engineer what had happened, find the source of the destruction.

It had been one of Captain Klimovich's prize captures from the war. During their retreat from Labkovicy, the Russian armored column had encountered their own light-infantry column racing in for what they thought would be a mop-up mission. Instead, the infantry was forced to lay down cover fire for General Novikov as his tanks withdrew. The light infantry made a heroic stand before abandoning their positions, leaving behind several of their weapons. Klimovich took them all, including two 2B14 Podnos 82-mm. mortars. One of them had been brought to his on-site residence by U-Haul, direct from Semenivka. He had assembled it that morning with the help of Tkach, but he had assumed the job of firing it himself. In case anything went wrong, in case it exploded, in the event of his capture, the mission could still continue with Sergeant Chorna in command.

Three days earlier, Zinchenko had found the perfect place from which to fire the weapon at the wall behind the Long Barracks. There were two, actually: a shed for the groundskeeper and the sloping bank beneath a footbridge that crossed the artificial lake in the center of the facility. The footbridge was in view of two separate security cameras; enhancement might reveal whoever was hiding in the shadows. It would serve as a backup, if needed. It wasn't. An investigation revealed that the groundskeeper had pro-Russian leanings, spoken softly but spoken aloud under the influence of drink at the local bar. Romanenko made certain that he was ambushed outside the bar the night before and beaten into unconsciousness, his swipe card stolen. The crate was moved there, unopened until just before it was needed. Anyone who might go in there would not have had the tools necessary to raise the bolted lid.

Koval had worked out the trajectory on his computer. All Romanenko had to do was hit the wall or roof at the rear of the building. All the authorities had to do was find the Russian mortar. Opinion would be divided as to whether Moscow had sent in Special Operations personnel to attack the industrial showpiece of the new, modern Ukraine . . . or whether partisans had employed a stolen weapon to make it look as if Russians had attacked. The division would only help Romanenko: law enforcement would be split between watching surveillance videos and departure points for *everyone*. That was one reason the lockers had been placed inside the Long Barracks. When the TSL Global workers were interviewed, no one would be able to say, "Yes, we saw soldiers there."

Throughout his career, Romanenko had met many officers, many troops, many politicians, and many officials from both Russia and Ukraine. He had been on exercises with units from other republics of the fallen Soviet Union. Never in his experience had he met anyone as impressive as Captain Klimovich. Almost supernaturally calm, the man, a heroic warrior and a master technician, had devised a brilliant scheme . . . and this phase was just a part of it. No one man could fight a war or battle single-handedly. But there were some struggles that could not endure without single men, inspiring leaders like Klimovich. There was not a lot in Romanenko's life that the forty-year-old major could say he looked forward to. This operation was surely one of those, but the highlight of it would be finally meeting the captain when it was all done. Even if fierce patriotism hadn't driven him, the opportunity to shake the hand of that great man would have.

To think that a fiend like Putin was said to be a hero, Romanenko thought as his beloved countryside flashed by. He is a hollow shell, a chest, a face, empty swagger. He is a throwback to the czars at whose boots the Russian people yearn to kneel.

Ukrainians knew it. And, soon, so would the world.

CHAPTER TWENTY-FIVE

Fort Bragg, North Carolina
June 3, 10:00 AM

The Joint Special Operations Command, or JSOC, was a twelve-person contingent with a five-person support team. They trained in readiness at Fort Bragg, lifted off five miles away from Bragg's Pope Air Field, and were available to be detached on request by Op-Center at any time of the day. The only caveat was that the Posse Comitatus statute precluded the team from deploying in the continental United States without a presidential waiver, a procedure that was as time-consuming as it was formal. It had not yet been an issue; when it was, as Dawson once put it, "those who need to know also need to look the other way."

Upon returning to Bragg from New York, Volner immediately felt the uncommon cool and clean taste that followed the storm and the tornadoes he'd just missed the day before. He went directly to where the team was drilling in a two-story "shoot house," conducting an exercise in initiative-base tactics. It was all about moving and shooting, or not shooting, depending on the threat and the target. Sergeant Charles Moore had laid on the extra drilling with the expectation that they would be going to Crimea on a mission.

Volner waited outside, talking to Roger McCord at Op-Center on a secure line, waited for the men to finish their drilling. Volner had already alerted Moore by text that they'd be going on mission.

After giving Volner a little space to decompress from what turned out to be a kill mission, and to reengage with the team, Moore put on his chronic look of concern.

"The mission is only for recon," Volner told the men as he gave them a general briefing. "At present, the status in the arena is Threatcon Normal."

Moore frowned. "Until we touch down and that level skips right up to Delta."

"Which is why we drill," Volner said.

It was a simple, obvious, and deflecting answer, but Volner didn't want to be drawn into further debate. Especially when Moore had a point. The team would be inserting themselves into a very narrow buffer zone between "Mad Vlad" Putin, as they called him, and an enemy. But while Moore was a natural cynic-in-training who was about to graduate, Volner preferred to be an optimist.

The team retired to their barracks, several of the men passing near the major and offering silent support for the call he'd been forced to make the day before. They gave him a smile of approval, a thumbs-up, and then restored his space.

Except for Moore, who shambled beside him like a bear.

"Everybody okay at Lejeune?" Volner asked suddenly.

Moore looked at him. "What're you, reading my face now, Major?"

Volner shook his head. "I saw the tornado on the news last night, noticed the heavy wind damage in our lot, couple of Special Ops recruiting trucks with broken windows, signs torn down. I know it was worse ninety miles southeast."

"Yeah, my buddies there are fine," Moore said. "Buildings took some hits, basements flooded, they lost power for a couple hours, but no serious injuries."

"Glad to hear it."

"But you're right," Moore went on, "I was just thinking about that, about how you can train like we do and meanwhile a tornado can drop on your head and you're shit outta luck." He shook his head. "Funny how the world is."

"Unpredictable," Volner said.

"Yeah." Moore regarded his companion. "Speaking of which, I wish I'd been there to support you, Major. I should've been."

"Thanks, I spoke up for you but . . . Dawson. He did okay."

"Hell, sure, he's all right . . . for West Point."

Volner smiled thinly. "The man jumped down a staircase, right where he knew I might be shooting, and protected the ambassador. I've got my issues with Brian Dawson, but yesterday he aced it."

"I still wish I'd been there to assist," Moore grumped. "Helluva get, pair of Russian hatchets."

It was more than just a professional sentiment. Volner and Moore couldn't be more dissimilar, but there was a real bond between them, forged in combat, burnished in peace. Volner, clean-cut and slender; Moore bigger and broader, his craggy features topped with dense, salt-and-pepper hair. The two men also hailed from different and highly competitive services, but they had quickly become good friends and had remained effective co-workers for more than three years. Volner had been an Army major, Seventy-fifth Rangers, for just two years, while Master Gunnery Sergeant Charles Moore, United States Marine Corps Special Operations Command, had been wearing his uniform for nearly two decades.

They meshed well, their team was a trim unit, and the only question mark going forward would be Paul Bankole. Op-Center's international crisis manager always went with the team, and this was his first assignment since they lost Hector Rodriquez. The familiar interactions were always difficult for a new man; it was tougher for a new man who was replacing a deceased and well-liked member of the team. Bankole had been appointed only three months ago; most of the platoon knew him only by sight. He would be arriving in late afternoon by the same UH-72A that had brought Dawson. Bankole had texted earlier that there were still considerable mission parameters to plan and review at Op-Center.

For now, though, like Volner himself, the team had an open space around them. He would have the team gather their gear, stow it in the ready room, and relax. They needed that before they got on a transport and headed east—into a David and Goliath situation where a slingshot could send the entire region to war.

CHAPTER TWENTY-SIX

Op-Center Headquarters, Fort Belvoir North,
Springfield, Virginia
June 3, 10:57 AM

Paul Bankole had always thrived on risk.

Perhaps it was in his genes. His father was a doctor, his mother a nurse in Enugu; they found themselves in the newly declared Republic of Biafra at the onset of the Nigerian Civil War. The Bankole family were loyalists who nonetheless remained for the duration of the thirty-month war: the siege of the tiny nation had resulted in widespread famine, disease, and injury. When it ended, they fled to the Dominican Republic and then to Atlanta. Paul was one year old. Ironically, his birth against the backdrop of a makeshift morgue—photographed by a reporter for *Newsweek*—made him a poster child for the global Biafran Airlift that ran blockades to bring in food, water, and medicine.

Like his parents, who worked for a free clinic in Atlanta, the boy grew up taking on difficult challenges. It was as if he sought them out, whether it was playing football at an inner-city school or, later, serving with the élite SEAL Team Six. In his last tour, he operated extensively in Syria and Iraq, in black ops, taking down ISIS leaders in increasingly risky raids.

After the firefight that left him with two bullet holes in his right arm, one in his right hip, he spent just over a year in the wounded-warrior battalion at Balboa Hospital in San Diego. He recovered physically faster than he did mentally. It wasn't just having to accept that his old life was gone. He watched the news of the terrorists of Boko Haram ravaging his homeland and he wanted to go there to fight. That, too, could never be. It took him a while, but eventually he came to terms with the fact that his wounds were so severe that he'd never serve with the teams of any kind again. Upon his discharge from the hospital, Bankole was stationed at Navy Personnel Command in Millington, Tennessee. He was grateful to be breathing: his Algonquin friend Keme Decontie had died in his own bloody arms. And a new-found faith had given him a new perspective.

Bankole had discovered Buddhism while he was recuperating, and he had taken to it as if it had always been a part of his life. He was willing to bet it was part of his previous life—that's how sure and absolute the fit was. Bankole came to understand that his wounded body was something that he should allow to heal as he strove to find truth and achieve happiness without substantiality and self-entity.

He loved those highly spiritual concepts, and he loved the language. And dwelling less on his body had allowed him to recover better and faster. Bankole was convinced that being open to "the universe" had brought him here. Why else would this opportunity have come to him, through someone who knew someone

who knew Chase Williams? And at a time when the need at Op-
Center was so great?

Bankole smiled. He had asked that question then, but not
now. The teachings of his beloved *Diamond Sutra* reinforced the
idea that theories are inadequate expressions of truth. Though his
job required him to speculate daily, he'd found that intuiting
what to do rather than *thinking* about what to do served him—
and his colleagues—far, far better.

He sat in his office, reviewing history, local religious and
political affiliations, protocols, Russian and Ukrainian troop deployment. He memorized the names and numbers of the people
he was to contact on the ground. When that was done, he went
to the Geek Tank to work with Aaron and Ambassador Flannery, making sure the hardware and software were functional. If
the JSOC lost contact with their one Ukrainian speaker, they
were—in a word—screwed.

"Paul, you want to come to my office? I'm here with the ambassador and Allie Weill."

It was McCord. Allison Weill was the cartographer from
the Geek Tank, though that description didn't describe the scope
of her knowledge. In addition to basic maps, she was schooled in
raster-based and vector-based GIS, geospatial data structures,
and advanced spatial data analysis. Privately, Dawson had described her as "the lady you want to be stranded on a desert island
with if you want to get *off* that island."

Tucking his tablet under his arm, Bankole walked down the
corridor with the slightest limp, the result of two hip reconstruc-
tions. Though he had been with Op-Center for several months,

he still didn't feel fully integrated into the group. Everyone had been welcoming, especially Chase Williams—but the ghost of his predecessor was like mist. It was everywhere, clung to everyone. Bankole didn't force himself; acceptance would come.

Weill's back was to the door as he entered. She turned and smiled. The young woman was reportedly descended from Corporal Richard Warfington, one of the noncommissioned officers who traveled with Lewis and Clark on their historic journey to the Pacific.

"Good morning," Allison said to him.

"Good day," he replied.

The two had spent several nights the previous week working on maps of the Mafraq al-Saeed region of the Shabwah province in Yemen for the CIA. Op-Center was helping to identify Al Qaeda operatives and command centers in the Arabian Peninsula. Those strikes had been one hundred percent successful, based on place-and-route algorithms Allison had created to predict leadership movements.

"Hi, Paul," McCord said.

The office was smaller by half than Williams's office, with only room for one good chair. Allison was in that. McCord was standing behind his desk; Ambassador Flannery was in his seat.

"We've got—not a helluva lot to love here," McCord continued.

Bankole laid his tablet on the desk. Allison connected it to hers, and a map of Ukraine filled the screen.

"Allison, walk him through it, please," McCord said.

She expanded a view of the eastern region.

"The Crimean Peninsula," she announced. "Ten thousand square miles, all of it controlled by Russia or Russian-allied forces—except for this tiny piece of land known as Arabatska Strilka, the Arabat Arrow. It's roughly sixty-nine miles long by a hundred and sixty-seven miles wide." She zoomed in again to reveal a Rorschach-like image that could have been a straight-ascending jet and contrail viewed from the side or a chimpanzee with a very long tail holding a baby monkey.

"That's where you and the team are going," McCord told him.

"Geopolitically," Flannery added, "of all the bad places to be, this is the best."

It took Bankole a moment to figure that out. "How 'good' is not the worst?"

"You will find many places to get ashore on the northern half of the peninsula, which belongs to Kherson Oblast, Ukraine, and faces the Sea of Azov," the ambassador told him.

"The terrain there is flat, *very* flat," Allison said. "Just grasses and lagoons. The Arrow is a fairly recent geological development, a pileup of sand and shells washed up from the sea about a thousand years ago."

"People live here?" Bankole said, marveling at the bulk of the Arrow, which was mostly the narrow section.

"About thirty-six hundred citizens do," Flannery said. "Mostly in two northern villages, Shchaslyvtseve and Strilkove. These are natural-gas transit centers—workers and engineers always coming and going. If you dress like the locals, no one will give you more than a passing glance."

"Eighteen of us arriving in a group will attract attention," Bankole remarked.

"You won't be arriving as a group," McCord said. "I've been talking to Mike Volner about this. You will lead the first landing, consisting of six JSOC troops, Volner will lead the second, and the five-person support team under Sergeant Moore will come in last. Each team will have a separate cover story—students on tour, which will explain why Mike's group doesn't speak the language; your group will be geologists, which will give Junior Warrant Officer Canter a chance to use his master's degree; and the third group will be journalists."

"I want to be with the journalists," Flannery said suddenly.

The other three looked at him. He was intently studying the tablet in front of him.

"Mr. Ambassador—" McCord began.

Flannery cut him off. "As of two years ago, communications in that region were spotty at best," the ambassador said. "And, even if your satellites are as powerful as Mr. Bleich says they are, the Russians have put relatively sophisticated wireless interceptors in place."

"Aaron assures us that they won't be able to read his signal," McCord replied.

"That may also be true, but they will know that there is a signal, an encrypted signal, one that no one on that peninsula is likely to be sending," Flannery said. He sat back and shook his head. "Putin has undercover operatives in the north, sympathizers—we knew that in 2014. Drones in the sky and eyes on the ground were how he received most of his intelligence." He looked up at McCord. "You brought me here for my help, my opinions. My opinion is that someone who speaks Ukrainian and Russian must be with you."

"I'll have to discuss that with Chase—"

"I can and will go myself if I must," Flannery said. "In fact, I can probably get there before your team does." The ambassador's voice had a resolute quality none of the others had heard before.

"I'm listening," Bankole said.

"Thank you," Flannery said. "This madness, something that a rogue element of the Ukrainian military is apparently planning, is a threat to a region I love, to an area I have been working for years to protect." He looked at Allison, then back at McCord. "Am I . . . is this too highly classified?"

"Ms. Weill is cleared," McCord said. "Thank you for checking."

"My apologies, Ms. Weill," Flannery said. "Diplomats are cautious sorts."

"I fully understand," she replied with a reassuring smile.

Flannery collected his thoughts. "We have seasoned Ukrainians—we don't know how many or exactly where they are—who are looking to provoke Vladimir Putin," the ambassador went on. "We don't know whether their apparent plan to strike Sudzha is the real target, whether it's a feint, or whether it's just one of many. Someone has to be there to listen and interpret and, perhaps most important, to make educated guesses." His gazed shifted to Bankole. "Can any of your people do that?"

"We are world-class guessers," he said. "But we're not in your league."

"Then I don't see that there are any options," Flannery said. His eyes returned to McCord. "I assure you, I can do this," he said.

"You went down a flight of stairs," McCord pointed out.

"As Ms. Weill noted, our destination is very flat," Flannery said. "No slopes. No cliffs. No stairs."

"Forgive me, but you are . . . sixty? Sixty-one?"

"Sixty-two, which proves that I look younger, more vital, than I am."

Allison chuckled. McCord frowned.

"I am under the age of retirement, and unless it's raining I take daily hour-long walks in Central Park," Flannery went on. "Don't make me cry ageism. I can do this."

McCord sighed. "I can't authorize this. That will have to come from Williams, and Paul will have to recommend it."

Flannery looked at him. "Mr. Bankole?"

The international crisis manager took only a few seconds to decide. "Roger, I've got a bum leg. If I can boat, wade, and walk to wherever we have to go, so can the ambassador."

"Thank you," Flannery said.

Bankole was still looking at McCord. "So, we're ashore on the Azov in the northern section of the Arrow. What happens next?"

McCord replied, "You—you go south," he said, still somewhat in disbelief. "You move carefully into Russian-annexed territory like you're handling nitro."

"You won't find it very difficult achieving that part of the journey," Flannery said.

"Hopefully not," McCord agreed. "Akira Kôchi is having the requisite documents printed. Passports, itineraries, student and press IDs—"

"Bribes," Flannery firmly interrupted. "Documentation is important, but euros, dollars, or yen are better. They will certainly get us past any checkpoints between the north and south."

"Very good to know," Bankole said, grinning.

Allison raised a hand. "I don't suppose there's any chance that I—"

"We are finished here, thank you," McCord said to everyone. His eyes settled on the cartographer. "Except for you. We have to go over potential routes on the Crimean Peninsula itself."

She gave Bankole a had-to-try look as he left with the ambassador.

"Is there anything you'll need before I go see Chase?" Bankole asked.

"You understand why I insisted?" Flannery replied.

"Yes, of course. It makes sense, and I'm extremely grateful."

"Good," Flannery replied, wincing. "Painkillers," he said. "That is what I very much need."

CHAPTER TWENTY-SEVEN

Sudzha, Russia
June 3, 8:46 PM

General Yershov's farewells with Lelya were always brief, not because he didn't care for the woman but because he did. The older he got, the more difficult it became.

Yershov was already in a reflective mood just from packing. He could have had an aide come and help, but that had never been his way. Even when it was a canvas bag carefully filled to fit a footlocker, he had taken that time to think about each journey, every journey he had undertaken before. The comrades who did not come back. The wives and children and parents they had left behind. He had met many of those families. The effects were cumulative. They inhabited his soul every time he packed his trunk.

It was difficult packing with those invisible reminders of the uncertainty of his profession. It was difficult knowing that he might never lie beside his beloved Lelya again. But he went for a cause he believed in, the holiness of his great mother, the nation that had bred—and been nurtured by—generations of Yershovs.

An embrace, a brief kiss as if he were going to the General

Staff Building, and then he was out the door and into a waiting staff car. His trunk would follow in the black minivan parked behind it.

"Anatoly?" his wife called after him.

He stopped, turned. "I'm proud of you," she said. "Never forget that."

Yershov smiled, and did allow himself a lingering look at the dacha as they pulled away. It was the dream of every Russian to live in such a place, and he did. He smiled, because it dispelled all those many ghosts. He smiled because he thought, The next time you lay eyes on your home, this task will be behind you. The new leaves will have withered and fallen, there would likely be snow, the night would be nearly constant . . . but he would be back. And, perhaps, this other demon, the shame suffered by General Novikov, would finally be placed in its grave.

The journey southeast from St. Petersburg to Sudzha was five hundred miles. Yershov was driven from his dacha to the Leningrad Naval Base, a touchstone of the Baltic Fleet—its name unchanged despite nearly a century of political upheaval. He was to be flown south on an Mi-24PN attack helicopter, the fiery warhorse of the skies. The aircraft made a short refueling stop at Kubinka Air Base outside of Moscow before continuing to its destination.

From the skies, Russia was in bloom, a cresting, surging sea of green canopies and pastel fields. Yet there was a pall when he came in sight of Crimea. Nothing had changed visually, but the helicopter was in its slow descent, radio chatter had decreased, the clouds thickened as the microclimate of the sea took hold, and the crew of two were more alert. NATO and Ukrainian drones were known to operate in this region, and sharp eyes watched the radar screen for any sign of an aerial intruder. Even the four-barreled 12.7-mm. Yakushev-Borzov Yak-B Gatling gun and the 30-mm. GSh-30K twin-barreled fixed cannon seemed a little more alert. No one manned the machine guns mounted at the cabin windows, which could be used for suppression firepower if needed, but even their benign posture could not conceal their lethal potential.

The lower-altitude turbulence rocked Yershov's trunk in the cargo hold. It was as if those spirits locked in his memory were trying to get out. Peering ahead, he focused on the Sudzha, which grew in size and clarity as they neared.

It was even greater than the days-old photographs had suggested. In that time, more aircraft, more armored vehicles, more personnel had arrived. This was not just a forward base; it was the proud beating heart of the new Russian military—a younger, more streamlined, more up-to-date military that was no longer using spit to hold together a crumbling Cold War infrastructure and rusting vehicles.

This was the kind of command any general would be proud to lead—though Yershov still hoped that President Putin would have a change of heart and send this iron wave out to meet the enemy. In his mind, Yershov had replayed that meeting many times, trying to determine whether there had been something in Putin's eyes or tone, a gesture, anything that had intimated a course of action different from the one he was stating.

"War without war, conquest without loss. A siege of the mind."

Was that a brilliant tactic or an impossible hope? Why send a general of Yershov's background and temperament if not to prepare for a crushing military action?

Because, with me, the president can have both, Yershov had decided. He could turn a drill into an assault with a single "Go" order.

The helicopter landed off tarmac, near the command center, concealed from the western side by the sprawling complex of buildings. Yershov's eye was drawn to four new Uran-6 de-mining robots with bulldozer blades and trawls. They were designed to replace a bomb squad of twenty and could be operated from a distance of one kilometer. It was one of the first pieces of equipment President Putin had authorized in the rebuilding of the Russian military. Behind his medals, pride filled the general's chest.

The acting commander—Colonel Dyomin, a one-eyed veteran of Afghanistan—met the general with a sharp salute and a firmer handshake. They started toward Yershov's quarters, but the general asked, instead, to be taken directly to the SIC—the Surveillance and Intelligence Center—for immediate briefing.

The staff in the dark room snapped to in a way that Yershov recognized: *The new commander is coming, make a brilliant first impression.* He relaxed them with a gesture and, making his way around the circle of monitors clustered in the center of the room, he was introduced to the intelligence chief, the middle-aged, soft-spoken Major Pavel Zharov. Yershov asked for a tour.

"We have drones over Crimea at all times," Zharov said, indicating flat-screen monitors with aerial imagery. "Two"—he indicated the screens—"have infrared capabilities. This station receives reports from the twenty-three operatives we have spread throughout the region, both undercover and sympathizers in territory that is presently controlled by Kiev."

It was not lost on Yershov that Zharov had emphasized the word "presently."

"These three stations receive intelligence from the armored columns and from the air," the major went on. "The channels are always open."

Yershov understood that comment, too. The troops wore radios, and the radios were required when they were in uniform. There was very little talk about personal matters, unless they wanted those distractions known to command. This was a first-line installation. Professional demeanor was required at all times while on duty.

"What is this?" Yershov asked as he noticed a series of grids on the next two monitors. They looked like lie detectors.

"That's new," Zharov said proudly. "Aerostatics."

"Blimp surveillance," Yershov said admiringly. "Audio?"

"Yes, General. The two DP-29 units were launched three days ago and are the most sophisticated listening posts on the planet. These are unmanned, but the Dozor class will carry a small crew and a marksman for targeted strikes."

At Zharov's command, the technician handed him a tablet.

"All the data from these shakedown missions is stored on this device and shipped to Moscow for further evaluation," the major said.

"Why not send it electronically?" Yershov asked. "Kiev has

American-made electronics—surely they can intercept the signal from the blimp."

"Incoming signal-acquisition software makes hacking dangerous for the enemy," Zharov said. "The blimp can pinpoint and listen back at them. They learned that very quickly when they intercepted us relaying their precise location to Moscow. They stopped tuning in. But they would be able to hack our signals to Moscow, so we will send the weekly records on these."

Yershov took in the major, the monitors, the room beyond with a feeling of immense pride. He had not been entirely sure that this post wasn't a demotion, on some level. Now he knew better. President Putin had entrusted him with the most valuable military assets in the Russian arsenal.

Zharov brought up video of the blimps being launched from the airfield. The black envelopes with a modest red star on the side were roughly the size of a freight car. But, despite the shouts of the crew managing the guy lines fore and aft, the balloons were extremely quiet.

"Those are the propulsion?" Yershov asked, pointing at two small ducts in the rear.

"Virtually soundless lateral-ducted fan air accelerators," he said. "At night, unless you happen to look up and it blots the stars, you wouldn't know it was watching."

"And there is no infrared—" Yershov realized.

"No fuzzy images, only crisp audio," Zharov said, smiling.

They continued the tour, and the general took in every detail as if his brain were a computer and his eyes were high-definition cameras. He felt as if he had been transported to his youth, to a younger version of himself—yet with his wisdom and his experiences intact. It was a brilliant feeling, one he knew he should probably never experience again.

He had been given the keys to his nation's future in the region, and there was no circumstance in which he would allow the Ukrainians or their allies to damage them. None.

Assembling his top eight officers for dinner in the modest dining hall of the command compound—with Zharov to his immediate right, a place signifying the importance he placed on intelligence—Yershov listened to the general plans for maneuvers, which would begin just before dawn.

"I do not need to know the location and nature of everyone, every device that is not only listening and watching," Yershov told the men, but he was primarily addressing Zharov. "What I need to know is every person and every asset that goes into motion when we begin our maneuvers."

"We have operators in the front lines," said Colonel Ivan Isaev, who sat to the general's left. "Seven Special Forces squads integrated into the local populace or posing as hikers, surveyors—"

"There is something being planned," Yershov interrupted. "I was personally informed by Minister of Defense Timoshenko and by Mr. Putin himself that the Cyber-Surveillance Directorate of the GRU has uncovered what we believe is an imminent plot against one of our bases—most likely this base, given its proximity to the front and its importance."

He waited for those words to register before continuing.

"Our agents in Moscow and America have been risking their lives shutting down the enemy's spy network. One of our top men *lost* his life on that mission in the heart of New York City." Yershov fell silent as the main-course plates were removed, then motioned for the staff to wait for him to call them. He folded his hands before him. "I have been charged—personally, by the president—with making our forces here as battle-ready as possible as swiftly as possible. I intend to carry out those orders. And I have one order of my own. You have no doubt, all of you, heard of tank commander Captain Taras Klimovich, the so-called Fox."

There were nods and general murmuring among the eight other men.

"He has been in hiding," Yershov continued. "But I believe that if Kiev is going to move against a facility deep with armored assets he will be involved. He must be. He is their best tactician *and* field officer."

"Indeed, he is a hero to them, a legend in the military," Isaev remarked. "Why would they expose him?"

"You mean they would keep him safe like Gagarin after he became the first man into space, not risk having him killed on a second trip?"

"That, General, and not risk having him captured and humiliated," Isaev said.

"What you say is possible," Yershov agreed. "But I have read all about this man. Before the battle at Labkovicy he was a highly visible leader, an inspiration to his men and to all the Armed Forces of Ukraine. I might almost say there was a touch of narcissism."

"Like Rommel?" Isaev suggested.

"This Fox and Hitler's Desert Fox seem to have much in common, no?" Yershov said.

The men laughed. The names made that obvious.

"If there is a tank component, I do not believe he will stay hidden," Yershov said. "I want him. Major Zharov, can your blimps search for particular voices, speech patterns? There must be recordings?"

Zharov didn't answer immediately. He idly touched a dessert spoon.

"Major?" Yershov pressed.

"May I speak frankly, sir?"

"I would appreciate that," Yershov said. He looked around the table. "You are each specialists here. I do not know your jobs in detail. I rely on your candor."

There were a few nods, but most of the officers remained silent, wary. They were professional officers. In any military, outspoken or contradictory officers did not rise. Some, like Erwin Rommel, did not survive.

"General Yershov, with respect, a solitary-target application of my resources, of Colonel Isaev's men, of our satellites, would consume a great many assets for possibly negligible results," Zharov said. "And other dangers might slip through."

"The GRU has watched his family without success," Yershov said.

"I understand that, sir," Zharov replied. "What I would suggest is that we reverse-engineer the search. Assign a few eyes and ears to watch their forward armored units. Move through the entire array in an organized cycle. If any vehicles move toward the east, we can key on their communications and follow them backward. Somewhere there will be a source. Most likely encrypted, but that in itself will tell us where he is. Then we watch that place from the ground, from the sky, from space. We watch for *him*."

Yershov considered this. He was impressed that the man had crafted this plan over an empty table setting.

"Thank you, Major," the general said. "A very sensible approach. Do it." He signaled to his adjutant, who stood at the rear of the hall. "But after dessert," he said.

The men exhaled like a beach ball deflating here, then there. Relaxed expressions returned to their faces. Yershov missed none of it. It had been an important first exchange with his command: he wanted them to know that he not only expected results but expected officers who were more dedicated to the mission than they were to rubber stamps and promotions.

The rest of the meal was as relaxed a gathering among officers as any could recall, with every man eager to be about the business of organizing the full, integrated, and powerful activation of Sudzha Base.

CHAPTER TWENTY-EIGHT

Op-Center Headquarters, Fort Belvoir North,
Springfield, Virginia
June 3, 2:30 PM

By the time Matt Berry arrived from the White House, Op-Center was already deep in preparations to send Volner's team to Ukraine. He was shown to Williams's office as Bankole was making the case for Flannery to accompany the team.

"Paul, we've both been with wounded men," Williams had said. "I don't have to see the way he's protecting his left side—I can see it in his eyes. This man is hurting."

Neither Flannery nor Bankole had denied it. Nonetheless, they pressed their argument. Ultimately, Williams had relented and left it up to Volner to make the go, no-go call.

"If you can take the bouncing and turbulence of the Clipper, then you can probably endure the boat ride," Williams decided. "But that is his call, upon the advice of Sergeant Carson."

Levi Carson was the team medic. Though he didn't have veto authority over personnel, his advice weighed strongly on any decisions Volner made.

The men had departed then, after which Williams sat with Berry, Anne, Wright, and Dawson to review the plans as they existed to that point. The general strategy was firmly in place. Volner and Bankole would work out the rest, with Flannery's input, during the flight to Amasya Merzifon Airport, a military air base in Turkey near the Black Sea. The details that remained were to arrange the journey by sea through the Kerch Strait into the Azov.

Berry excused himself to brief Harward, who would relay the information to the president.

Lunch was ordered, and the team had their first break since morning.

"You look the way I feel, Chase," Dawson said as he unwrapped a taco.

"Oh? How do you feel?" Williams asked, not yet touching his cheeseburger, only picking at the fries

"I have never, not here or in the military, gone into a powder-keg situation with less information than we have now," Dawson said.

"Which is *why* we're going," Williams reminded him. "To get intel."

"Right," Dawson said. "Gathering intel about a powder keg *in* a minefield." He shook his head. "That's got to be a new kind of rose-colored crazy, and I've been accused of some stouthearted calls."

"I know," Williams said. "Russian maneuvers ramping up on one side. A possibly rogue, surgical Ukrainian military operation likely setting up on the other. NATO on a war footing, continuing to load Poland with materiel in the event of a Russian attack—a small army right on the doorstep of both sides. And our team winding its way through the middle in a hemisphere where Putin watches everything." Williams looked at Berry. "What do you think?"

"I don't like the other choice—doing nothing," Berry said.

"Agreed," Williams replied. "Though Putin could make an argument, one that would play across the globe, that we're participating in whatever is being planned in Crimea."

"But your team will withdraw at the first sign of movement," Berry said. "Yes?"

"That's the plan," Dawson told him. "Assuming they don't get pinned somewhere, in which case we don't dare go in to extract them."

Williams's phone had beeped. He saw that it was McCord and put him on speaker.

"I just got word on what caused the Bionic Hill fire," the intelligence director informed him. "A blast from a Russian mortar. They found shell fragments in the ruin, and a mortar in a nearby shed."

"Markings?" Willams asked.

"Scraped off," he replied. "They're going through security footage, but whoever fired it did due diligence. There are definitely blind spots."

"Roger, it's Brian," Dawson said. "How does someone smuggle a mortar past security?"

"Trucks full of crated equipment come and go all the time," McCord replied.

"It would've been stupidly easy."

"Any idea who fired it?" Williams asked.

"Not yet," McCord replied. "And it may not matter."

"What do you mean?" Williams asked.

"Whether the Russians did it or the Ukrainians did it to make it seem like the Russians did it, all the Ukrainian public west of Crimea will hear is 'A Russian mortar was fired,' and they'll be inflamed."

"Which would suggest Ukrainians looking to raise sentiment against Russia," Williams said.

"It doesn't need raising," Dawson pointed out. "It could just as well have been the Russians looking to anger the Ukrainians into launching a reckless attack—bigger than the one that's being planned."

"Why would Russia want a bigger attack?" Williams asked.

"Looks better to have that many more flaming Ukraininan tanks and artillery," Dawson said.

"It could also be the Ukrainians using a distraction to cover their tracks," McCord suggested. "Or they may simply have wanted to obliterate that building and whatever they were doing there. Blaming it on the Russians was just a bonus."

"Good point," Williams said.

"We're trying to find out more, but the truth is no one even knows for sure who was working in that back room."

"Do we know anything else about who Galina Petrenko or Fedir Lytvyn may have been working with?" Dawson asked.

"Nothing," McCord said. "We know they used burners. Fedir's only had local embassy contacts on it."

"I've been wondering about something," Dawson said. "There's been a lot of talk about NATO being an empty suit, that if Putin attacks a member nation the United States would never become involved militarily. If something does get triggered, will Putin take a shot at Poland or another member to see what we do?"

"Sort of the way Saddam Hussein fired Scuds into Israel during the Gulf War, trying to provoke them," Williams said.

"Exactly," Dawson replied.

"I've been leaning in that direction since this started," Wright said. "Something that forces international involvement and, in lieu of war, lands Putin a treaty that legally gives him a new, more favorable map."

"You know, that could explain the secret involvement, perhaps, of members of the government in Kiev," McCord suggested.

"How so?" Williams asked.

"There are many members of the Ukrainian Parliament who were frustrated by our inactivity while Crimea burned," McCord said.

"We sent them arms through Turkey," Dawson grumbled.

"We sent rifles and semiautomatics on a fleet of fishing boats," McCord jumped back. "I'm with Jim on this. My sources tell me that some members of Parliament actually found the delivery system insulting, as if we were saying that's the proper conveyance method for a peasant population. There's a bloc in Kiev that still wants us to commit at a higher, more visible level."

"By getting Putin pissed enough to attack a NATO member," Williams said.

"That's right," McCord replied. "And it's three years later, when their frustration has metastasized into anger and impatience."

"Flirting with World War Three because you were insulted by arms shipments," Anne said.

"Look, I'm not *justifying* it, Anne—" McCord said, his voice rising.

"I wasn't implying that—"

"But many of my colleagues inside the Beltway are looking at this very, very warily—that everything we've seen could be a provocation directed at Putin but really aimed at us. He overreacts, we're forced to get involved. You want to talk paranoid? My counterpart at the CIA thinks Putin is actually orchestrating all of this, financing the rogue Ukrainians, to cause a rift in Kiev and use that as a reason to move in from Sudzha, 'stabilize' the region, and ensure peace on the border—from thirty, forty, fifty miles into Ukraine."

"Which he will then annex," Anne said.

"Unless NATO ousts him," McCord said. "Which it probably won't. Hence, a treaty. Hence, a new map with him not moving backward."

"I'm not buying this as Putin's idea," Dawson said. "The killing of the two agents doesn't fit that scenario. I think this is just what it seems like: a bunch of crazy Ukrainians who have had it with Putin *and* Kiev. A sort of military coup without the coup. We just don't know what the bigger picture looks like, if there even is one."

"I hear both of you," Williams said. "We have to proceed

under the assumption that there is a military plan afoot. Which is why, for a change"—he glanced back at Berry—"I'm with the president. We have to be very, very careful about what we say and do. My divining rod here is Ambassador Flannery. This is a man who knows the region and the people, and he doesn't fool easily. He is very concerned, which is why we need Volner and Bankole *and* him on the ground there. Until we hear from them, let's keep watching for signs of deployment large or small on either side of the border."

The meeting broke up without a consensus, which was the norm for the team . . . for any committee in any government. Anne was the last to depart—with a sympathetic glance back at Williams as she closed the door.

The director sat back. He tried to eat, gave up. Trying to profile leaders and assemble clues that might define plans—it was all too damn speculative. And then lives were gambled on imperfect conclusions. It was like playing stud and betting everything on just one card. Frankly, he liked it better when he was in the field, following orders, with a target to take out. There were rules of engagement, objectives to be achieved, and officers who, if they had opinions, didn't offer them unless asked.

This job made him respect men like Flannery even more—the "geopolitical jugglers," as Wright had once dubbed them, which was why he had deferred to the ambassador's agitation and his insistence that he go abroad. That was really the tipping point for Williams: the older, injured man had made that request without knowing fully what hardships might follow. He didn't know because Volner and Bankole hadn't finished formulating the plan. If a veteran like Flannery was *that* concerned, then Williams should be, too.

Williams angrily tossed the takeout tray into the trash. Thinking of the danger, fear, and deprivation he had known at times in his military career, the burger, the forced air of the office, the fact that he could walk outside into safe, warming sunlight made him feel decadent. The old excuse—"You've paid your dues"—didn't find purchase when he thought of the sixty-two-year old in harm's way.

Fortunately for Williams, there was a solution and he applied it now, turning to emails. When he was at the Naval Academy in Annapolis, an ensign in their Germany and the Nazi Experience class had asked the professor a question:

"I don't know how I could have handled nine days of the Dunkirk evacuation," he'd said, "thinking of all the troops that were trapped there."

"Thinking," the teacher, USMC Major Tara Fitzpatrick, had replied. "Sometimes it's best not to."

CHAPTER TWENTY-NINE

Atlantic Ocean
June 3, 1:22 PM

There was a Roy Rogers lyric that Mike Volner's maternal grandfather, Albert, used to sing to him when he was very little:

"I'm back in the saddle again . . ."

It was the only part of the song Albert knew, and he kept repeating it, adding an "oh" before each refrain Volner had been too young to realize it at the time, but Albert and his Grandmother Eugenie were the only stability he had in his life. He lived with them from the time he was eight. Following a rancorous divorce, Volner's father, a college professor, left the country and, four years alter, was killed as a bystander by a car bomb while teaching in Pakistan. His mother fell prey to the ravages of solitary drinking and prescription painkillers to the point of having to be institutionalized. That was when the living arrangements with his grandparents, in Germantown, outside Philadelphia, became permanent. Visits to Independence Hall, Valley Forge, Gettysburg, set him on the path to enlistment and his career.

The military stopped well short of being a passion for Volner.

He didn't like going around in uniform, being peppered with the well-meant but unsolicited "Thank you for your service" comments from waitstaff and bank tellers and total strangers. He was raised with a respect and a love of America and what that stood for, even the old movie and TV cowboys, and this was the best way he felt he could serve the nation.

"At least until the job of Lone Ranger opened up," he had told Grandfather Al when he went off to Iraq for his first tour.

He had no less respect for the man sitting to his left, Ambassador Flannery, than he did for the generals at Belvoir or Bragg. This man not only loved his country; he loved another nearly as well. That took a special kind of heart, and being here took a unique kind of courage. Especially because the rocking, rattling ride that marked any trip on a C-17 was obviously causing him pain. Sergeant Carson had rebandaged Flannery's torso to mitigate the pain but still allow him to breathe, and prescribed a powerful aspirin, instead of painkillers, so he'd be alert.

"As long as you don't puncture a lung, you'll be okay," Carson had said in the medical bay at Belvoir.

"How will I know?" Flannery had asked.

With a crooked grin, Carson had replied, "Sir, you won't have to ask."

Op-Center had acquired its own transport for long-haul trips, a matte-gray, unmarked C-40A Clipper. The Boeing aircraft was a workhorse for both the Air Force and the Navy, and this particular plane had seen service for the latter. The population at Pope Airfield took verbal jabs at Volner for using an "enemy" aircraft, but they cared for it as if it were their own. From

Williams's point of view, the Clipper had a value among the green-money voters in Congress: it exceeded international noise and environmental standards, which had the practical benefit of making it more fuel-efficient and allowing it greater range. The aircraft could carry up to a hundred and twenty-one passengers in a standard two-three seat arrangement but also had a combi configuration that could accommodate three cargo pallets and seventy passengers. Volner liked having the ability to evac civilians or other military personnel if necessary. It could also land on shorter runways than a C-17 or an equivalent behemoth required, such as their current destination in Turkey.

Once they were airborne, sitting three across, Volner had huddled with Bankole to review the plans to get to the Arrow. They were looking at networked tablets, which showed a map of the region. Flannery sat on the aisle.

"The area of the Black Sea we have to cross is a little over three hundred miles," Volner was saying. "I can get us a fishing cruiser out of Samsun that can accommodate all of us and our gear below deck. It can do sixteen knots—a little over eighteen miles an hour, which gets us to the strait in about sixteen hours. Plenty of time to rest, and we don't have to worry about going through a Russian radar net."

Flannery was listening and nudged the major.

"The Russians know about the black ops," he said, using the name for the secret fleet that crossed the Black Sea. "They knew about it in 2014, at the height of the gun running."

"Did they harass the boats?" Bankole asked.

Flannery shook his head. "There were too many ringers

making their way into the Azov from Turkey, Bulgaria, and Romania. Some of them were paid, some of them were actual fishing boats. It would have tied up too many assets for Mosow to form an airtight blockade. They buzzed aircraft, shot at a few, brought down one civilian aircraft as a warning—which is why the shipments weren't made by air."

"The Russians aren't fighting a war right now," Bankole pointed out.

"And Kiev isn't on an embargo footing," Flannery said. "They're purchasing arms from Belarus, Brazil, other nations. The Russians are likely to leave us alone."

Volner had assumed as much from the DOD intelligence reports on the region, but he was grateful for Flannery's participation and insight, and thanked him.

"We get an air-to-air refuel out of Ramstein and will be landing at Trabzon Airport on the eastern Black Sea," Volner went on. "From there it's a short bus ride to the vessel. Our captain will be Kaan Hamzaçebi. " He brought up a picture of a swarthy man in his forties, with an eye patch and a full beard. "He served in the Turkish Naval Forces, lost an eye while testing an air-cushioned landing craft. He's got a small pension and a big grudge against the Undersecretariat of the Sea and the Australian firm that made the vessel."

"Do you know the man?" Flannery asked.

Volner shook his head. "But he's marked A2. The brass at Bragg trust him."

"Then why not A1?" Bankole asked.

"In the event of a conflict with the Republic of Turkey or the

Christian population, he would still side with Ankara over any opposition," Volner said.

"Member of the Syriac Orthodox Church," Bankole said, reading his dossier. "'Syriac,' as in 'Syria.'"

"That's right," Flannery said. "But allied with Oriental Orthodoxy and following some of the oldest Christian doctrines. Traditionally, they tend more toward monastic ideals than war."

"I'm looking forward to meeting him," Bankole said.

Volner looked over. He knew from the man's dossier that their new Op-Center liaison was a Buddhist.

"May I ask, sir—and you'll forgive my ignorance or tell me if I'm out of line here—but how do you reconcile war and faith?"

"I'm still working on that," Bankole said, laughing.

"One of the big questions of modern times, isn't it?" Flannery interjected.

"Like Captain Hamzaçebi, I had a good deal of hospital time—a period when I was angry, despairing, depressed," Bankole said. "In Buddhism I found a philosophy of personal responsibility that fit my own belief system. There's a concept called *Sarambha*, which means that any human who acts on ideas that are considered destructive—*dosa*, for example, hatred—experiences the resulting violence as a means of self-harm. It prevents you from achieving enlightenment. It's sort of like a kid who eats too much sugar: that's going to delay a host of developmental ideals."

"Except that there's no parent to wag a finger at you," Flannery suggested.

"Oh, teachers will, and should," Bankole said. "But, ultimately, your own spiritual growth or lack thereof is on you." He

238 JEFF ROVIN AND GEORGE GALDORISI

pointed at the tablet. "I read about a great many religions while I was in the hospital, and I'm willing to bet that this man has the same conflict."

Flannery smiled. "Would—" He stopped, winced as the aircraft bounced. "Would that we all had that same level of questioning."

Volner felt left out of this conversation and discreetly turned back to the map to look over the Kerch Strait and the Sea of Azov section of the journey. There were still tactics to be considered, decisions to be made. Though they would continue with Hamzaçebi to the Arrow, Anne would be making all the arrangements for their landing. Studying the map, Volner was beginning to wonder if a southern landing in Russian territory might not make more logistical sense than a longer journey south.

Flannery noticed his attention to a map of the region.

"You're thinking of an early anchor?" the ambassador asked.

"We land in Turkey shortly before dawn," Volner said thoughtfully. "We reach the strait just before sunset. We arrive in the Azov after dark. I'm not sure we gain anything by traveling farther north and involving locals only to travel south."

"The Russians patrol those waters with some frequency," Flannery said.

"'Some frequency' still leaves us windows," Volner said, requesting updates from Op-Center. "And those lost hours could matter." He looked over at the international crisis manager. "Yes?"

Bankole nodded. The thought of going back into potential action, a riskier landing, awakened some tameless part of him that had been dormant for years. He did not fight it down.

"Now all I have to do is make it worth Kaan's while," Volner smirked, rubbing his fingers together.

"I was hoping a discourse on religion might sway him," Bankole half joked. But only half.

"Mr. Ambassador," Volner went on, "we'll get satellite data of the Russian naval patrols. Putting that aside for the moment, where is the ideal spot to go ashore in the dark?"

"A great many Russians, well-to-do Russians, use Solyane as a health destination," Flannery said.

"Fishing?"

"Some pleasure boats," he said. "Will yours pass?"

"I don't know," he admitted. "Solyane is one of the three cities on Arabat Spit—the only one in Russian-held territory."

"That is correct, though there is an ongoing dispute about Sevastopol."

"I want to avoid suspicions and disputes," Volner said.

"Solyane is a very small location with miles of beachfront," Flannery said. "Though I have another suggestion." He leaned over and scrolled south on the touch screen. "Arabat Fortress. It was built around the seventeenth century by the Turks, taken over by the Russians in 1737—another reason Putin lays historic claim to the region—and has been a part of virtually every war until now. It serves little strategic value, and at night I cannot imagine there would be tourists."

"Just the sea patrols," Volner said.

Flannery nodded.

"Looks good to me," Bankole said. "We could walk to the peninsula from there, probably conceal ourselves before sunup."

"It's where we want to be," Volner agreed.

Bankole contacted Op-Center to get current surveillance from the National Reconnaissance Office and to find out how many fishing boats worked the southern Azov.

Volner went through the cabin informing the team of the change of plans, indicating that they should look at the maps of the reason to familiarize themselves with the coast and also the northern edge of the Crimean Peninsula itself.

"Chances are good you will need to know that region in the dark."

The gregarious quality that often accompanied the onset of a mission evaporated quickly as the team hunkered down to study. The only sound was the slightly muted bellow of the two large and powerful CFM56-7 engines and the rattle of the gear stowed aft.

Volner could also hear his heart in his ears, only part of which was due to the altitude. Unlike the others, he was aware of the hair-trigger politics of the region and the reality that recon could quickly turn to self-defense, with rules of engagement that were sharply against them. . . .

CHAPTER THIRTY

Semenivka, Poltava Oblast, Ukraine
June 3, 10:00 PM

It was the confirmation Captain Taras Klimovich had been waiting for . . . the words he had been hoping for.

An indispensable operative working in the woods outside Sudzha had reported that an Mi-24PN attack helicopter had landed just a few hours before at the airstrip of the new base. According to intelligence from St. Petersburg, the likely occupant was Colonel General Anatoly Yershov. The report had been pieced together from two separate and discreet sources: the forward observer at Sudzha himself, and a deep-cover welder at the Leningrad shipyard, a soldier who had gone to Russia with forged documents when the first stirrings of war erupted. The two men didn't know about each other, but Klimovich knew them both.

The reports confirmed Klimovich's own suspicions that this was the man Putin would send. A seasoned tank commander and the obvious choice to firmly reestablish the honor lost by his predecessor, General Novikov, whose name and career the Fox had destroyed.

Or, rather, enabled the general himself to destroy, he thought. Pride goeth before destruction, and Novikov had a medaled chest full of it.

And Putin—the modern czar also had his simple, predictable ways.

Putin does nothing that is complicated, the Ukrainian officer thought. He does not have the capacity to think in any direction but a straight line, *through* something.

Putin would try and do that via his proxy Yershov. A perfect pair to take the bait that Klimovich had prepared.

It was late, it was dark and moonless, and it was time to move. The officer smoothed his mustache, then checked his appearance in the full-length mirror in the closet. It wasn't vanity, not really. But appearances mattered, and he was pleased to see that he still wore the uniform with crisp ease. This would be the first time he had gone out in uniform in months. He had been wary of being spotted by satellite, by unmanned drone, by traitors—any of the assets the Kremlin retained in the region. Now there was no longer any reason to hide. At some point—and that time would come very, very soon—he wanted Yershov to know that the Fox was here . . . and on his doorstep.

He will bite, the captain thought confidently. A man like him must.

Klimovich's part of the plan was simple. He would rejoin his command, a tank corps that did not exist on any listings or charts in Kiev and was known to only a handful of high-ranking loyalists in the Ministry of Defense. It was based in the town of Kharkiv, in the Slobozhanshchyna region of eastern Ukraine—

just twenty miles from the Russian border. It was an old factory, an apparent graveyard of more than four hundred tanks, supposedly abandoned. To any Russian surveillance, it had the carefully maintained appearance of a metal graveyard.

It was anything but that. For well over a year, under the cover of night, shielded by the factory walls and the inordinately high grasses, the vehicles had been scrupulously maintained. Ordnance and supplies had been relocated to the heavily fortified compound, which was monitored 24/7 by unseen patrols and cameras.

When Klimovich arrived, when his old tank crews made their way there—some on leave, some retired, a handful forced to go AWOL from current assignments—this dead army would spring to life. And, alive, it would move toward the unsuspecting Russian border like ghosts from a war gone by.

It would be a shock to Moscow to see half of those tanks alive and on the move. The word would go out, by morning, that the Fox was taking his command on maneuvers in Ukrainian territory.

Then it would be up to Yershov. If he moved, Klimovich would slow. If he didn't move, Klimovich would begin to assert indomitable control over the western fringes of Ukrainian territory. Then, when Putin felt the teeth of the Fox near his throat, he would have three choices: do nothing, which was unthinkable; commit airpower, which would be restricted from crossing the border—a provocative ploy he had tried against Bulgaria in 2016 and which drew wide international censure—or, if they did, risk being fired upon; or send his tank corps to form a barricade on the other side.

Putin would have to commit his tanks.

And when Yershov moved out, Klimovich's other team would move in. A seven-man team that Yershov, Putin, and Sudzha would never see coming . . . and, if everything went as planned, would never see leaving, either.

Klimovich went downstairs to a waiting police car—driven by one of his old lieutenants—and, after an embrace, they set out on a mission the Fox had designed to inflame a population that had been kept down for far too many decades.

CHAPTER THIRTY-ONE

Sumy, Ukraine
June 4, 12:35 AM

The train station in this northeastern Ukrainian city presented a sharp contrast to the architectural splendor of the Kyiv-Passazhyrskiy Railway Station. It is a long rectangular structure, three stories high, that looks as if cinder blocks had been piled on a foundation of sandstone. The saving grace is the big windows, which—when it is sunny—blanket the interior with light.

The train was typically but not inconveniently late. Major Romanenko and his team emerged on a seasonably chilly night and, separating, took different routes on the short, southward walk to the Yubileinaia, a high-end hotel. The six men had four separate rooms there, all on the ground floor, and each arrived with different cover stories; however, none of the staff inquired. Since landing near the front line of war, the hotel had been busy and turned an unseeing eye to whoever came and went.

"It's like my grandfather used to say about hotels in Morocco and other neutral states during World War Two," Tkach told Romanenko when they entered the suite they shared. "Always changing hands, ready to move whichever way the new conqueror decreed."

The team members showered and ordered room service over the course of two hours. During that time, Romanenko and Tkach had the additional task of checking the backpacks and duffel bags that had been delivered to their room earlier in the day. These were marked "Crimea Geological Survey." The bags and the logo were scuffed to make them look field-worn.

In a duffel bag, each man would find a Fort-14TP handgun; a compact Fort-221 assault rifle; a half-dozen RGD-5 hand grenades that had been found in a small arms cache left behind by Russian forces; and a Kevlar vest. The backpacks contained extra ammunition. One grip, larger than the rest, contained a UAG-40 grenade launcher, the latest production model. It was a sleek, compact work of military art. Setting it on its collapsible stand, Romanenko stepped back and took in the charcoal-black barrel. It was the first time he'd smiled since destroying the Long Barracks.

The man who had delivered the bags showed up at 3:45. All of the men had been told to make their way to Romanenko's room before then, when the halls were quiet and empty. All six team members were drinking coffee when he arrived.

The man was an imposing figure, normally standing six feet three; his work boots gave him another inch. He was broad-shouldered and dressed like a laborer except for the distinctive black beret—a sign of allegiance to Captain Taras Klimovich.

Two years and two months before, in an act of stunning self-sacrifice, Admiral Volodymyr Berezovsky, the fifty-seven-year-old chief of the general staff of the Ukrainian military, had publicly sworn his allegiance to the pro-Moscow movement in Crimea. The Ukrainian president, Viktor Yanukovych, dismissed him at once. Only the president and select members of the government knew that the defection was a sham and that Berezovsky had resigned in order to gather whatever intelligence he could for Kiev.

It was Berezovsky who, upon the death of agents Petrenko and Lytvyn, had been forced to get close enough to the newly operational base in Sudzha to send reports to Captain Klimovich. And to leave a package in the woods outside Yunakivka, in Ukrainian territory. One that Russia would never forget.

Romanenko and his team saluted the former officer. The steady gray eyes glistened at the tribute. It had been an extremely challenging twenty-six months, a time when his family in Ukraine had been subjected to ridicule and shame. But those days, that psychological prison sentence, was about to come to an end.

"Captain Taras Klimovich sends compliments to Major Romanenko and his team," Berezovsky said, returning the salute.

"We are deeply honored," Romanenko replied.

The admiral peered through the half-open bedroom door, saw that the gear he'd brought to the room had been divided among the men and was stacked crisply on the bright-red bedspread. All that was missing was the materiel he had left in the field over a period of weekend leaves lasting several months— weapons that would have made travel through the forests awkward for the team.

"I am happy to report that the captain has arrived safely and without incident in Kharkiv," Berezovsky told them. "He has been to the factory, preparations have been completed, and twenty-one hours from now the entire command will move east." He paused for a moment to look into the eyes of every man present. "There has never been a moment like this in our nation—or in the history of any nation. An army will rise and, with it, the spirit of a people. And yet you six are the heart of this mission. Whatever happens, while the Russians are distracted and confused in the northeast, it is your strike against Sudzha that will be a knife in their heart.

"I am also pleased to tell you—and I have just returned from that location—that since the arrival of the new commander there appear to be no perimeter changes," Berezovsky went on. "If the armored columns are drawn away, and you follow the training video—or whatever you call that creation—you should have no difficulty getting inside."

The men were silent. They had drilled for this—the maneuvers were in their muscle memory. Even surprises, holes left by the failure of Galina Petrenko and Fedir Lytvyn to acquire information—even that would be overcome, they were determined, by darkness, by teamwork, by the blunt surprise of their audacious plan.

Now the import of the moment, of the approach of H-hour, made its way into their souls. When they struck, the Russians would know at once that they had fallen for a feint designed to leave the base vulnerable. When they struck, Moscow would realize that the entire attack plan had been announced beforehand, laid out in the leaked virtual film—but they had been unable to make that simple connection. Both the military and the intelligence network would suffer a global humiliation and personnel changes that rocked the Kremlin.

Then, with luck, anti-Russian members of the government would have the public support to act, and to act decisively. The time would be right to take Kiev from the moderates and retake Crimea from Moscow.

Romanenko was shown a map of the location of the two heavily wooded locations with ordnance the admiral had left for the men. When Romanenko had memorized the locations, the map was burned. Then Berezovsky broke out the bottle of vodka he had packed for a toast.

"To the cause," he said simply, as the men raised two glasses and a bottle cap while the others passed the bottle itself.

There was a round of embraces, after which the admiral said his leave ended at ten and he had to hurry to rejoin his command on the Azov. However, he paused at the door and looked back at a clock on a lamp stand.

"In less than twenty-four hours from now, you will make history," he said. "I am proud to have met you all."

And then he was gone and the door clicked behind him, and six men stood with the vodka and their thoughts—but only for a moment. Romanenko turned and regarded the clock.

"It's four oh one," he announced. "The countdown has begun."

CHAPTER THIRTY-TWO

Washington, D.C.
June 3, 7:07 PM

"How the hell do you do it, Matt?"

Brian Dawson's question to Matt Berry was rhetorical, but Berry answered anyway.

"Because I love it."

The men sat across from each other in a small booth at the Nookery on Connecticut Avenue NW. For a metropolis keenly sensitive to political correctness, the near–double entendre of the name of the singles bar was refreshing. It had received a lot of attention before it opened—"It's a place to plug in your tablet and read," Heather Jacks, the proprietor, had insisted—and it had grabbed an overflow of hip young clientele from day one. Dawson and Berry were not that, but the owner was Berry's cousin and they always managed to get a table.

Berry had briefed Trevor Harward before leaving Op-Center. Williams and his team had just reviewed and approved the change of plan suggested by Mike Volner, and Anne had finally confirmed all the necessary arrangements in Turkey. Kaan

Hamzaçebi had not been happy with the idea of going ashore so deep in Russian-held territory, but an extra five thousand U.S. dollars assuaged those concerns.

Harward had expressed the same concerns as Hamzaçebi, but then Berry had expected that. If he said "light," the NSA automatically said "dark." The call had been on speaker, so the others knew where Op-Center stood. The president would be informed, with all the red flags Harward could muster. If this went south, it was all on Chase Williams.

Williams had seemed unconcerned and sent everyone home.

Dawson picked at his Wisconsin Salad, which was a few vegetables on top and a lot of cheese below. "I still don't understand," he said. "My head's full of what-ifs, and I can't stop chewing on them. What if the Russians attack in Ukrainian territory? What if the Ukrainians attack in Russian territory? What if the Ukrainians attack our guys? What if the Russians do? What if our team is captured by Putin's troops? What if our guys shoot and kill Russians?"

"All of that? It's out of your control now, Brian," Berry said. "The apparatus is in motion."

"Yeah," Dawson said. "And a bunch of those turning gears have my initials on them. Lives depend on how it all comes together."

"You saved a life yesterday, about this time. Can't you feel good about that?"

"I should, but that was yesterday. I'm concerned about tomorrow."

"Understood, but the pros are in the field, they've got the ball," Berry said. "It's on them now."

Dawson shook his head. "I can't be that detached. You learned to be when you were a divorce attorney, I understand that. But when I was with Fifth Special Forces, I was B-Team leader for a reason: someone else had to make that go call. I always wanted a little more time to work it out."

"Like with Carolina?" Berry asked.

"Did I tell you I saw her today?"

"You didn't have to. It's all over your face."

"Oh. Yeah, I couldn't pull that plug, either."

The men ate in silence for a moment.

"With me, it's more than detachment," Berry said. "Even when I had my law office, I tried to find the pluses."

"Pluses? In emotional upset?"

"It's a divorce, Brian. Someone is always gonna be hurt. I tried to make it a controlled crash. I was part attorney, part shrink, part confessor. And it was interesting work. What's the song—you look at life from both sides?"

"Joni Mitchell, 'Both Sides Now,'" Dawson said.

"Well, in one hour you're for the man, the next hour you're for the woman, and once I was for the kids of a cabinet member. That put me on track to where I am today. It was quite a kaleidoscope. I'm only sorry I missed out on gay divorces."

"Why?" Dawson asked.

"First generation, history being made."

Dawson sipped his Bud Light. "Is that what I was, Matt?"

"What do you mean?"

"A kaleidoscope, a weekly psychedelic display?"

"No—it was daily, as you may recall," Berry said around a mouthful of a side of Frito pie.

"Screw you."

"At its height, twice daily," Berry pointed out.

Dawson scowled. "It was a shitty time—"

"*Was.* It's been over for nearly two years and look how your face just soured. Christ, it melted."

"Can't help it," Dawson said. "I'm having trouble getting past the fact that she's happier with that Australian rancher than she was with me."

"I told you then and I'll repeat it now," Berry said. "You pick at that scab and it'll never heal. Anyway, don't look at it as having lost a wife," Berry went on, smiling broadly. "You gained a friend."

Dawson made a face. "You needed a squash partner who was six four and built like you."

"You're hurting my feelings," Berry drawled.

Dawson continued to fork at the grated cheese. "My *point*, when I still had one, is that you liked that work and you like this work. Maybe you thrive on confrontation—and don't take this personally—when the stakes are on someone else. Spouses, Chase Williams—

"It's possible," Berry admitted. "I like going to horse races at Laurel Park, too, as long as I don't place any bets. Maybe you just get too involved in this stuff."

Dawson made a circling motion with his finger. "Return to where I mentioned the lives that are at stake. When I think back,

you know when I was happy? Flipping burgers at a fast-food joint
when I was a teenager. Every now and then I had to slide over
and drop fries in the oil, then back to the grill. Task—done.
Task—done. Nothing stayed with you except the smell of the
grease."

"So? Go back to cooking burgers. It's a brave new world,
Brian, where people with top security clearance make strawberry
shakes and kids without a college degree hack the FBI from a
table you just served."

Dawson finished his salad and nursed his beer. Heather
came over to make sure everything was all right.

"Fine, cuz," Matt said. "Brian's just being introspective."

"Well, order dessert or introspect at the bar," she said. "Louis
needs the tips."

"We'll have the check, thanks," Berry said. "I have my kung-
fu class at eight."

Dawson smiled up at Heather as she walked away. It was
too bad she was married. He could have helped screw up another
woman's life. He looked back across the table.

"I do admire your initiative, Matt," Dawson said. "All I
want to do is go home and watch a ball game."

"That's okay, too," Berry said. "As long as you're happy."

"Right," Dawson said. "That's the missing part."

Berry regarded him for a long moment. "What's the missing
part here? What's got you so down? And don't tell me it's women."

"No," he said. "They're a low-level buzz, like tinnitus."

"Then what? There have been risky missions before, potentially more dangerous than this."

"True," Dawson said. "But however I look at those gears you mentioned, the moving parts in this operation, they all mesh just one way."

"And that is?"

Dawson said, "Lose-lose."

CHAPTER THIRTY-THREE

Op-Center Headquarters, Fort Belvoir North,
Springfield, Virginia
June 3, 8:33 PM

There was one person who didn't take Chase Williams's advice.

Williams and Anne had gone home shortly after the rest of the team. They didn't want to leave, but they knew they had to be fresh for the arrival of the JSOC team in Turkey. Neither knew how much sleep they would actually get, or if they would even try, or if they would be able to stay away from the command center. But just being out of the subterranean network of offices, away from machine-cooled, forced air, away from the anxiety that naturally permeated the corridors, would do them good. Both were reachable at all times on any number of secure lines and devices, and they could be back at the office quickly. In the old days, under Paul Hood, there had been a night command, fully staffed; now there were only monitors to get in touch with Williams, Anne, and the others. Being under the radar had its fiscal downside.

Roger McCord, however, had decided not to leave. There

were too many missing pieces in Crimea, pieces he felt were out there if he looked in the proper places.

"You're the intelligence director," he told himself as he sifted through data from national and international assets. "You shouldn't *have* blind spots."

Especially when the goddamn target had given them part of a road map: the virtual end-game. And a potentially related attack on Bionic Hill, he thought.

The problem was, this team—and it had to be one, however small—had covered their movements well before anyone knew they were there. And missing names, destinations, materiel— what was called the "negative space" in the narrative—wasn't small. Op-Center didn't know whether that video showed the entirety of the plan or only the access point. Was there a second part? Was biological or nuclear material involved?

Or is this just a band of patriots looking to jumpstart a Reconquista using sheer brass? It was hardly unprecedented. That act itself was named largely for the bold moves made in the eleventh century by the Spanish hero Rodrigo Diaz de Vivar—El Cid, the Lord—against invaders from Africa. The superior, entrenched Moorish forces were driven back in part by a noble leader, in part by an aroused population. That was how a knight, not a prince or a king, became the national hero of Spain.

A century later, the same template played out in Russia, as Prince Alexander Nevsky united warring princedoms to battle Teutonic invaders. His peasant army beat back the heavily armored knights on horseback, defeating them on the frozen surface of Lake Peipus.

It was not impossible that someone in Ukraine was proud, patriotic, and vain enough to attempt the same thing, either from the safety of Kiev or at the head of an élite paramilitary squad. Every generation has its brash hero, from William Barret Travis at the Alamo, who drew the first recorded line in the sand, to Chase Williams's own personal hero, the ungovernable General MacArthur, who vowed, "I shall return," and did, McCord thought. Ukraine has a heroic void, and this would be the time to fill it.

Especially given the news that, after emptying its first sovereign fund to pay for its adventures and make up for chronically low oil and natural-gas prices, Moscow was tapping the second and last of its financial cushions. The National Wealth Fund reserves were supposed to be for emergencies, not to fill budgetary shortfalls. Burning through funds at its current rate, by the end of 2019 the totality of Russia's federal resources would be five hundred billion rubles scattered throughout a variety of banks and institutions. At the current rate of exchange, that was significantly below eight million dollars. With a declining ruble, Russia would be broke. While Putin might be willing to play brinkmanship, the world couldn't allow that: a bankrupt Moscow would leave the nation effectively in the hands of the military and the black market, with widespread destabilization on the border of China. The Kremlin would expect, and rightly, some kind of Crimean resolution to be forced on Kiev long before that happened.

Armageddon is headed our way, full tilt, because you can't find a bunch of foolhardy Ukrainians, McCord thought with frustration. He was frustrated about that and he was frustrated because he was getting tired. But he was like a dog with a bone. There had to be *something*.

He looked at a current satellite map of the region, which displayed the new Russian base and the old Ukrainian forests.

Somewhere there is a bottleneck, McCord thought. To get to one of the two army bases, to come at Sudzha or, possibly, Voronezh from the west, there has to be one route that's most advantageous. And he couldn't entirely rule out the naval base at Sevastopol. He *would* not rule it out.

But the search for a chokepoint was a dead end. As with D-Day, or Hannibal and his elephants, or George Washington crossing the Delaware to attack the Hessians at Trenton, the attack might come from an unexpected place at an unanticipated hour and with unconventional firepower.

Maybe that whole damn virtual-reality program is a red herring and they're going to piss on the naval base from drones.

McCord sat back angrily in his swivel chair. The history courses in the PhD program in International Affairs had been loaded with successful surprise attacks. His own experiences as company commander in Fallujah and as a battalion exec in Ramadi had reinforced his understanding that, while it was occurring, history was about a complete *lack* of understanding and perspective. Context came later. The trick was imagining a context with sufficient antecedent and wisdom to predict what was going to happen.

And then it was still just that: profiling and prediction.

McCord was unhappy, and he became increasingly so as the

night grew old. There was an axiom in the intelligence community: Something is out there, you're just not seeing it.

What had he overlooked? There were Ukrainian heroes, there were traitors, there were all stops in between. Where to focus what few hours were left?

None of the algorithms worked. Nothing. He tried Havrylo Koval with any military personnel. He looked for Koval in surveillance footage from Bionic Hill. He found him, but never with anyone. He searched for the deployment of 2B14 Podnos in 2014, for any Russian retreats where they might have been abandoned. He checked for stolen inventory, but Russia was a sieve for black-market armaments. All he found was lists of the materiel they had.

Agents. Double agents.

Kiev hadn't been forthcoming about who was in the field. They surely had them; they simply didn't trust NATO enough to share. Not until the organization, and the United States, did more to openly provide them with infantry arms and heavy ordnance.

Someone is behind this, McCord thought. Someone is drilling. Someone will be in the field, may already be in the field. That was what Bankole and Volner were going to find out. Someone in my position should at least be able to provide goddamn direction!

He started with a proposition he had visited earlier, that the attack on Bionic Hill was meant to disguise whatever drilling had been going on there, destroy any evidence, and arouse local passions. The Russians might have targeted it if they knew the team was drilling there—but more likely with a fire and barred exits, or, even more likely than that, with an assassination like those they'd already committed. Bionic Hill was also a campus, for God's sake. Anyone could have had access.

Eliminate the Russians and you have Ukrainians. The question was which Ukrainains.

The ones who were already there, he thought. Suppose they were the ones who did this?

They might go to ground until the investigation was through. But then there was a risk, however slight, that they'd be caught, transportation centers shut down. They would likely blow the walls down and immediately head to their target zone while the training was still fresh.

Or one would. The others would have gone ahead, lest the trigger man was captured.

That made sense. It was *how* Special Forces deployed: they didn't drill, then take a week off, then go ahead and attack a high-risk target. They left almost at once.

Assuming that Sudzha was the target, how would they have moved forward? McCord wondered.

An airdrop was unlikely: the Russians would be watching for that, and it would be easy to detect. Separate vehicles by road? Very possible. Train? Also possible. They would have trained with the weapons they would be using so they would be utterly familiar. The question was, would they be carrying those weapons or would they have been shipped ahead? Shipped ahead, they could abort if the cache were uncovered. Carrying them, they would be forced to fight.

The big drawback to vehicular traffic was that everyone in the front seat was visible to security cameras, and every security camera had infrared illuminators for night traffic. The United States had given Kiev this and facial-recognition software to watch for politicians, military figures, and journalists who were known to have Russian sympathies. The so-called chicken-wire net—Ukrainian officials were fond of branding enemies—had nabbed a number of troublemakers who, in the United States, would have been defended by the ACLU or some other rights group. That was not a consideration in Ukraine, not to the extent it was here.

Trains and buses were covered. The only time anyone was visible was at the terminals.

That only leaves me with several hundred possi—

He sat up suddenly.

Maybe not.

Having one of Aaron's people hack the e-ticket train and bus database in Kiev was unlikely to turn up anything. A careful operative would have purchased tickets in advance, for cash, on site. They wouldn't have trusted an outsider: it had to be someone in the know, someone who was trusted. One of them.

Maybe all of the travelers went to the station at some point, individually, McCord thought. Maybe one or more had been there hours before, maybe made a point of "missing" a train they never intended to catch as a reason to hang around, watch for potential trouble such as police or military personnel. McCord didn't think they would go to their final destination separately; it would be too dangerous to communicate by cell phone, and it was essential that they stay in touch in the event of a change of plans.

But . . . there was one thing they couldn't cover.

Someone would likely have gone there at some point, days or weeks before, to see where the security cameras were in order to know how to avoid them. Yet to spot the cameras this person might first have been caught by one or more of them. And, somewhere during a long trip east from Kiev, that same individual might have gotten out to stretch. And certainly to depart. Was it possible to avoid every camera along the way?

McCord contacted a source on the graveyard shift with the National Police of Ukraine in Kiev. Elena Reva was a computer specialist who collected one hundred dollars weekly from the CIA. Since 2014, Op-Center had thrown in another fifty. The woman was neutral in war but not in finance.

McCord asked for, and got, the daily code to access stored and current footage from the rail line.

He didn't bother looking at any of it. He ran it through Op-Center's sophisticated digital analyzer, looking for faces that appeared repeatedly. The expected ones showed up: engineers and conductors, commuters who got on and off within an hour or two of Kiev. There were tourists who came and left Kiev days apart.

But then there was someone who stood out. Someone who was clearly casing the station, because he had no luggage, nothing to read, and came and went within an hour. This same someone—nearly eighty-percent possibility—showed up today at one of the easternmost stops on the rail line: the city of Sumy.

He contacted Elena, asked for access to the footage there.

Some negotiation was required—an additional two hundred dollars—but he got it. He didn't bother explaining that this was for the security of her own nation. All he cared about was the Op-Center team.

The same man showed up, on foot, with a considerable duffel bag, walking through the deserted nighttime streets. McCord had no idea who he was or where he was going. The destination wasn't as important as the identification.

Excitement rising, McCord went back to access what Op-Center had earlier, material that had been downloaded and saved: the security footage from Bionic Hill.

This man was there, too. Driving into the front gate weeks earlier. It wasn't enough to get an ID, only to confirm that he was most likely part of whatever operation was being hatched there.

And if the train IDs are this same man, it is an operation that's already in motion dangerously close to the border.

He set to work trying to figure out who the hell this was and when he was planning to act. It was Bruce Perry III at the Department of Naval Intelligence—an old friend and colleague—who finally made the ID for him.

McCord immediately phoned Williams with a suggestion that wasn't going to sit well with anyone at Op-Center or in the field.

But there was no way around it that McCord could see. And, worse than the risk it posed for Volner and his team, the danger to the region was even greater.

CHAPTER THIRTY-FOUR

Kharkiv, Ukraine
June 4, 3:45 AM

Havrylo Koval was overwhelmed.

The road to this event had been longer than the road to this place, though the latter felt interminable. Seated beside Ivan Glinko, all Koval wanted was to communicate with Romanenko or any member of his team. But that was forbidden. In the aftermath of the attack on the Long Barracks, it was impossible to know who would be listening to or triangulating mobile devices. Glinko occasionally shut his iPod to turn on the news, but there was nothing to hear.

They made their way northeast slowly, circuitously, with Glinko never revealing where they were going. His orders were to tell no one and, as he pointed out, "No one includes my passenger."

"Even though I will find out soon enough?" Koval had complained.

Glinko had shrugged. "Maybe I am being tested for trustworthiness, for other tasks."

The man had a point. Koval had no idea what his relationship with the team leadership might be.

The main road, the side roads, the country roads droned on. Koval half expected to be waylaid somewhere along the way by some outlying members he knew nothing about. All he knew was that there was an operational command center somewhere adjacent to Crimea and that he was being taken there. His job would be to make sure data flowed between personnel on a system that had been put together—as Romanenko had described it—"in the dark by the only tech people we could trust."

It was just after two in the morning when they reached their destination, Khariv, the second-largest city in the nation and a modern urban center Koval had visited once, years before, for a computer convention. The city was Ukraine's center for electronics, aeronautics, and nuclear-power research, and the home of the region's most successful IT startups. Koval took heart that whoever had assembled the communications network did a reasonable job.

The U-Haul continued through a Soviet-era industrial park that had managed the transition without missing a step; the journey carried them to a derelict section where tanks had once been manufactured. It sat dark and overgrown behind a high chainlink fence.

Koval sniffed at the open window. It seemed to come from a fan vent of the factory.

"I smell—an electronic fire," he said. "Or something like that."

Glinko shrugged, grinned, said nothing. Glinko turned off

his headlights as they pulled up to the main gate, which was padlocked. He just sat there, and after a few minutes someone came out to admit them. Even in the dark, Koval could tell that the young man was dressed in the dark-and-light-blue camouflage pattern of the Ukrainian tank corps. The man's name was embroidered on his right pocket and the traditional patches were on both upper arms, with one addition: a large metal badge on the left lapel, the head of a fox.

"Oh, Jesus," Koval said with sudden understanding. He looked back across the rows of abandoned tanks. "Oh, Lord."

Glinko laughed in his belly as he drove in.

The gate was closed behind them, and the driver waited until the soldier directed them to an area between the factory and the dark, ramshackle administration building. Gravel and metal debris crunched under the tires as they proceeded, Glinko wincing with every sound. It took a few slow minutes for them to reach an open garage door below a sentry tower that was built like an old castle turret—with slots for rifles instead of bowmen.

Glinko pulled in beside an improbably out-of-place police car. He killed the engine and they sat there.

"Do you know for sure that this is what we're supposed to do?" Koval asked.

"It's what I was told to do," he replied.

After several minutes, a door opened at the far end, throwing a trapezoid of white light across several cars and a bare concrete floor. A man motioned them over.

"Let's go!" Glinko said as he popped the door and started

forward. Considering how long he'd been behind the wheel, the man was remarkably spry.

Koval joined him, trying to make out the figure silhouetted in the light. It took a moment for him to notice the edges of the famed mustache. Then the man stepped back to admit them, the overhead bulb illuminating his face. Now Koval was sure.

Three years ago, Captain Taras Klimovich had been on every news site in western Ukraine. He was respected by all, loved by Ukrainians, hated by Russian sympathizers. He had beaten their vaunted tank corps in a rout . . . but then he had vanished.

"You know who I am," the captain said as they turned toward an old concrete staircase painted green.

"Yes, sir!" Koval said almost jubilantly. "Where—where have you been these past years?"

"Planning for this day," he replied. He stopped and regarded Glinko. "Ivan, would you mind going ahead—make yourself a meal in the kitchen?"

"Of course, Captain!"

"Thank you, old friend," Klimovich said as the driver hurried ahead. "A good man," the captain remarked. "His late son served under me."

"I see," Koval said.

"Where have I been?" he said, continuing up the stairs. "I was in Semenivka, running this operation by courier." He grinned beneath the woolly mustache. "That, and refurbishing tanks at night, with a skeleton crew, takes time and patience. Your work came relatively late to the process—it was the last yet most essential piece in this ambitious mosaic."

"I assume, based on what you've said, that you—we—are undertaking a two-pronged assault against Russian forces over the border."

"Not quite so," the captain said, pausing on the landing. He regarded Koval. "I am planning a parade, one that will march right to the border, but not across, hoping to draw the Russian armored columns away from the base."

"No tanks," Koval reflected.

"I'm sorry?"

"When we were drilling with the virtual program, the major told me to pull the tanks from the last exercises," Koval said.

"We hope that they will not be a factor in Sudzha," Klimovich said. "It is our belief that the Defense Ministry has sent Colonel General Anatoly Yershov to command that post. He is a tank officer. He will want to engage, or at least come out and see what the 'legendary' Fox is up to, the man who defeated his beloved corps."

Klimovich had put a wry flourish on the word, indicating that he did not believe the legend . . . though he was perfectly willing to use it as bait.

"Without tanks," Koval said, "the major's team can get in and do considerable damage to the base."

"Considerable and humiliating damage," Klimovich said, focusing on the goal. "We want to inflict a global embarrassment on Putin. If he chooses to reignite the war, he will bankrupt his nation. If he chooses to negotiate, we will recover our nation."

Koval realized that his chest had tightened, his heart racing. "What if this officer, Yershov, attacks?"

Klimovich put an arm around the computer scientist's shoulder. "I am a tank commander, too, with several columns of tanks. We will strike him very, very hard."

"You intend . . . to just march out?" Koval asked. "Roll out?"

"A parade, like the Kremlin mounts every May Day," the captain replied, an almost mystical quality to his voice. "Hereafter, the fourth of June, at eight AM, will be *our* day. The day this mythical figure, the Fox, inspires a new patriotism. It will be a day of pride and liberation. And, to the east, each May Day that comes for Moscow will be a time of shame, of empty bluster." He shook his head. "Conquest cannot be sustained. Tyrants will always fail."

The men moved through the swinging door to an old-fashioned series of glass-walled offices overlooking the old storage facility below. There were pyramids of fresh munitions that were in the process of being shuttled by cart to the dark field outside.

"We have been warehousing these as well, aided by members of the military," Klimovich said. "I assure you, we will be ready just as Major Romanenko is ready. The rest will be up to you."

Koval's heart was beating even faster now—though he couldn't tell if it was fear, pride, or anticipation. He was a scientist, and the logical core of the man felt that this was an enormous risk on every front. Which is why, he thought, you did not conceive a project like this. He did.

The men continued toward the railing that ran along the perimeter of the building.

"There is an uplink in the former guard tower," Klimovich said, pointing to the southern side of the building. "You will sit in the office there, at the base." He pointed to metal door. "Please make sure, won't you, that everything works. When we leave before dawn tomorrow, and it becomes necessary to communicate, I will not speak with Major Romanenko and his team directly. The few essential details will be relayed through you. His team will maintain radio silence, of course, in case the Russians are listening through one of their new signal-acquisition balloons. But, for the sake of timing, you will communicate our progress to them so they will know when it is safe to move."

Koval was overwhelmed but—he decided—excited beyond evaluation for the chance to be a part of this. The plan began to coalesce in his mind, along with a sudden concern.

"Captain," Koval asked, "what—what are the chances of Romanenko and his team returning?"

The officer looked at him, his eyes alive above the high bridge of his nose. "There is a part of the mission of which you were unaware because it involves a deep undercover source," Klimovich said. "But I would say that their chances of returning are much better than you might think."

CHAPTER THIRTY-FIVE

Samsun, Turkey
June 4, 4:55 AM

"That is one very big *if*, Roger," Mike Volner said into the phone. Though his voice was even, as always, he was not a happy commander.

"Understood, and I completely agree," McCord replied.

Major Volner stood on the tarmac, his gear slung over one shoulder as he talked to Roger McCord. Dressed in civilian clothes, the other team members had already boarded the charter bus that Anne had arranged to meet them at the front of the terminal. No one curbside at Amasya Merzifon Airport would have seen the men emerge from an American aircraft. That kind of information might prove valuable to terrorists who had no dog in this particular fight. Volner wanted to finish this conversation before he joined them.

"But I've spoken with Chase at home, and we think it's the best course of action," McCord replied.

"That's an entirely new mission," Volner said.

"It isn't," McCord insisted.

"How do you figure that?" Volner asked. "We planned for recon to assess the situation. Now we're abandoning that, and our transportation, to hunt a man who might be part of a team that may be heading toward the Russian border."

"I didn't say 'hunt,'" McCord replied. "I said 'find.' This is *still* recon."

"You'll forgive me, but that's cover-your-ass talk, sir," Volner replied. "You are giving us an actionable target who, if they were the men drilling and headed to mission execution, are most likely armed."

"All of what you just described is possible," McCord agreed.

"Likely," Volner shot back.

"But there is no reason you cannot fulfill the original mission parameters while you're looking for whatever location this man is headed to. Observe and report. No need to engage."

Volner was silent. He brought up a map of the region.

"Major, we *have* to adjust here," McCord went on. "This team may be at or near a place where you can quite literally walk to Sudzha. We don't think he'll go in the daylight, and he doesn't appear to have left yet, according to surveillance. So you have a little time to prepare, to let us do more digging."

"What are the rules here, Roger?"

"Same as before."

"The rules of engagement," Volner stressed. "If this individual or team is in operational mode, if this is the attack they were training for in the virtual world, then are we supposed to report back and just let that assault transpire?"

McCord was silent.

"Roger?"

"This is *your* mission," the intelligence director said carefully. "You know what's at stake, you make the calls."

"Goddammit, *no!*" Volner snapped, finally losing it. "You are *not* going to cover your ass with mine. If I'm in the field and I make a call to shoot Ukrainians—allies—I'm the one who will get thrown to the wolves here."

"We are preparing to communicate with both Kiev and Russia should that transpire," McCord said. "There is no evidence to suggest that his is an officially sanctioned operation."

"Which makes us murderers, if there's a firefight. And that assumes the Russians don't kill us laying down a massive retaliation."

"Major, if you want to abort now that's your call, too," McCord told him.

"I do want you to know that Chase has spoken with Defense Minister Timoshenko before and we will initiate communication, without being specific, when you make contact with any Ukrainian forces that may be in Russian territory."

" 'Make contact,' " Volner said. "What am I supposed to do, ask politely that they stand down? Christ," he realized suddenly. "I'm going to have to have Flannery there. I'll need him to translate. How will he keep up?"

"Since we don't know the terrain well—the information is coming—I can't answer that yet," McCord said.

"You're shooting way too many blanks here," Volner complained.

"Understood, and I apologize," McCord told him. "Look,

I've been working up a new route for you that puts you outside Sumy. Chase is informing the airfield now."

"The—we're going back up?" Volner said.

"Hopefully, in thirty to forty minutes, according to Anne. Private hire direct to Sumy. Has the team—?"

"They're already on the bus," Volner said.

"You'll have to get them back."

"No shit!"

"Again, I'm sorry," McCord said. "Anne has already informed the bus company and is also arranging to have the boat go to and remain at the original location," McCord told him. "That will be your emergency evac if needed."

Volner had been at this long enough to know that plans changed. But they hadn't even prepped for Sumy.

"Hopefully," McCord said, "I can find these ops guys by satellite or thermal sig and give you additional info and assistance."

"Yeah, hopefully," Volner said. He allowed himself a moment to breathe and relax. "All right. I'm going to the bus. Get that data to me, local maps, too, and I'll arrange it with our fishing captain."

"Coming," McCord said. "Along with your flight info when I have it. Thank you, Major. Honestly, I'd rather be there than here."

"I do know that," Volner replied, his voice softer. "Out."

The JSOC commander knew that McCord was telling the truth. The former marine didn't want for courage, nor did he love the bureaucracy into which he'd been parachuted. He himself once said, "I still feel like I'm caught in shroud lines." But that didn't alter the fact that a mission that was so broadly defined and sketchy to begin with had just acquired several new ways it could go dangerously wrong.

Shrugging his backpack onto both shoulders, tugging down his Redskins baseball cap, and jogging toward the terminal, Volner remembered something else his Grandfather Albert used to say. It was a line from a cartoon show that the older man liked to watch, and he applied it to every new challenge the boy took on himself: "*You knew the job was dangerous when you took it!*"

Smacked by the cool air off the Black Sea, Volner savored the sea smell just before he climbed onto the bus.

"I'm told you're not to stay?" the driver said, looking down at him.

"Change of plans, but you're being paid," Volner said.

"I have been so informed," the driver said courteously.

"If you'll just sit tight, I want to talk with our people and the tour organizer a moment."

The man extended an arm into the bus and, following it, Volner addressed the team. "New schedule," he said. "Our hosts have decided to fly us over."

His expression told the men nothing, though they knew that whatever was going on had just heated up. As they began to quietly gather their gear, Volner motioned for Bankole and Flannery to remain seated. As the men filed out, he walked over and flopped beside the intelligence director. He networked their tablets as the map from Op-Center arrived.

"Is everything all right?" Flannery asked from two seats away.

"I'll explain while we go back to the terminal," he said. "Just sit tight."

"Easier said," Flannery remarked, leaning back gently and looking at the team without seeing them. Volner saw no enthusiasm, only concern—and discomfort. Even leaning back had caused him to wince.

"Trouble?" Bankole asked.

"Not if you prefer paintball to checkers," Volner replied. "We're flying north to intercept what may be the Ukrainian strike team."

"Op-Center's been busy," Bankole said.

"It's McCord—and he's only about fifty percent sure," Volner said.

"Is it that or is something else bothering you?"

"It's the bullshit," Volner said. He jerked his head toward the terminal. "I got a bunch of double-talk back there, about us being watchers but with the discretion to terminate."

"We were always going in armed."

"For self-defense," Volner said. "We have zero instructions about how to handle a Ukrainian attack against Russia."

"We've got time to consider that," Bankole said.

"Yeah. We do." His expression was steel. "We'll have to."

Bankole regarded the man as he looked back at the tablet and the map. "Mind if I ask you something personal?"

"Shoot."

"Mission creep has happened to me before," he said "and you, too, I'm sure. How much of your last mission is spilling into this?"

Volner nodded in acknowledgment. "A lot. I can handle a

change-up. Hell, I expect it. Still, we lost Rodriguez and he was top-of-the-line. I can't speak for you, but the ambassador—he's a concern."

"Then we leave him behind."

"I need a translator."

"Then I'll look after him, make sure we're accessible," Bankole said.

Volner didn't look up and he didn't have to say what was in his appreciative but humorless half smile: Bankole and Flannery were the walking wounded, one a theoretically recovered but untested veteran leading an older, wounded diplomat who had never seen combat. It was not a situation he could take far into the field.

But he thanked Bankole and expanded something on the map.

Looking at it, the intelligence director said one word: "Shit!"

CHAPTER THIRTY-SIX

Watergate Hotel, Washington, D.C.
June 3, 11:08 PM

Chase Williams hadn't realized where he was standing until Anne asked what "that" was behind his head. He raised his eyes from the tablet and looked behind him.

"Shower curtain," he said, turning from the sparkling expanse of white and walking back into the bedroom.

The Watergate complex is renowned for many things, infamous for one. Named for its location on the Chesapeake and Ohio Canal—"the Grand Old Ditch"—construction began in 1963, was completed in 1971, and a year later it was the site of the Democratic National Committee burglary that led to the downfall of President Richard Nixon. Williams lived in the residential section known as Watergate South. He had a view of the lower Potomac River. After two years, he could count on one hand the number of times he had seen the water in daylight.

Williams had come home to shower and clear his head, take care of the cat, then return to Op-Center. He had abandoned those plans, except for the cat, and had been about to

head back to his office when McCord called. The two men had
already spoken a few minutes earlier to "fine-tune the deployment," as McCord had put it, though both knew the mission
had become more than that. Williams had paused to text Matt
Berry, and now McCord was calling back with Volner's concerns. Anne had joined them after putting in motion arrangements for the JSOC team to fly to Ukraine. She had the aircraft
but was waiting to hear back from a city official in Sumy before
finalizing the flight.

"Roger was just telling me that he got pushback from Volner," Williams told her.

"But they're going," McCord added.

"You knew they would," Anne said.

"We all did," Williams clarified. "Roger was just the mes-
senger. And however we describe it internally, when I tell Berry
and Berry tells Midkiff, the bottom line is that what began as a
plan to move through eastern Ukraine, taking the temperature
from south to north, has morphed into something more than recon. Optimally, if it turns out that there is a rogue Ukrainian
unit headed toward Russia we're hoping our guys can intercept
them."

"With what instructions?" Anne asked.

"COD," McCord told her.

Commander's operational discretion was one of the most
dangerous acronyms coined in the rules-of-engagement play-
book. After years of having their hands tied by regulations that
refused to allow troops to fire unless fired upon first; that placed
"no shoot" restrictions in areas where civilians were known to

be located; that barred artillery fire against targets where there could be collateral environmental damage, such as hostile forces transporting oil or chemical weapons; President Midkiff had given the DOD some wiggle room. Officers could initiate an attack under the "urgent and immediate considerations" provision, but that would also be a mandated "multi-interview follow-up analysis," which was an official euphemism for "court martial."

"No wonder the major is pissed," she replied. "Frankly, gentlemen, I don't like this, either."

"It is not a likable situation," Williams pointed out.

"That's a dodge," Anne said.

"Do you have a better solution, Anne?" Williams challenged. "Should I pull them?"

"I don't know," she admitted. "We may have to wait, anyway, for this damn functionary in Sumy to get back to me— but . . . I just don't know. We still don't have any idea of the size of this Ukrainian force, do we?"

"None," McCord replied. "Though we assume it's squad-size, under a dozen men. Something that can move without attracting much attention and coalesce quickly."

"So we're evenly matched, but with a home-court advantage," Williams said.

"That's only while they're in Ukraine," McCord reminded him. "Once they're in Russia, they're equal—"

"Chase, even if they're forced to cross the border, they cannot fire at Russians," Anne cut in, hard. "That cannot be on the table."

"Even if it's to protect their own people?" McCord said.

"Which circles back to the idea that haste may not be the best policy," Anne said.

"Anne," Chase said, "I told Major Volner we'd take that possibility up with Minister Timoshenko if a border crossing was imminent."

"Do you think the Russian defense minister will wait for us to handle an invasion force?" Anne asked.

"For a trade-off of some kind, he may," Williams said. "I've texted Berry to see what the president is willing to give, if it comes to that."

"He may find a deal advantageous in lieu of a shooting war, Anne," McCord said.

"Even with a paramilitary unit in his country?"

"Yes," McCord said. "Dead Ukrainians are still dead Ukrainians, regardless of where they were shot. That may be all Ukrainian loyalists in Crimea need to turn violent."

"Timoshenko has a boss who may not be as sensible as you are," Anne said.

"All right," Williams cut in. "Both points taken, and all of it hypothetical. The *reality* of what we have is two teams whose footprint is relatively small and must remain as small as possible to avoid additional actors. I want to think about this, but next time you talk to Mike tell him that I will not only back his play, but I will take responsibility for it."

"That's admirable, Chase," Anne said, "but it won't help if something occurs that we haven't discussed—which is if either side grabs our boys. Neither player will give them right back, and

Midkiff will have your head after he denies all knowledge of anything."

"Ugly truth about politics," Williams agreed. "But it's the best I can offer until we know more. Roger, *get* more. All hands on deck."

"Chase, no one is slacking here," McCord said.

"I know that, Roger, but—Anne, get Brian, Jim, everyone to call in any favor they have, go to trusted confidential informants in Moscow, find out more about any of the players at Sudzha. Lean on Kiev, see if any officers have been flagged for—Christ, anything."

"Chase, we're already doing a lot of that and coming up empty," McCord said. "We've also had to be careful not to reveal too much of what we know. We don't want any of that getting to the Kremlin, in particular. Timoshenko could lay waste to everything around Sudzha, including our team, and call it 'maneuvers.'"

"I know," Williams said more moderately. "I wasn't questioning your methods. But our boys are in the dark right now, and the last time there was a hole in our—"

"Chase," Anne said.

The director fell silent and looked at her face on the tablet. It wasn't an admonition. It was concern. They were all still raw from the IED that took the life of Hector Rodriquez while he and Dawson were riding in that Humvee in Mosul. Dawson survived, and bitter survivor's guilt was one reason Williams had let him go on about women and more alcoholic downtime than before. As long as it didn't affect his job performance, as long as he saw Meagan Bruner once a week for what he called "my extended debrief," Williams remained silent.

"Right," Williams said. But he didn't apologize. He wanted his intelligence director to be damned careful. "I'm heading back in a minute—"

"Chief, there's not really anything you can do here at the moment—"

"It's unseemly," he said, not sure where the word came from.

"Should we call in the others?" Anne asked.

"Not yet," Williams said. "Let's wait until we have an ETA for the team in Sumy."

"I'm gonna beat the bushes some more," McCord said.

The intelligence director jumped off the conference as though he couldn't get away too fast. Anne stayed.

"More than intel, I wish we had time to—"

She was interrupted by the music from Williams's smartphone. It was lying on the bed and he went over to answer.

"It's Dawson," he told her as he picked up. "Go ahead, Brian."

"I'm at the Nookery," he said. "Too loud, I'm headed outside. But I just got a message from Matt that . . . sending. Will discuss when I'm away from here."

Dawson hung up and Williams went back to his tablet, opened the secure link to Op-Center. Anne was automatically networked, and he downloaded a file marked "NSA-6/3/22:44." It was an intercept from a Russian blimp operating in the border region near Kharkiv, with a label that was caption-translated:

Military-caliber long-range FM Wireless Audio-Video Transmitter and Receiver. Test Signal, WGS84 50°

0'16" N, 36° 13'53" E 50.004444, 36.231389 Geo URI
geo: 50.004444,36.231389 UTM 37U 301613 5542798

"Any idea what that is?" Anne asked.

"A new, content-free signal that someone had to know would be picked up," Williams said as he asked the tablet to pinpoint the coordinates.

"Kharkiv," Anne said thoughtfully when a map appeared. "That's not far from the base in Sudzha."

"No, it's not," Williams said. "Neither is Sumy."

The phone sang again and Williams grabbed it, put it on speaker. "Brian, did Matt have any context?"

"He said it's Kharkiv—"

"Yeah, we've got that," Williams told him. "Any information exactly where in Kharkiv?"

"Not yet," Brian replied. "All they said is that there are no military units in that sector."

"You better meet me at the office, Brian," Williams said as he and Anne exchanged looks of grave concern, expressions that finished Dawson's sentence the same way:

"*. . . no military units in that sector that we know about. . . .*"

Swiping away the connection, Williams grabbed the sports jacket he'd tossed on the bed and slammed the tablet back in his shoulder bag. As he hurried out the door, he realized where "unseemly" had come from: it was something his mother used to say when his father was working on something in their Valley Stream, Long Island, home—the lawn, a snow-covered walkway, washing the car—and he was on the floor reading a *Classics Illustrated* comic book.

Williams had been four or five at the time.

As he hurried to the garage, he couldn't help wondering how many mothers were presently "running" how many government agencies throughout the nation's capital. . . .

CHAPTER THIRTY-SEVEN

Sumy, Ukraine
June 4, 9:06 AM

Route H-07 was the main highway to and from Sumy. Following a relatively straight northeasterly course, it made its way into Russia, through the town of Sudzha, and on its way—not always in a good state of repair, frequently crumbling, but navigable in the right vehicle.

Major Romanenko didn't intend to take it past the border. Koval had rented a canvas-backed truck favored by the pro-Moscow paramilitary units that operated in this region, like the infamous *Okkupaj Pedofilyaj* thugs—"Occupy Pedophilia." Based in nearby Belgorod, which was also just over the Russian border, these ski-masked youths patrolled at night in "white justice vehicles" and "white train cars"—descriptive of their ethnicity, not the actual color. They carried grips filled with guns, knives, crowbars, pliers, and cameras to record their activities against the gay population of Crimea and northeastern Ukraine.

Romanenko and his team had no interest in the neo-Nazi bands; they were one of many that preyed on homosexuals, Jews, the wealthy, the old, the anti-Putinists, the pro-Westerners. He and his men would create the impression of the singular brutality and madness of that group, because ordinary citizens would keep their distance . . . and sympathetic Russian officials would be inclined to look the other way.

"It is a dirty business," young Tkach had said when the plan was laid out back in Kiev. As the most Western-influenced member of the group, he had the most trouble understanding inbred, generational insanity. He was a fierce patriot by the example handed down from his grandfather and his father, one who had grown up without the Soviet yoke; that was the only hatred he possessed, and he was uneasy even at play-acting this part.

Romanenko had instructed him to look past his distaste for the half-hour ride to the point where they would park the truck and continue to Russia as smoke and the onset of darkness hindered the enemy.

Romanenko had received the single "Go" signal on his computer, a broadcast that lasted two seconds, a distinctive C# to Eb progression on the musical scale that matched the recording on his computer. It was the only time those notes would be used. They were not a progression that occurred in any other prompt, or one that was likely to be sent by anyone who happened to intercept their signals or learn of their plan.

It meant that Captain Klimovich would be ready to move in two hours, and that Romanenko should watch the feed from Kharkiv: that would be the signal for his team to depart.

He informed the men by hotel phone. In a half hour they would leave as they had arrived, individually, and make their way on foot to the Sumka River. During the spring, the banks were a popular destination for locals and tourists, and they would not be noticed there. They would take an early lunch—during which they would follow events in Kharkiv on their phones, something many others would be doing—after which they would walk the bridge to the vehicle-rental facility on the opposite side, on Lermontova Street. That was where Koval had made a reservation, confirmed, for the truck. After that, they would pick up several afternoon newspapers to have at the ready, if needed.

The day threatened rain common enough in this part of the world—in which case the men would have skipped lunch and posed as tourists, taking pictures and making the best of the bad situation. But the clouds passed and the sun emerged, though a chill dampness lingered, some of it coming from windblown fountains. It felt, smelled, and tasted as if it arose from a freshly dug grave, an unpleasant blend of muddy earth and ancient air that carried the tinge of petrol, incinerated trash, and mold. Every smaller Ukrainian city had its distinctive sensory personality; all it took was a change in weather to stir it up. Only the occasional smell of gardens planted here and there along the river walk disguised the subtle but pervasive atmosphere.

The men were in sight of one another along the gently curving river. They were just finishing their lunch when the descending Bb to G# signal arrived. Each man turned to the app for local Sumy radio.

". . . astonishing scene playing out in the industrial park there, as—a dozen? More? At least twelve tanks have rolled through the gates of an abandoned factory and into the busy lunch-hour streets of Kharkiv. There are unconfirmed reports that the column is being led by an officer who has been out of the public eye since the invasion three years ago—there is video now, and it clearly shows a man in a blue camouflage uniform standing in the open turret of the lead tank. Thirteen of them? There are thirteen tanks, and they are apparently under the command of the corps commander whom the press nicknamed the Fox, Captain Taras Klimoshenko, though a positive identification has not yet been made. This is simply—I used the word 'astonishing,' and that is the only word to describe this parade of vehicles making their way to the east, not pausing for traffic but moving slowly enough for everyone to get out of the way.

"Police are frankly baffled, they do not know what to do, have nothing to confront . . . tanks. The one officer who tried to block their passage was forced to dive away at a gesture from the commander, who indicated that they were not going to stop. And they did not stop. They are not stopping, according to this— again, *astonishing* video I am seeing live from Kharkiv. . . ."

Romanenko listened a little longer than confirmation had required. He listened to let the pride he felt infuse his blood, his breath, his sinew. He allowed his own imagination to fill in the news words as he shut the streaming audio.

"The question on everyone's mind is why? What is the purpose of this display, which seems to have a very direct goal in mind? Is this a parade or is this something more? Would a man of the stature of the Fox come out of retirement simply to march through the streets of the second-largest city in a nation oppressed by a thuggish, bullying neighbor?"

The answer, of course, was that no one watching the return of the Fox and his ghost command would ever glean the true purpose of the tank column.

No one, including the man at whom it was directed.

CHAPTER THIRTY-EIGHT

Sudzha, Russia
June 4, 12:11 PM

General Yershov was peering through field glasses, watching tank maneuvers on the airstrip, when an adjutant came running up to him.

"General, sir, you must see this!" the young man said breathlessly, thrusting a tablet into the officer's hands.

Yershov had to maneuver slightly to recover the signal. The portable, mobile HF whip antenna that he used to communicate securely with the tanks was no help; even their powerful new satellite uplink was spotty due to the high hills of the eastern Russian Plain.

When the jerky image finally flowed, it was a live feed from Ukraine's largest TV channel, 1+1. The picture showed tanks moving slowly through the city, followed by an increasing number of civilians . . . and, in front, a police escort.

"What is this?" Yershov asked, searching for the volume.

The adjutant swiped the screen, turning up the sound. It hadn't been low; the voice of the on-the-scene reporter had simply been drowned out by the crowds and the sound of the helicopter providing an overhead picture.

". . . the war hero the Fox has made no statement, and there is no indication as to his reason for this display," the woman was saying. "The military has made no public or private comment about this display, and all we know is what we can see: that this tank column is moving east, in the direction of the Russian border."

Yershov's phone chimed. He practically threw the tablet back at the adjutant as he answered. The general's forehead was flushed, his breathing hard, as he let the words and the image sink in.

"Yes?" he said without checking the identity of the caller.

"You saw, no doubt?"

It was Minister Timoshenko.

"I saw, I see," Yershov replied hotly, turning back to the tablet, which the young man cradled before him. "Did you have any idea of this?"

"We knew nothing," he said. "The president is not pleased with that fact."

Yershov motioned the aide away and walked to where he was out of earshot. "What—?" he was about to ask what Putin wanted him to do. Instead, he asked, "What do you want me to do?"

"They cannot be thinking of an attack," Timoshenko said. "That would be suicide."

"Suicide is a tactic," Yershov pointed out. "So is martyrdom." Reason began to return as his tactical mind engaged. "This man has . . . he has been in hiding, planning this, waiting. It has to be."

"Waiting for us to destroy him?" the minister asked.

"No," Yershov said. "Waiting to cow us. Waiting to show that the battle we lost in Labkovicy sapped our courage, our will."

"That may be *his* message, but our desire is to—"

"It doesn't matter what we want, what we know," Yershov interrupted. "You and I know about the crafting of the Dark Zone policy, but the people will see it differently both in Ukraine and in Russia. We will appear to be *exactly* what he is depicting: afraid to engage. If we don't go to the border, he will say we are fearful. If we go only to the border, he will say we are fearful. If we cross the border—"

"Then we will be in open defiance of the president's orders, unless he issues new ones," Timoshenko said, a nervous flutter in his normally obsequious voice.

At that moment, Yershov lost even a mote of respect for the man. In a single, inspired move, Captain Taras Klimovich was paralyzing and shaming the entire Russian military . . . but only if they let this stand.

"Minister Timoshenko, I must go to the border," Yershov said, affirmatively . . . and defiantly.

"General, that decision is not yours to make."

"The conduct of these maneuvers, ordered by the president, is entirely within my authority," he replied.

Timoshenko was dully silent. Yershov was already making his way to the command center when he motioned over the officer who was in charge of the drilling.

"Colonel Dzhamanov," he said, "prepare Columns A and B

to move out, and bring in the—I will take one of the BTR-82s . . . number two."

"Seconded from sentry duty?" the older officer confirmed.

"Seconded from sentry duty *at once*, Colonel!" Yershov replied. It was the most powerful vehicle he had outside the main and secondary battle tanks, and he wanted to be seen as well, standing in an open turret behind a mighty 1×14.5-mm., 1×7.62-mm. machine gun.

"Yes, sir," the man said, saluting impressively as he turned to go.

"General, I heard that—I urge you to be careful. Very careful," Timoshenko said.

"There is a difference between careful, which I am, and careless, which I am not," he replied. "Please inform the president that I am still on maneuvers, expanding the reach and pace of the Dark Zone in accord with his stated goals and my sacred duty to safeguard the interests of the republic."

"I will convey that message . . . if Mr. Putin asks."

That last statement was a frank admission that whatever Yershov did was on him. He did not need to hear any more and killed the call. The minister was interested in maintaining his position, not in the honor of Russia. With no record of the call, he could claim responsibility if Yershov caused the Fox to back down . . . or claim to have advised against this approach if it ended in something other than a bold stalemate.

As Yershov waited for the low-lying armored personnel carrier, he wrestled with the one demon he did not want to be present, the thirst for vengeance, payback for the dishonor of Colonel

General Nikolai Novikov. In his heart, Yershov felt there was no greater prize he could bestow on his predecessor than the pelt of the man who had toppled him.

And then the general was on board the rumbling, roaring vehicle as its eight great tires turned toward the command that awaited in the dusty haze at the end of the airstrip.

CHAPTER THIRTY-NINE

Samsun Airport, Turkey
June 4, 7:00 AM

The arrangements for the plane had been easy. The arrangements for clearance were not.

Anne understood that Sumy was a private airstrip and, absent standard security or a customs accommodations, clearance for any foreign plane had to be secured from the local government that managed the field. She had anticipated that this would require a document to be filled out and filed, with a passenger manifest, any cargo, and a purpose for the visit.

She had half expected that it would have to be filled out in Ukrainian. She was reticent to contact the embassy in Kiev, lest they start asking questions and began working their own agenda, such as currying favor with Kiev by slipping them classified intelligence. It was done all the time, and most of the time lives weren't on the line.

Anne had translators at her disposal, but finding them and securing their services in the small hours of the night took time. The group profile had shifted to all geologists, searching for untapped areas of groundwater, and the cargo was scientific equipment. That was in one of the bags Volner carried. If the others were checked, Moore carried thousands of dollars in American currency to help them make it through; he also carried a loaded Colt Close Quarters Battle Pistol to ensure that they did.

When the document had been completed, it had to go to a civil servant, who would call the airfield with a landing code and a time of expiration. In this case, they had a civil servant who chose not to answer his phone. In a public emergency, a police officer would have been dispatched. That couldn't be done for a group of geologists.

So she waited, which was something she didn't do well. When Williams arrived, he tried to convince her that there was nothing she could be doing differently.

She understood that, but the pressure was finally beginning to lean hard on her. Like Williams, she got very quiet under pressure . . . as if any movement would cause a bunch of rubberbands to snap and take out eyes here and there.

While Op-Center waited, the team also waited; energy boiled off like the morning mist. Fearing that jet lag would take hold and the men would lose their edge, Volner told everyone to review maps or walk outside the terminal in order to stay sharp and focused. Bankole sat on a bench and meditated. Flannery slept beside him, waking whenever he accidentally pulled his side.

Volner tried not to think of all the warning signs that were screaming "abort." Instead, he sat on the floor of the large terminal building strategizing with McCord and cartographer Allison

Weill. With Anne tied up with the unexpected, he had to deal with plans that hadn't yet been settled.

"Roger, the airport is pretty far south of where you think the target is or was staying," the major said.

"But you're near the H-07, the main automotive artery," Weill told him. "If you can secure transport, you'll cover that distance in about fifteen minutes."

"Eduardo is trying to secure a bus like the one that was waiting for you there," McCord told him. "Wrong hour of the day to be doing that. He's obtaining home numbers, trying to wake someone."

Eduardo was Anne's executive—and only—assistant, who held a master's in Logistics and Supply Chain Management. As efficient as Anne was, the young man was unstoppable.

"I'm wondering if there's another way," Volner said. "I see there's a river, the Strika—"

"Too shallow in spots, even if we could arrange transport," Weill told him.

"Crap." He shook his head. "Twenty miles on foot, with our gear, across city streets and then uneven terrain in the dark to avoid a checkpoint—that's a good twelve, thirteen hours—longer if you have to factor in waiting for dark," Volner said. "We can do that, but Flannery and Bankole can't."

"We'll find a vehicle," McCord promised. "There are dairy farms, private shipping centers, moving companies—you throw money at a problem, it gets solved."

Once again, Mike Volner had a stronger than uneasy feeling about sending his people on a mission that had logistical issues to settle before they could even address the prime objective.

"It's Hector and it's that deadly-force judgment you had to make in New York," he told himself. The corrosive nature of doubt was worse than the reality of "shit happens."

Alerted by Op-Center, McCord also watched the events unfolding in Kharkiv. He knew, with certainty now, that the two eastward military adventures were related and most likely off the books. He saw the secure alert that Russian maneuvers had been "expanded" in the direction of the Ukrainian tank columns. There was, as yet, no comment from Kiev.

If it's a rogue operation, the military must be seeing the grassroots enthusiasm on the ground, wondering if they should join in. They have to decide whether to embrace or reject.

The reality of being caught in a reckless, hair-trigger crossfire had been a concern. The prospect of being in the middle of an all-out shooting war merited careful monitoring. Volner went over to Bankole and folded him in. Williams obviously had the same thought and, with Dawson and McCord, was on the next call.

"We're going to watch for any additional troop movements," McCord said. "So far, we aren't picking up any change in DEF-CON status on any other Russian or Ukrainian base."

"They probably don't know about the team on the plains," Dawson noted, "and I'm guessing they'll let the tank commanders chest-thump for now."

"Most likely," Bankole agreed. "Until they do find out about the boys headed for Sudzha. Then hell comes to the border from north to south."

"In any case, Major, I will back whatever call you make," Williams told him.

"Thank you, sir," Volner said, though he knew that would hold very little sway if things went south and he was ever court-martialed. Williams was a civilian, and Volner was the ranking military officer. Williams also had as many enemies in the armed services as he did allies. Still, it was good to hear.

After five endless hours, and a brief but heartfelt apology for the process, Anne had secured permission for them to land. But by that time the private Gulfstream she had engaged had run out of time to make the six-hundred-mile trip before having to fly to Ankara. She always had a backup, in this case a Bombardier Learjet 45XR that was hangared in Bingöl, Turkey. She hired the jet, after Eduardo had made certain that it would have no trouble setting down on Sumy's 8,202-foot runway.

Before the jet had finally been fueled and the team was on board, nearly seven hours had been spent on the ground. It was a perfect contrast between bureaucracy and action: the flight itself, the heartbeat of the mission, was just under two hours. The team wished it had been longer: the Bombardier was a corporate jet, with seductively cool air circulation and deep leather seats. Everyone slept, even Volner, though he was awakened by a ping on his tablet.

"Mike, we have something," McCord told him.

The major was instantly alert as a satellite image appeared on his screen. He took it in at once, surmising that the road on the left was a part of the H-07 and that the open field to the right was the southwestern fringe of the Russian Plain.

"Theirs?" Volner asked.

In response, McCord sent over an NSA image of the field with seven late-afternoon shadows thrown toward the east. The time stamp was two hours earlier—ten minutes after the picture of the truck had been taken. The intelligence director sent over an image taken a few minutes later. The seven shadows had moved farther east.

"We have to assume it's the squad that drilled with the video," McCord said.

"How far to the truck?" Volner asked.

"A little over twelve miles," he said. He sent another image. "It was ditched before the Russian checkpoint, which you can see here."

Volner studied the image. It indicated what McCord had said, but nothing more.

"What are you thinking?" McCord asked.

"We've got about four hours of sunlight when we land," Volner said. "I can't imagine these men moving across the border in daylight."

"We also can't rule it out," McCord replied.

Volner wanted to hit something. He needed actionable intelligence, not what-ifs. They could be farmers, for all he knew. "Ask Anne if we can get—I don't know, a bike, an ATV, something to reach that truck, assuming it hasn't been found and towed. Then—"

"Brilliant," McCord said. "You put the bike in back, return and collect the team."

"Yeah."

"What about theft guards on the vehicle?" Allison asked.

It was a question McCord expected from a Millennial who had never seen a vehicle older than his driver's license. Volner had been raised by grandparents who owned a farm.

"That thing is about twenty, twenty-five years old," Volner said. "Moore can hotwire it in his sleep."

"I'll let Anne know what you need," he said.

"And I'll let Sergeant Moore know he's got lone-wolf action," Volner said. "I do believe he will remember you in his prayers."

"Back at Bragg," McCord said.

"Back at Bragg," Volner said, solemnly repeating a phrase that was as much a prayer as a declaration.

CHAPTER FORTY

The world was born in fire. His nation would be reborn, starting with fire.

Romanenko had left the truck parked off-road, in a small parking lot, with a sign in Russian and Ukrainian that said Do Not Remove—P.O. They would need the truck to get away from the storm they would unleash. Given the deep history of anti-gay sentiment in both nations, the major was certain no one would be inclined to remove the truck. Given the violence of Putin's cross-border thugs, no one would dare.

The region was technically outside the limits of the Yunakivka, but the small Ukrainian city was a jumping-off point for people visiting the border regions, which were studded with woodlands, open fields, and nature preserves. A few people were walking and, behind the men, a young family was having melon at one of ten picnic tables. There were fresh springtime buds and plantings, and Admiral Volodymyr Berezovsky had disturbed none of them. He had buried the six items behind a boulder—

recognizable by an "X" chipped in the rock side facing them—in ground that melting winter ice had made especially soft. Walking over and squatting behind it, unseen by the picnickers, Tkach and Zinchenko were able to remove the items using just the latter's knife.

They were individually wrapped in waterproof oilcloth. Tkach handed one to Romanenko, who carefully undid the string and removed the weapon inside. It was a high-powered incendiary grenade, pin-activated, and about the size and shape of a thermos bottle. The major wrapped it and set it back with the others, kicked the dirt back in place with his foot, just enough to conceal them in the event a police helicopter or a military aircraft passed overhead. He checked his watch.

"Find the spots that will work best," he told his team as he looked around. "I would say the trees about twenty meters away—the one with two dead oak trunks in the center." He looked back toward the north. "Those picnic tables. We go in ninety minutes."

"If people are present?" asked Marchuk.

"We must hope there are not," Romanenko said. He looked at his watch. They had eighty-eight minutes. This was going to be the slowest, most frustrating period in his life; anticipation couldn't overcome the anxiety of the operation's failing to come off as planned. Romanenko had no precedent for this. Battles were won or lost; that was the nature of war. But he had never been in command of fully half the battles in a war, as he was now. He wanted nothing less than to overachieve, to impress the Fox.

And in daylight, he thought, always having embraced that aspect of the challenge. He would create his own night with the incendiaries.

The men walked a bit, Romanenko waiting for the next signal from Kharkiv. It came after an hour, another musical progression that indicated that Koval could see the dark, distinctive clouds of smoke on the horizon. Yershov's armored column was approaching the Russian border with Ukraine and was near or at the point of no return. Even if he left now, he would not be able to reach Sudzha in time to aid in its defense. Romanenko checked radio reports from the city. They corroborated the computer scientist's information.

He lifted his arm and circled his upraised hand, signaling Tkach and Zinchenko, who had remained near the pit. They retrieved the devices and stored three of them in empty backpacks carried by the brothers Pavel and Mikhail Lomov. They would be responsible for setting the grenades when they reached their destination.

The brothers started ahead so the canisters would be well away from the staging area when the pins were pulled.

The winds had kicked up—fortuitously, Romanenko thought—and the tables were empty, as was most of the field. Tkach took one device to the tables. They would catch and burn easily. Zinchenko took two others to the small woods. The new buds on the trees would take longer to incinerate—but the dead stumps would feed the fire for quite some time, especially with two devices spaced roughly ten meters apart.

And then it was time.

Romanenko joined the others on the northeastern side of the fire zone while Tkach and Zinchenko pulled the pins. They set the canisters down and ran. Ten seconds after being triggered, the grenades erupted with a sound like a balloon popping. An egg-shaped ball of flame rose from each, hovered in the air for a brief, weightless moment, and then rushed outward in all lateral directions.

The team jogged ahead, Romanenko bringing up the rear, looking back as he trudged forward. Ugly black waves rolled outward and billowed upward, driven by the winds, forming a dark scrim with remarkable speed. The tables burned, the dead wood and the healthy trees burned, even the grasses burned as droplets of accelerant fell from the air and set them ablaze. The fire in the picnic area was quickly swept toward a low hill of high grasses. Birds rose from them only to fall from the sky, their bodies afire. Arboreal mammals choked and dropped and burned. Soon the sky itself was tarnished by the fringe of the rising smoke and the deep-orange flame.

When they had put some distance between themselves and the fire, the Ukrainians stopped to change and bury their civilian clothes, putting on black pants, sweaters, and ski masks. They were about to cross over into Russia. Though the woods were patrolled, they were relatively porous and any soldiers who were out here would probably be watching the fire to make sure the wind didn't change.

The team started out again without urgency—cautiously, Tkach on point watching for the lone Russian UAZ-469s or drones used for sweeps of the frontier.

The admiral had reported that the area around the Russian base was rich with dry grasses and dead trees that had been nicked or felled by bulldozers during construction and left to rot.

Romanenko smiled as he thought of the enormity of that fire. And not just physically.

CHAPTER FORTY-ONE

Sumy Airport, Ukraine
June 4, 4:08 PM

"We were lucky we landed when we did," the pilot said to Bankole as the men exited the jet.

"Why is that?" the American asked the veteran Turkish flyer.

"There is a brushfire to the east, blowing smoke this way," he said. "I may not myself be able to leave quite yet."

Bankole checked with Op-Center to find out if they knew anything about the situation and to see if Anne had found a motorcycle to rent.

"We just saw the fire less than a kilometer from where the truck is parked," McCord told him. "As for the bikes—Anne?"

"There's a Hertz-affiliated annex, but no bikes," she said.

"We need a Volkswagen," Volner said.

"Got one!" Moore shouted from the front door of the terminal.

A fellow New Yorker, Private First Class Dick Siegel, had gone out with him. Parked curbside, out of the way of traffic, was a perfectly maintained 1971 red Dnepr with dual leather seats. It obviously belonged to one of the staff members.

"One problem, Sarge," he said. "It ain't for rent. And it ain't yours."

"We'll have it back in a half hour," Moore said. "And there's no time to discuss it with the owner, who'd never let this baby go."

Volner came out, followed by Bankole and the others. The international crisis manager had just told the major about the fire and he could see it now, burning in the area where they were headed.

"They set that for cover," Volner said.

"Sir?" Moore said, half turning.

"Do it, Sergeant," Volner decided.

It took Moore less than a minute to flip out his pocket knife, find and detach the wires leading to the ignition switch, and put them on his tongue at the same time that he pressed the starter button. The motorcycle growled to life.

"They don't make 'em like this anymore," he said.

"Thank God," Flannery remarked, though he was openly impressed by Moore's technique.

"Dick, leave your gear, on shotgun," Moore said, handing his grip to the PFC and slipping on his sunglasses.

"Sergeant?" Volner asked.

"It'll save time if I have someone drive it back instead of loading it in," he said.

Siegel nodded. He handed his backpack to Corporal Al Fitzpatrick and boarded, the weapons pack over his shoulder— and Moore took off.

Someone ran out from the terminal, shouting. At a nod from Volner, Flannery took the man aside and quietly explained what had happened—and that he would be paid for the loan of the motorcycle. And any damage, he added, noticing the man's concern.

The two American soldiers blazed onto the H-07, heading north.

"That old truck—you can do the same, yeah, Siegel?" Moore asked, shouting to be heard over the engine.

"Who're you telling how to hotwire?"

"A kid from Staten Island," Moore shouted back. "How the hell do I know what you did out there?"

"Same as in Brooklyn, only to date hotter women."

Moore let that pass as he wove through the slowing traffic as sirens sounded from behind and ahead.

"You're not comin' back, are ya?" Siegel yelled.

Moore shook his head. "You see how greasy that smoke is, low in the air?"

"Yeah."

"The major noticed it, too," Moore yelled. "That's military grade. Our target was creating a diversion. He'll have all eyes west while he heads east."

"You gonna track him?"

"The name's Moore, not Daniel Boone," the sergeant replied. "I got another idea."

Siegel grunted. "This'll leave a lotta unhappy people back curbside."

"They'll be unhappier if I sit on my ass," Moore said. "It'll open the door to a lotta war if we *don't* find these guys."

They reached the abandoned truck in less than twenty

minutes, spotting it from the highway and speeding into the parking lot before the authorities had been able to weave through the traffic and close the exits. Siegel hopped off and lashed the grip to his abandoned seat. Then he climbed into the truck.

"You gonna wait while I—?" Siegel began, but Moore cut him off.

"Nothing I can do if you can't start her," the sergeant said, flipping the younger man a friendly salute then turning the bike in a tight circle so it was facing back onto the highway. He paused to pull out his handkerchief and tied it around his mouth and nose before roaring off.

Traffic was nearly at a standstill as wipers struggled to sweep the oily soot from windshields and the smoke itself impaired visibility. Moore kept low, continued to duck and weave, and rode on the shoulder wherever possible. He knew from the maps where the Russian checkpoint was, knew how to recognize if not read the warning signs, and intended to take the last exit before reaching them.

It came up after less than half a mile; incongruously, it led to a shopping area just on the Russian side. To the southeast was a field with a large wooded area about another half mile away. According to the GPS in his Op-Center-issued worldwide smartphone, every move he made after leaving the highway was in Russia.

He skidded to a stop at the bottom of the off ramp and walked the motorcycle back toward H-07, still in Ukraine. The highway was ground level and he crouched there, beside the bike. He killed the engine so that he could watch *and* listen.

There were two missed calls from Mike Volner. Moore pulled the handkerchief away and phoned him back.

"Where are you?" Volner asked. It was a question, not a criticism. Moore was glad the major was on board.

"I'm off the highway at the border, just southwest of a shopping area," Moore said, breaking out his binoculars and looking east. "Must've gotten great black-market deals before the invasion."

"I see it," Volner replied. "We'll be there as soon as Siegel arrives. What does it look like there?"

"You've got a lot of thick woods," Moore said, "and I—I also see what looks like the base on the other side of a deforested area in the distance. Smoke isn't blowing this way and I can see most of the field, though the sun's at my back and the lights getting a little long here and there'll be deep shadows pretty soon."

"What *can't* you see?"

"Whatever is presently in one of the first of the large wooded areas—grids R1 and 2 on the map," he said after checking the display. "Next area, couple miles, is R3."

"That's the base, or at least the start of the fence," Volner said.

"Hold on," Moore said, peering southeast through the glasses. "Shit, I see 'em. I see *someone*."

"Where?"

"Ahead of me about a half click on the south side of the R2 woods, about to enter Russian territory," Moore said. "I just saw the tail end of a group—three guys, moving through an open patch. No uniforms, all black. Oh, and, Major? I do believe they have incendiaries, or, at least, they did."

"I recognized the smoke," Volner said.

"Which means they may be planning to light up the base."

"I figured the same thing," Volner said. "Can you track them safely?"

"Yeah, but it occurs to me that when you guys arrive the Ukrainians are *not* going to be happy to see someone driving their own vehicle up their asses," Moore said.

"I'm counting on it," Volner replied. "I want to adapt the standard hostage-negotiation drill: get Flannery to engage in some urgent diplomacy and . . ."

Moore didn't hear the rest as a helicopter passed low overhead. He ducked behind the bike, out of sight, and snapped a picture of the red-and-white Mi-8. He sent it to Volner.

"Sergeant?" Volner said. "What was that?"

"Chopper just went overhead. Just shot you the image."

There was silence, then muted conversation at the other end.

"Flannery says it's the Interior Ministry, Anti-Terrorism Division," Volner said. "They must be looking for the arsonists."

There was another silence as Moore watched the helicopter poke and nose along the treetops. The shadows were large below. He couldn't see anything there. He was sure the soldiers had gone as low to the ground as possible.

The helicopter made a hard turn before the border and headed east, looking for Russians who might have crossed over.

"Chopper's peeling off, but those guys—I see them again, and they're booking now. Sir?"

"Yes?"

"I think the time table just got accelerated. I'm going to try and keep up."

Volner told him he was not to engage, but Moore couldn't hear over the roar of the engine.

CHAPTER FORTY-TWO

Op-Center Headquarters, Fort Belvoir North,
Springfield, Virginia
June 4, 9:30 AM

Everyone was on deck in the large conference room located down the hall from Williams's office. There was an uncommon tension in the room; this mission creep had an even less pleasant feeling than the operation that had cost Hector Rodriguez his life. Unlike that situation, it was a successful sortie that had ended with an accident.

On this one, everyone had their eyes open—figuratively, at least.

It had been a sleepless night for many of them, and most of that had consisted of the most tedious kind of intelligence work: waiting for people to get back to them. Anne and McCord had taken the brunt of that; Williams had been able to nap on the couch in his office, others at their desks.

They were watching the live feed from the field, having been patched in by Volner after Moore and Siegel took off. They could hear Volner and the squad, but their own conversation was muted. The only member on the call was Paul Bankole.

"It doesn't sound like the government helicopter saw them," Bankole said.

"I wish they had. Then it'd be their problem."

"What's your recommendation?" Williams asked him.

"My gut says stand down, this is a bad political situation and a damned risky military proposition," he replied. "My brain says that if we've got a shot at stopping these guys we take it. Which is what we're doing until someone here or there pulls the plug. And you've got, I would say, about five, ten minutes before we head out."

"Understood," Williams said.

"We have to notify both governments," Dawson said.

"Notify them about what, exactly?" McCord asked. "The sources that got us here will be compromised if we say too much. And they'll want corroboration about any evidence regarding the Ukrainian squad. What do we have, exactly?"

"We have a team in harm's way," Anne said. "I hate to be the bad oracle here, Chase, but we have Sergeant Moore in pursuit and likely to make contact, in Russia, before the others can get to him. And apart from Flannery talking to them—if he even gets that chance—we still don't know what Mike is supposed to do when the team gets there." She looked at Williams. "This started out as recon in Crimea, then recon north of Crimea, and now they're racing to intercept—patriots, terrorists, whatever you want to call them."

"That's the problem, Anne," Wright said. "We *don't* know what to call them. We don't even know, for sure, that they're rogue."

"Jim's got a point," Matt Berry said. "The president's on the same page here: this is equal parts confusion and ignorance. Hell, the government there can't agree on whether or not to embrace Captain Klimovich, for God's sake, and he's got a tank column fifty strong less than a mile from the Russian border!"

"Kiev can't endorse the Fox because there's a Russian column less than a mile from the Ukrainian border," McCord said. "He's literally a loose cannon, one of two who are presently in the field."

"And Kiev—at least officially—still only knows about one of those," Berry said.

"But they're almost certainly coordinated," McCord said. "Think about it. Klimovich is a distraction for Russia and the media. The fire is a distraction for local resources. Everyone is looking somewhere other than where an actual attack will probably occur."

"We think," Wright said. "We *guess*."

"Goddamn politics," Dawson said. "Here's the one thing we do know. Mike and his team are the only ones who can stop those guys, the actual attack squad, without causing massive retaliation and slaughter from one side or the other."

"*If* someone crosses the border," Anne said.

"We just heard Sergeant Moore say they were racing toward it," McCord said.

"But Moore doesn't know for sure whether they're Ukrainian troops, as we suspect, or possibly even Russian mercs or Special Ops who are returning home, which is what the NSA has suggested," Berry said.

"Forgive me if I navel-gaze, but my concern isn't any of

that," Wright said. "If Moscow and Kiev want war, they can have it—if not here and now, then somewhere else, some other time. *My* worry is that we may do something inadvertent, or something we cannot avoid, an act that triggers one side or the other to act. I say we support Paul's gut and abort. This is *not* our fight."

"And there may well be a fight," Anne said. "With casualties. For what? Because two other nations have a grievance that doesn't affect us directly? Those combatants aren't just going to stop because we say so, because we have a diplomat."

Williams looked over at the signed photo of MacArthur. "A doctor who sees someone injured in the street, a cop who's off duty—there are moral responsibilities that transcend doctrine. We keep going," he decided. "I'm going to talk to Minister Timoshenko."

"And tell him what?" Anne asked.

"That we believe Captain Klimovich is there to do exactly what he's done, pull the heavy guns from Sudzha."

"Which means you'll have to tell him about the paramilitaries out there," McCord said.

"Correct."

"But the Russian troops at Sudzha may not be able to stop them in time, or at all," McCord went on. "The Ukrainians have drilled for this. They've got a game plan and—*and* if the Russians come running out, and *they* get hit with the incendiaries? Putin will crush the border. It will be Crimea north."

"Which leaves our team," Dawson said.

"Yeah, I know," Williams said. "Brian? Put the call through to the Kremlin—we'll need their translator. Paul?"

"I'm here, Chase."

"Thanks for your patience. We've got to try this, we've at least got to be there to stop the Ukranians. Hopefully, I can get Timoshenko to sit tight."

"I understand," he said. "So does the ambassador."

There was a solemn quiet as they listened to the arrival of PFC Siegel with the truck and the men loaded up. Williams wished Bankole luck.

"They're getting the minister from a meeting," Dawson informed him.

Williams nodded. He felt numb. Anne's look was anything but.

"This is a very, very fluid situation, Chase," she said. "Fluid like gasoline. I know you know that, but if—and this is a very real possibility—if our team intercepts and terminates the Ukrainian squad, there may be casualties on both sides. And, more than that, those who survive will be in Russian territory and in Russian hands."

"You're right," Williams said. "I do know that. And I'd love to have another—"

What he was about to say was cut off by a shout and the sound of gunfire.

CHAPTER FORTY-THREE

Sumy Airport, Ukraine
June 4, 4:44 PM

The clarity of the Ukranian master plan, the brilliant simplicity of the master plan, all became apparent to Paul Bankole as the truck sped onto the H-07—and then immediately slowed in a mass of traffic and ugly black mist.

Draw away the tanks. Draw away local resources. Make it difficult to approach the border from the west. Draw attention north and south—then slip a team into the east and give Putin a black eye. On his own territory, as he did to Ukraine. And at a time when any tantrum he might throw, however hard, would necessarily be brief because his nation was bankrupt.

After that skirmish at Labkovicy, those who had been paying attention realized that Captain Taras Klimovich was a formidable tactician. What they didn't realize was that his disappearance after the battle was also a tactical move, a retreat so that he—and presumably it *was* he, using his resources and reputation to win secret allies—could plan this operation.

It was neither necessary nor desirable for the government or

the military to have known. All that was required was the participation of key players here and there to help deflect attention
from the abandoned tank factory in Kharkiv, the careful leak of a
virtual program to see how Russia would—or wouldn't—deploy
its assets. For Klimovich, this was a no-lose scenario. Bankole
didn't believe he would cross the border. There was no need. If
Russia attacked Kharkiv, he would end up either victorious or
martyred. If the Russians didn't attack across-border, he showed
the bear to be without claws and he emerged the leading patriot
of his day, of his era, the most influential man in the region.

A little farther south, this fire—quite literally a fire wall—
to allow an élite team to approach Putin's proud new base, attack,
immolate the enemy using incendiary devices, and fade into the
dusk. Putin could rage, but the world would cheer the Ukrainian
heroes. Putin could attack, but a move into northern Ukraine,
not far from the border with Belarus, would almost certainly
drive that increasingly Western-leaning nation away from Moscow and result in a wider regional war—which, again, Putin
could not afford to fight.

There was no way that Klimovich's overall objectives could
be blunted, save one: if the attack at Sudzha failed to come off.

Perhaps that was the elusive quality that kept us moving
forward, Bankole thought, the seasoned warrior's sixth sense, a
sense of destiny even when the objective was neither clear nor
present.

Sitting on the floor in the back of the truck, the flaps drawn
shut, Bankole had expressed his thoughts to Major Volner. The
officer had been studying his tablet, looking at a 3-D view of the
region. He looked up sharply.

"I have a man taking fire," Volner said. "I heard him call out. That's my only interest right now."

"We don't know his situation," Bankole pointed out. It was an innocent observation with stupidly unanticipated results.

"We *know* he's been offline for five minutes, and I *will not* lose another man. Siegel!" The major turned toward the cab of the truck, directly overhead. The slot between the compartments was open.

"Sir?"

"Status?"

"Nobody's moving!"

"Off road, *now!*" he yelled. "We can take this incline—looks like bushes and rocks below. Small, erosion protection—go!"

Flannery was sitting beside Bankole. The international crisis manager felt the ambassador's hand on his forearm; until then, he hadn't realized how tense he was. Bankole nodded with understanding.

Small objectives, big objectives, he thought. Even in the military, he had been a big-picture man. In his new faith, it was the same: his eyes looked away from the world of desire to the realm of the higher deities. But it takes all kinds to make a world, and to make it function.

The truck nosed toward the south and then charged forward, braking sharply as it rode the slope to a mushy field and shooting over it hard and fast to keep from becoming mired. He heard the shouts of other drivers through the flap, but their voices were lost in the thick cloud of smoke. He heard the slap of squeaky windshield wipers and the oaths of the driver.

Then they smelled, then tasted, the smoke.

"Cover up!" Volner yelled, and every man used whatever he had to improvise a breathing filter—handkerchief, collar, cap, socks.

Bankole kept watch on Flannery, who had a large white handkerchief over his face. He could see it darkening as they rode through the smoke. There were coughs here and there, held breath, shouted updates from Siegel that either "I can't see shit!" or "I'm seeing a clearing!"

The passage was bumpy and interminable, as if they were lost in a limbo where even the sounds of sirens were muted. There were helicopters high overhead, from the sound of it; unable to come lower for fear of their engines choking, the occupants were most likely blind to whatever was going on below.

And then a cheer from the cab, and they were through it.

At Volner's command, one of the men peeked through the flap. "Just open field back there, sir."

"Siegel, get us *through* some goddamn woods *now!*"

"They're thick, sir! We can get into R1, but I'm not sure we can get out!"

Volner swore. "Don't stop the truck," he said, then turned to the twelve other men in back. "Hunter, Canter, Bankole, Flannery, you stay here. The rest out now, with me. Double time, safeties off at the sound of gunfire!"

Like paratroopers, the eight team members went out the back with practiced precision and raced ahead of the bouncing truck.

CHAPTER FORTY-FOUR

Sudzha, Russia
June 4, 5:01 PM

Lying in a furrow where he'd ditched the Dnepr, Moore had two reasons to kick himself.

First, he should have realized after the flyover that a flashing red motorcycle would be presumed to have been sent by the ministry. A single bike would have a better chance than a helicopter of getting in and out of Russian territory, unseen, and bringing back intel. Especially if there were no drones in the region, or there were drones but too many trees.

And an unarmed drone wouldn't be helpful here in any case, he thought as he hunkered down.

Second, he shouldn't have raced ahead and flashed the sons of bitches. His intention had been to cause them to drop, as they had with the helicopter, give Volner time to catch up. But flashing them—

See reason one, he thought now.

The good news was the Ukrainian troops couldn't proceed as long as he was ahead of them. The bad news was the Ukrainian troops couldn't proceed as long as he was ahead of them. And they had, now, no time to waste.

Gunfire pinged the earth around him. The shots were coming from slightly different positions. They were moving to encircle him and close in, while he couldn't move anywhere. Though he had weapons, they were all in his backpack, which was still tied to the bike. His phone was on the other side of the bike. At least the major would be able to pinpoint his location . . . if the Ukrainians didn't get there first.

You're gonna have to get your semi at some point, he thought. *Some point soon.* He was looking back, wondering if he could possibly make it to the other side of the bike, use it for protection the way cowboys used to do with their horses.

Coin toss, baby, he thought. Hold out or wait for the cavalry? He was okay dying with his boots on, but he'd hate to run for his backpack and get tagged just as help arrived. His last thought would be a word that used to get his mouth scrubbed clean.

He listened for the truck and heard nothing. That wasn't good.

He jumped as a bullet pinged in the shallow trench he was in. They were gaining height on him. It might be only seconds before they could shoot down.

He swore. He was going to have to—

"Stand down!" he heard from somewhere in the distance . . . and in blessed, blessed English.

He heard muted chatter in what he assumed was Ukrainian. He knew what they had to be thinking: Who are these assholes, and do we take this other asshole hostage?

That instant of distraction, when he suspected they had to be reconnoitering their own rear, was when Moore moved. He bolted from the trench and crawled like a bloody gecko on a screen to the bike. Gunfire bit the ground behind him as he flipped over the chassis, slapped a hand on the backpack, and, bending low, felt for the zipper. He pulled it back as bullets banged off the underside of the Dnepr and deflated both tires with a poofing hiss.

He felt the barrel of his XM8 assault rifle and slipped the 5.56-mm. weapon toward him. He suddenly felt very, very whole. He felt protected. He crouched there and waited.

From this position, he could see the enemy. He could see them down low now . . . one man gathering together three packages.

He used his foot to feel for the phone. He found it, dragged it toward him. Bracing the weapon against his shoulder, his right hand trigger ready, he used his left hand to text the major:

```
          Incendry iminnt
```

He wasn't sure if Volner would get the message, and he wasn't sure which way the Ukrainians planned to fire them up.

Just then, everyone fell very quiet as they heard the truck pull up. The Ukrainians had to assume it was backup—though arms were patted and fingers were pointed as they recognized the vehicle.

Then he heard a voice in Ukrainian coming from the direction of the truck.

Flannery.

Whatever he was saying, the men were talking about it.

Two of them were growling at the others—one of those was the man with the incendiaries. He shook his head violently and, with the other dissenter, they started crawling deeper into the wood . . . toward the Russian base.

Moore sprayed the area several yards ahead of them with gunshots. The men dropped as their comrades returned fire, forcing Moore to abandon his position as the bike was chewed to sharp-edged ruin. That flurry drew reports from Volner's team, the shots passing overhead—but not by much. Everyone went down. The woods were suddenly silent again.

Flannery resumed. Now all the men but one thought it best to turn back. That one was still the man with the incendiaries. He pointed ahead. He seemed intent on going there and, unwrapping what Moore now saw was an industrial-size incendiary grenade, he pulled the pin and rose enough to hurl it behind him.

As he did, his forehead exploded forward, *toward* Volner and his team. Moore's eyes shot east.

"Russian sniper!" he cried.

That was a concern, though less so than the fact that as the Ukrainian soldier went down the pinless incendiary went with him.

Everyone ran, including Moore, heedless of the sniper and with the kind of survival panic he had seen only on the *Animal Planet*. There was no further fire from the Russian; as everyone circled west, the trees erupted into a fireball. A shockwave of heat preceded it, causing the sweat on Moore's neck to superheat and burn, turning the MAW and the phone both hot as griddles and propelling him to greater speed.

There were shouts from the American team as Ukrainians appeared.

"Drop your weapons! Now!" was the main one, which Flannery translated. Though Moore couldn't imagine that was needed.

Away from the fire and concealed from the base by a now familiar oily black smoke, he made his way, on surprisingly wobbly legs, in the direction of the voices.

Moore winced as hot sweat seared his eyes. He could barely see the Ukrainians being rounded up by his teammates.

"I oughta have your ass!" the major barked when he saw his sergeant.

"You might wanna hold off on that," he said. "I thought I was gonna die out there."

Volner's angry expression cracked, and he gave it up altogether. He hugged the sergeant, who held tight.

"Me, too," Volner said as he stepped back. "Glad you didn't. Get in the truck and—you got your phone?"

Moore wagged it.

"Update Ops—and one other thing," Volner said.

"Yes, sir?"

"Figure out how you're gonna pay the air-traffic controller for the bike."

CHAPTER FORTY-FIVE

Valuysky District, Belgorod Oblast, Russia
June 4, 5:33 PM

From the head of his armored column, Colonel General Yershov watched the tanks of Captain Taras Klimovich moving east along the T2104. He had stopped following the press reports, turned off the radio in his headset, stopped listening to the cheers of the easily moved and deluded people of Kharkiv, of Petrivs'ke, of Bilyi Kolodyaz', of every city and town through which the young Ukrainian tank commander passed. Klimovich wasn't even a *smart* officer, for Yershov didn't need to watch the news to know where he was. Like a whale, his position was given away by the gulls circling overhead—in this case, the press helicopters.

What are they expecting to do? Yershov wondered. *Record your march into Russia or capture your retreat from conflict?* There was no scenario on earth in which, on an open road, that approaching column could match the strength or firepower of the Russian column.

But then it really didn't matter to the general what was on Klimovich's mind. What mattered was that Russian honor be maintained and in one case restored. Vladimir Putin would not lose face in a brash assault on Russian sovereignty, and the reputation of Colonel General Nikolai Novikov would regain some of its luster with the defeat of the Fox. One tread, one gun, one foot passing over the border would result in a decisive and overwhelming defense of the homeland.

Yershov thought, in passing, of the obvious futility of the captain's position and wondered if he had lost his perspective or embraced his infallibility, or both, during his three years in hiding.

There was a voice in his headset. It was the driver signaling Yershov on the inter-vehicle information system.

"Minister Timoshenko for you, highest priority," the young man said.

"Thank you," Yershov replied, switching to the secure channel. He believed—he prayed—that this was an order from the president himself to do whatever was necessary to stop the Ukrainian column. Yershov could not imagine Timoshenko himself assuming such a responsibility.

"General, you are to return to Sudzha at once," the minister said without inflection or preamble.

Yershov was surprised—and confused. "Minister, the tank column from Kharkiv—"

"Is a distraction to which you have submitted," the minister replied. "Your base was the target. The attempted siege has been averted while you were in the field."

Yershov felt his body empty of soul, his mind lose its capacity to think. He saw the puffs of smoke from the approaching tanks, heard the distant treads . . . could swear they were voices, laughing at him.

"The president has demanded that upon your return you submit your resignation," the minister went on. "Colonel Dzhamanov has already been appointed acting commander."

"Already," Yershov said dumbly. He was not even to be allowed the dignity of a handover.

"General, turn your tanks around at once!" Timoshenko barked.

"Yes," Yershov replied. Numb, dull fingers changed the digital setting to give the command.

There was a lurch as the armored personnel carrier swung to the south to pivot, leading the tanks the way a caterpillar pulls its own body.

Ahead, in the slanting sun, lay the breadth of all of great Mother Russia, with its myriad people and time zones, climates and ethnicities, history and future.

A future in which he would have no part.

He had lost a nation, he had lost his president—Putin had *abandoned* him—he had lost his standing and his work. He would also lose his dacha, which was only for the wealthy or the privileged. He was, now, neither.

He stood in the open hatch, because if he descended into the darkness now he would never get up. Instead, through tears, he looked at his country and he thought of his wife, and he told himself that he must be strong for her. Not because *she* needed it, but she would need him not to come apart. It would not be fair to ask her to carry them both.

We will have no more than we began with, he thought, a small flat in a large city where I am anonymous.

He could do that if they were together. He could survive that if he held on to one thing more: that somewhere, someday, a tank commander would look into this story and understand. A colonel or general who would do for him what he had attempted to do for Novikov. . . .

CHAPTER FORTY-SIX

The advance toward Russia ended as planned, in proud Pryko-lotne, a railroad center that Captain Klimovich intended to become the new forward post for his tank corps. Given all that Havrylo Koval had seen today, he did not doubt at all that it would come to pass.

There had been no word from Major Romanenko's team, and no news about an attack on Sudzha. But there had been news reports about a second fire burning inside Russia, and that personnel from the base were in the process of extinguishing it. It sounded very much as if an incendiary device had gone off—and, for whatever reason, it marked the ultimate forward advance of the team.

Koval felt sadness for them, but not surprise. From the beginning of the virtual drilling, he had sensed that Major Romanenko was operating on tenuous hope and an abundance of military swagger. Not that he couldn't have pulled it off: he and his team appeared to believe they could. And they came close. But close was not victory. Koval wondered now if Captain Klimovich had ever truly expected them to succeed in damaging the base. This had been about shaming Russia, and the turn-back of the enemy column seemed to indicate that it had worked. The only reason to leave was if something had happened near or to their home base.

Though there were renewed cheers from the street as word of the Russian retreat spread, it was strangely quiet in the factory tower. Koval finally had a chance to wonder what was next for him.

It would be professionally challenging and personally rewarding to continue doing this, he thought. Designing simulations to drill the Ukrainian military, to use surgical strikes and highly specialized teams to blunt the monolithic Russian war machine.

He thought that Klimovich might ask. Koval *hoped* he would.

The computer scientist leaned back in the creaking office chair and picked up the bowl of *schav*, the sorrel soup that had been sent up five hours before. It had been hot then, the way he liked it, and was mournfully cool now, but no meal had ever tasted so good.

We have done it, he thought proudly.

He wondered how many people could say that with as much heart as those words came tonight.

CHAPTER FORTY-SEVEN

"They *did* it!"

The voice of Chase Williams hung in the air of the conference room for only a moment before it was swallowed whole by cheers. There were a few high fives and fewer hugs, but the mood was ebullient.

Voices of congratulations were shouted at the speaker on which Paul Bankole had made the report.

Part of the joy—a large part—was relief. It was the kind of job that Op-Center had been designed to do, but it was a job that had more moving and unknown and makeshift parts than any it had faced since the halcyon days of Paul Hood, General Mike Rodgers, and the bold Striker Special Operations force.

"Paul, can you hang on a moment?" Williams asked.

"I'm at a hospital in Sumy getting checked out for smoke inhalation," he said. "We all are."

"We're gonna make sure you get out okay," Williams said. "Right, Matt?"

"State is my second call, after Harward," Berry said as he left the room.

The White House deputy chief of staff was followed by Dawson and everyone, except Anne and Williams. Anne was about to leave when Williams motioned for her to stay. She shut the door and sat back at the table.

"Paul, it's just Chase and Anne now," Williams said.

"Hi, Anne. Thanks for everything you did to get us here."

"To put you in harm's way? Paul, it's what your government does best."

"I can't answer for the government, but I can answer for this team," Bankole told her. "I have never seen anything like it. And, honestly, I hope I never see it again."

He laughed, but underneath it was a thick coat of sincerity.

"Paul, how is the ambassador?" Williams asked.

"He's being rebandaged and he may have busted his wrist getting out of the truck," Paul said. "He climbed over me to get to the Ukrainians and try to talk them off the ledge. He was in this up to his chin."

"But you got everyone out?" Williams said. "Save that one?"

"Save the leader," Bankole told him. "The Russians took him out. They showed remarkable restraint."

"Why shouldn't they?" Anne said. "They didn't want a flash point with Ukraine any more than Kiev did."

"Not as long as we were there to take the bullets for them," Williams added. "Speaking of the Ukrainians—?"

"Gone like they were never here," Bankole said. "I managed to grab a few pictures in the truck when their masks were off. But once the authorities met us on the field, south of Yunakivka, that was it."

"I wonder how much they knew," Williams said.

"Flannery doesn't think they knew much, given what they were saying in the truck," Bankole said. "They were surprised when the ambassador told them about Captain Klimovich and the tanks. They refused to use one another's names, though I'm sure the military will make them public when they put these men on trial."

"They'll have to, won't they?" Anne said. "Moscow will demand it."

"After the Kremlin demands extradition and a trial in Moscow or Sudzha," Williams said. "Those kids are never going to see daylight—if they aren't sentenced for treason."

"I'd guess prison, not death," Bankole said. "I don't think Klimovich will abandon them. I don't think Ukrainian patriots will, either. It'll be a delicate balancing act to appease that side and Putin."

"Once again, the soldiers do the heavy lifting and then the politicians who started it finish it," Anne said. "Hey, Paul. I can arrange for the return trip as soon as I hear from State that there are no hang-ups with—"

"I've been informed—*pre*-informed—by the major that that will not be necessary," Bankole told her.

"Oh?"

"The fishing boat," he said. "If it's still there, they want to cruise the Black Sea back to Turkey before coming home. I really have been looking forward to meeting the skipper."

"Why is that?" Williams asked.

"Kaan Hamzaçebi sounds like a very, very interesting man," Bankole said. "A sea voyage and a chat about religion could do us all a world of good."

"I'll make sure it's there," Anne said, and looked at Williams. The director nodded

"Let me know if you need help getting to the Azov," Anne said.

"Oh, and Sergeant Moore needs about six hundred American to pay for a bike he wrecked," Bankole said.

"I'll have the U.S. embassy in Kiev send someone with the money," Williams said. "Op-Center's got an alumnus there—legal attaché named Lowell Coffey II."

"Talent rises from hereabouts," Anne said.

Williams thanked Bankole again, and told him to thank and congratulate every member of the team. He ended the call and sat back. He looked at his watch.

"Is that AM or PM?" he asked.

Anne smiled. "Y'know, I'm not even sure."

"Well, I better figure it out," he said. "I want to know if it's breakfast or dinner we need to be catching up on." He frowned. "Hey, didn't you have—?"

"A doctor's appointment? That was yesterday. Moved it to next week," she said. "So. You buying?"

"Op-Center's buying," he replied, rising unsteadily and stretching. "We earned this one."

With Anne leading the way, Williams followed into the sunless light that was the subterranean home of Op-Center.

"There's just one thing," he said as they left. "Something I want McCord to check on."

CHAPTER FORTY-EIGHT

John F. Kennedy International Airport, New York
June 6, 12:03 PM

Georgi Glazkov was sorry to leave Hong Kong, but at least he left with a successful mission against the family of that wet-behind-the ears college student Chingis Altankhuyag. A lovely psy-ops move, no bloodshed.

And he was excited at his new post. He left the Air China 747 and, with the patience of his trade, the assassin made his way through customs. With the smiles of his trade, he went past the agent without incident. With the relaxed anonymity of his expression and dress, he looked every inch the avuncular figure he wished people to see, someone's uncle looking for family—though in this case the family was someone who had been described to him in a coded text while he was still in Hong Kong, a portly young diplomat who was supposed to look like his favorite nephew. He would be here to help Georgi get established in his new city, a replacement for his friend Andrei Cherkassov.

With a single carry-on tossed over his shoulder and one large suitcase on wheels, he looked for the man—and saw something that he was not expecting, a quality that was not good in his profession.

Standing near the exit of the airport was a uniformed driver holding a placard with his full name on it. His real name, not the name under which he was traveling.

Looking around, he saw an area where he could break silence and call the embassy. He did not know if the man he sought was here—but he had to know why the embassy had shattered protocol like this. His fury was difficult to tamp down as he stood in a corner beside a closed rental-car counter.

With angry, trembling fingers he punched in the number of the Russian Consulate.

An older couple dragging luggage walked by, and Georgi turned slightly from them as the phone beeped at the other end. He didn't want anyone to hear. Airports, he knew, were crawling with intelligence officers.

The assassin desperately wanted a cigarette, but that would attract attention and then law enforcement in this ridiculous city. He waited impatiently.

"Welcome to New York," he heard the woman say.

Georgi looked into the lean, pale face of NYPD bureau chief Irene Young. He nodded his thanks warily. The woman remained standing there, the man watching them both from a few feet away.

"Olga gave you up," the woman said. "Set foot in my street and you're a dead man."

Then, stepping away, and with Brian Dawson smiling at her side, the two continued to the exit and the line of squad cars waiting outside.

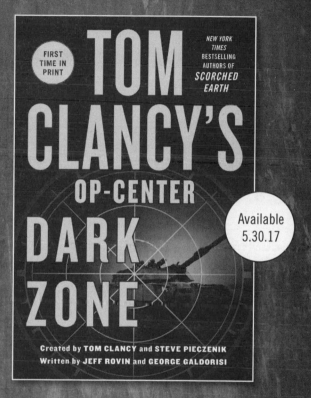